Praise for *One Man's Justice*

"Akira Yoshimura has long been an esteemed and bestselling author in Japan. . . . The quiet, calibrated prose used to tell of murder and retribution in *Shipwrecks* (1996) and *On Parole* (1999) succeeds brilliantly again in *One Man's Justice*. His patient accumulation of tiny, meticulous details has a cinematic effect and brings to mind the great Japanese filmmaker Yasujiro Ozu, to whom nothing was too small to be significant."   —*The Dallas Morning News*

"Meticulously researched . . . *One Man's Justice* is the journey of a man forced to hide, a man surrounded by people scared, and slowly ashamed of being linked to a war criminal—the transformation of a proud lieutenant of the Imperial Army into a scared human being."

—Associated Press

"Yoshimura has extensively researched both the air war and the Tokyo trials, but the heart of the novel describes Takuya's life on the run in a burned-out, half-starving, demoralized country. The physical and psychological details of that ordeal, presented in a clean, spare style, are telling."

—*Los Angeles Times*

"There's no doubt that Yoshimura is a very considerable talent. One looks forward to seeing more of his scrupulous, intense fiction in English translation."   —*Kirkus Reviews*

"Yoshimura creates a window into the life of ordinary citizens struggling with destruction, poverty and shame. And as peace settles in, he shows us how even the darkest hatred fades to leave behind ordinary men struggling with their pasts."   —*The San Diego Union-Tribune*

Praise for *On Parole*

"From the start, Yoshimura exhibits the technical excellence that has made him a bestselling author in Japan. . . . His spare, sensual prose has all the intensity of poetry."

—*Publishers Weekly* (starred)

"A brilliant dramatization of the implacability of fate by an exceptionally good novelist." —*Kirkus Reviews* (starred)

"Here is a novel crafted in excruciatingly exact detail: Line by line, moment to moment, *On Parole* reveals almost cinematically the minutiae of one man's existence. Yoshimura is a master at leaving almost nothing to the imagination in this calibrated account." —*The Dallas Morning News*

"Elegant, spare language and flawless craftsmanship—powerful and beautiful." —*BookForum*

"An austerely graceful book, which should help cement Yoshimura's reputation here and bring over more of his twenty bestselling novels in its wake."

—*The Washington Post Book World*

"A neat novel . . . There's nothing picturesque about the story, and it's a measure of Yoshimura's mastery that we're still disturbed and fascinated, even without the interest of a wholly alien world. The more Yoshimura writes about, say, railway timetables, the more we're transfixed by what the man on the train might do next."

—*The New York Times Book Review*

"A masterful commentary on the fragility of the human spirit." —*Booklist*

"A riveting tale of crime and punishment." —*Library Journal*

Praise for *Shipwrecks*

"Haunting and austerely beautiful... Makes you wonder why it took so long for an American publisher to discover him."   —The New York Times

"Extraordinary in detail and verisimilitude... A haunting read."   —*Los Angeles Times Book Review*

"Many Japanese authors have gained popularity in the West with novels not nearly as accessible and moving as this one.... If he has more fiction of the caliber of *Shipwrecks*, it deserves to be made available to a much wider audience."   —*St. Louis Post-Dispatch*

"Seamless interweaving of description, characterization, and narrative, and an enduringly powerful image of a vanished time and place. More, please, of Yoshimura."

—*Kirkus Reviews* (starred)

One Man's
Justice

Also by Akira Yoshimura

SHIPWRECKS
ON PAROLE

AKIRA YOSHIMURA

One Man's Justice

Translated from the Japanese
by Mark Ealey

A HARVEST BOOK
HARCOURT. INC.
San Diego New York London

Requests for permission to make copies of any part of the work
should be mailed to the following address:
Permissions Department, Harcourt, Inc.,
6277 Sea Harbor Drive, Orlando, Florida 32887-6777.

This is a translation of *Toi Hi No Senso*. Original Japanese edition published by
Shincho-Sha Co., Ltd. English translation rights arranged with Akira Yoshimura
through Writers House, LLC/Japan Foreign Rights Centre.

www.HarcourtBooks.com

Library of Congress Cataloging-in-Publication Data

Yoshimura, Akira, 1927–
[Toi hi no senso. English]
One man's justice / Akira Yoshimura; translated from Japanese by Mark Ealey.
p.   cm.
ISBN 0-15-100639-3
ISBN 0-15-600725-8 (pbk.)
I. Ealy, Mark. II. Title.
PL865.O72 T6413 2000
895.6'35—dc21 00-046142

Text set in Goudy
Designed by Linda Lockowitz

Printed in the United States of America

First Harvest edition 2002
A C E G I K J H F D B

One Man's Justice

Chapter One

The boy's eyes were no longer on Takuya.

Each time the train lurched, the boy's head, filled with ringworm, was buried in the gap between Takuya and the middle-aged woman standing in front of him. Takuya would lean back to create enough space for the boy to breathe. The boy looked up at Takuya repeatedly. There was a shadow of resignation in his eyes, a recognition of his powerlessness in the mass of adults, as well as a flicker of light, an entrusting of his well-being to this man who kept shifting back for him. Before long, however, the boy's head dropped. The strain of leaning to one side may have been too much for him, for now he hardly moved his head when he was pressed between the adults. The woman standing in front of them seemed to be the boy's mother, and Takuya could sense that he was holding on to the cloth of her work trousers.

The car was packed with people and baggage. Some had pushed their way in to stand between the seats, others perched on the seat backs, clinging to the supports of the luggage racks. No one spoke, and all that could be heard was a baby's intermittent hoarse crying.

The train slowed down. The sound of the wheels jolting over a joint in the tracks began at the front, rattled their car and clattered on to the rear of the train. There was a hum of voices as the passengers realized that they were approaching their destination, Hakata.

Takuya turned to look out the window. He wanted to be delivered from the suffocating atmosphere of the train, but at the same time he felt reluctant to step onto the platform in this city.

The train slowed more, shuddered slightly and came to a halt. The air filled with voices as people transformed the cars into a bustle of activity. The boy winced as he twisted around to face Takuya. Resisting the human tide, Takuya held the boy's gaze until he saw that a space had opened in front of him. Satisfied, he forced his way between the seats next to him to jump out the window and onto the platform.

Takuya looked around the concrete platform. The station was more or less as it had been when he left this city seven months ago, but scorched iron girders stood here and there, and the crossbeams of the roof's steel skeleton were exposed. He shuffled with the crowd across the platform toward the ticket gates.

Leaving the station, Takuya saw people milling around and peering into a cluster of makeshift wooden stalls. The hawkers' voices were animated, but the people on the street moved lethargically from one stall to the next.

The thought that someone in this crowd of survivors

might recognize him made Takuya take the path that ran along the railway tracks for a short distance from the market to a stone bridge over a little stream.

A desolate expanse of charred buildings opened up in front of him. Once again he was astonished that so many homes could have been reduced to ashes in a single night.

Takuya set off along the road through the charred ruins. Though he had spent the last two years and four months of the war here, he had not expected to ever set foot in this city again. He knew deep down that it was unwise to go anywhere near the place.

The reason Takuya had left his hometown to come here by train, ferry, and then train again was a postcard he had received three days earlier. It was from Shirasaka Hajime, a former army lieutenant. Shirasaka had been born in the United States, but returned to Japan with his parents before the war, graduating from a private university before joining the Imperial Army. He had belonged to the same unit as Takuya, the Western Region Anti-Aircraft Defense Group, under the command of the Western Regional Headquarters, and his knowledge of English had led him to stay on after the war as part of the staff winding up headquarters affairs in liaison with the Allied Forces. The postcard, scrawled in his typescript-like handwriting, had mentioned that he was keen to see Takuya again, and suggested he come to visit soon.

Takuya was bewildered by the message. He had been in the same class as Shirasaka as a military cadet, but they hadn't been particularly close. In fact, at times Takuya had felt something akin to repulsion at the occasional man-ifestations of Shirasaka's foreign upbringing. In those days

Shirasaka had seemed keenly aware of Takuya's feelings and made no attempts at friendship. Having been born and raised in America, a hostile country, Shirasaka was mocked and berated for his strange accent, and he was often on the receiving end of disciplinary action. Takuya didn't think this at all strange, in fact it mildly pleased him. Shirasaka was a tall, well-built man. These were certainly desirable attributes in an officer, but when Takuya thought of how this was the result of an ample American diet, he saw it as proof of an insidious disassociation from the Japanese people.

On orders from the commander of air defense operations at headquarters, Shirasaka had served as interpreter in the interrogation of captured American B-29 pilots who had bailed out when their bombers were shot down. Takuya had also been present, and had been surprised at Shirasaka's fluent English, which only aggravated his ill feelings toward the man. Shirasaka's English was completely different from what Takuya had learned as a student, and for the most part was unintelligible to him. Takuya could tell that the years he had spent in America had profoundly affected his character, and his natural way of conversing with the American fliers made Takuya doubt Shirasaka's trustworthiness. He would shrug his shoulders and shake his head without saying anything, and the Americans would look at him imploringly, appealing to him in muffled tones.

Takuya's feelings about Shirasaka had not changed since they had parted ways. And his impressions gained credence from the self-importance he had detected in ethnic Japanese American military interpreters on two other occasions. He imagined that Shirasaka would have used his English skills to ingratiate himself with the American military, and would doubtless be leading the same uninhibited lifestyle as those Japanese American interpreters.

Takuya tried to read between the few short lines on Shirasaka's postcard. Since the start of the Allied Occupation, all mail had been censored by the Supreme Commander of Allied Powers in Japan (SCAP), and mail and documents from the staff handling the affairs of the now defunct headquarters would surely be strictly monitored. That Shirasaka had sent such a deliberate message to Takuya, with whom he had not been particularly close, must mean that he wished to see him urgently. As an interpreter, he would be in a position to assess developments on the Allied side, so it was possible he had come across information that concerned Takuya and was trying to pass it on.

After reading the card over and over, Takuya had headed for Fukuoka, where Shirasaka was helping to wind up the affairs of the Western Command.

Walking along in the spring sunshine, he looked down at the road under his feet. He could see hairline cracks from the searing heat of fires that had raged after the incendiary attacks. In places, holes in the asphalt exposed the soil beneath. Scorched roofing iron and rubble were piled on both sides of the roadway, and the occasional ruins of square concrete buildings and the tops of underground warehouses were all that was left standing.

In stark contrast to Takuya's parting impression seven months earlier, Fukuoka had acquired the settled desolation of a wasteland. Maybe it was because the burnt ruins were starting to return to the earth, or because all projecting objects had been removed, but this huge scorched plain seemed almost to shimmer in the heat. The sound of a piece of

roofing iron that had come loose would approach on a gust
of wind, then disappear into the expanse beyond the road.
Here and there windblown piles of sand stood out in the
arid lifelessness. Then, to the south, came the foreboding
sight of two gently sloping verdant hills. The hills were split
to the east and west of a central ridge called Abura-yama,
a vantage point from which the distant islands of Tsushima
and Iki can be seen on a fine day. According to legend,
during the reign of Emperor Shomu a monk named Seiga
established a temple there and became known for the ex-
tract he made from the fruit of trees in the surrounding
forest. The thicket where Takuya and his companions had
executed the Americans, near the crematorium at Sanroku
and not far from the hills in view, was linked inextricably
to his memory of this city.

Shifting his gaze out to sea, he caught sight of a convoy
of four U.S. Army trucks moving along the coastal road,
the beams from each set of headlights dancing in the clouds
of dust thrown up by the vehicle in front. Some people said
that the Americans drove with their headlights on during
the day to flaunt the U.S. military's affluence, and there was
no denying the compelling nature of those shafts of light.

Ahead of him Takuya recognized a watchtower protruding from the burnt-out shell of a fire station. The building,
or what was left of it, had a rough whitish look not dissimilar
to that of unglazed pottery. Most of the outer walls had
crumbled away, and rusty, glassless window frames hung
loosely from the surviving structure.

Beyond the ruined fire station Takuya was stopped by
the sight of a bank of pink cherry blossoms. At the top of

the road, up a gentle slope, was the former regional command headquarters building, encircled by a belt of cherry
trees in full bloom. After the scorched desolation he had
just walked through, Takuya found the vibrant pink of this
hill strange to behold. Perhaps because it was surrounded by
blossoms the old headquarters building radiated elegance
rather than foreboding, as though it were a stately western
manor. This gentle hill seemed somehow removed from the
passage of time.

Takuya glanced to either side of the building. Sitting on
the ferry and swaying inside the train he had felt a faint
distrust of Shirasaka's motives. It was easy to imagine Shirasaka, in the course of working with the Occupation Forces,
developing a relationship that went beyond tending to the
affairs of the former Western Command. Takuya thought
that the postcard might even have been sent on the instructions of the Americans, to lure him into the open. He had
decided to come here despite his apprehension because he
assumed that even if there were some basis for his fear, the
situation would not have reached a critical stage.

Since the middle of the previous November, the newspapers had been full of reports of Japanese servicemen being
tried and then executed by military tribunals for crimes
committed overseas against prisoners of war. Even so, Takuya surmised that if the Occupation authorities were suspicious of him, they would have instructed the Japanese
police to arrest him by now. And even if Shirasaka's card
had been sent on the orders of the Americans, it was likely
that they only wanted to carry out some routine preliminary
questioning.

Moreover, Takuya felt sure that what they had done could not have been discovered by anyone on the outside. They had planned everything so carefully and so secretly that no civilian could have witnessed, or even been aware of, any part of the proceedings. There was no way, he thought, that this deed, carried out within a rigidly closed military system, could ever leak to the outside world. If the fact that executions had taken place were discovered, the headquarters staff would be culpable to varying degrees, and almost all of them would likely be implicated. That in itself, Takuya thought, would keep their lips sealed.

He concentrated his gaze on the low hill. It seemed deserted. There were no people or vehicles in sight anywhere around the building, nor on the road chiseled into the front face of the knoll. His eyes riveted on the hill, he started walking forward. To one side a bent and broken water pipe protruded from the ground. Water flowed down the road, filling a hollow in an exposed patch of dirt and spreading out in a fan-shaped arc. Faint signs of moss could be seen just below the surface of the little pool, and at the bottom grains of sand glistened as though washed to perfection.

Takuya walked up the slope, stopping at the stone pavement in front of the building. The cherry blossoms were just past their peak, and petals covered the ground.

The reception desk was unattended and the utter lack of sound suggested that the building was deserted, but a message on the wall, written on straw paper with an English translation typed beside it, invited visitors to make their way directly to the second floor.

Takuya stared ahead down the corridor. Hardly any of the windows had panes of glass and many had been boarded over completely, leaving the corridor dark and foreboding. The room Takuya had used was on the left, at the end of the corridor, but he felt no desire to go that way. He walked up the stairs to find the second floor bathed in sunlight. From there he followed the arrow written on a piece of paper stuck to the white wall. It pointed toward the section of the building where the offices of the regional commander and chief of staff had been located, and where the remaining affairs of the Regional Command were likely being attended to.

He paused before the door marked with a piece of paper bearing the word "Entrance." This chamber was connected directly to the chief of staff's office and had been used as the tactical operations center. Worried that members of the Allied military might be inside, Takuya stood glued to the spot, trying to sense what was on the other side of the door. He could just make out voices, but couldn't tell whether Japanese or English was being spoken.

He reached for the knob and opened the door. Some old desks had been brought in and arranged in an L-shape on the right-hand side of the room. A man wearing a navy blue suit and an open-neck shirt was sitting with three men in uniform behind the desks. They hadn't noticed Takuya's presence and seemed to be poring over some documents. The man in the suit lifted his head and turned to look at Takuya. Immediately he stood up and walked around the desks toward the visitor.

He had longer hair now, so for a moment Takuya didn't

recognize Shirasaka. Distracted, the three uniformed men turned as one to look toward Takuya, who recognized them immediately as non-commissioned officers from the old headquarters staff.

Gesturing as though to push him back, Shirasaka ushered Takuya out of the room and into the corridor, then guided him in the direction of the staircase before opening a door and beckoning him in. Shirasaka's hand movements and facial expression were new to Takuya. Evidently, in his association with the Occupation authorities he had regained his American mannerisms.

Shirasaka sat down behind the single desk in the middle of the room. Takuya put down his rucksack, placed his service cap on the desktop and sat facing Shirasaka.

From Shirasaka's expression Takuya realized he had been right to assume that there was nothing frivolous about the decision to send him the postcard. But they had gone to great lengths to ensure that every scrap of evidence was destroyed, so surely there was no chance they had been found out. It could only have to do with the matériel or facilities previously under the jurisdiction of the now defunct headquarters organization.

"Those American fliers . . . I'm afraid things have taken a bad turn." Resting his elbows on the desk and knitting his fingers together, Shirasaka explained how the former army major-general who had been commander in chief, his chief of staff, and a colonel who had been an aide-de-camp to the commander in chief were now being questioned by U.S. Army intelligence officers attached to the SCAP.

Taken aback, Takuya stared at Shirasaka.

Shirasaka told him how the former senior officers from

headquarters had been detained for almost a month now. The questioning focused on what had happened to the crew members who had parachuted from the B-29 bombers shot down the previous year. American intelligence was carrying out its duties under article ten of the Potsdam Declaration, covering detention and punishment of war criminals guilty of mistreatment of prisoners of war, and thus far not only had established the exact location of the crash sites of the B-29s downed by Japanese anti-aircraft units, but also had discovered that a total of fifty-eight crew members had survived the downing of their aircraft in the western headquarters administrative sector of Kyushu. On the basis of this knowledge, the investigators had gathered detailed information from civilian sources and learned that of the fifty-eight, seventeen had been sent to prisoner-of-war camps in the Tokyo area, and the remaining forty-one fliers had been handed over to the *kempeitai* by local police, and from there transferred to the custody of the Western Regional Headquarters.

By all accounts, the investigation team had carried out a rigorous interrogation of western headquarters staff, and now knew that the crew members had, to a man, been either formally executed or disposed of to the same end. The "bad turn" Shirasaka had referred to was that the headquarters staff had categorically denied issuing any orders to this effect, and insisted that the executions had been carried out arbitrarily by young officers.

"Incredible, isn't it," said Shirasaka, shaking his head.

Takuya was dumbfounded. He was shocked not just that things could have been traced this far, but that senior officers in the Western Regional Command, including the commander in chief himself, could have painted a picture so at odds with the truth.

During his days as the head of the Eleventh Army in China, the commander in chief had gathered a great deal of information about the movements of the U.S. Army Air Force units flying out of China, and had done his utmost to use this knowledge after his posting to the Western Regional Command. Surmising that the American buildup of air-power in China harbingered air raids on Kyushu, he commanded the anti-aircraft intelligence network to focus their attention on the Korea Strait. His deduction had proved to be correct, allowing for early detection of the American bomber squadrons heading for Kyushu airspace, thereby giving local fighter units time to effect the optimum defense and inflict heavy losses on the incoming bombers.

This success had greatly enhanced his profile within the army, where he was already widely renowned as a general of genuinely noble character. As composed and imperturbable as a man could be, he would respond to each request for a sample of his calligraphy by writing the Chinese characters for "Death, life, be as prepared for one as for the other." That a man of his caliber could have brazenly divorced himself from his responsibilities was beyond belief.

Demobilized on September fifth of the previous year, Takuya had gone back to his hometown. Soon after his return, he learned that the Occupation authorities had intensified their efforts to apprehend suspected war criminals.

On the eleventh of that month a warrant was issued for the arrest of those designated class A war criminals, on charges of having participated in the "formulation or execution of a common plan or conspiracy to wage wars of aggression." Former prime minister General Tojo Hideki had shot himself in a suicide attempt when he realized that American military police had arrived at his residence. The following day, it was reported that other high-ranking officials, such as former army minister Field Marshal Sugiyama Hajime, former minister of health Major General Koizumi Chikahiko, former minister of education Hashida Kunihiko, former commander of the Northeast Region General Yoshimoto Sadakazu, former commander in chief of the Kwantung Army Honjo Shigeru, and former prime minister Konoe Fumimaro, had taken their own lives. The newspaper coverage included the full text of article ten of the Potsdam Declaration regarding Japan's surrender, stating: "We do not intend that the Japanese shall be enslaved as a race or destroyed as a nation, but stern justice shall be meted out to all war criminals, including those who have visited cruelties upon prisoners."

On the tenth of October Takuya read an article stating that warrants had been issued for the arrest of three hundred former staff of prisoner-of-war camps on charges of mistreatment of prisoners. The same article, a release from the Associated Press office at General MacArthur's headquarters, stated that these suspects would be arrested by the Japanese authorities and handed over to the Eleventh Army division headquarters in Yokohama, and that no stone would be left unturned until those guilty of mistreating prisoners of war were brought to justice.

Included in an article six days later, below the headline "Bodies of Seven U.S. Airmen Discovered—Parachuted to

Ground During Tokyo Air Raids," was a statement from a spokesman of the Eighth Army Corps. It said that investigators had found the remains of two American fliers buried beside a Tokyo canal. Evidently the dead airmen had had their arms tied with thick rope and had suffered massive wounds to the neck and head. The clue that led to their discovery was provided by a young Japanese girl who, during the days of the air raids on Tokyo, had seen Japanese soldiers burying bodies wrapped in straw matting. The remains had been found in shallow graves full of muddy water, with the bodies clad only in flight jackets, sweaters and torn boots. It also stated that another five bodies had subsequently been exhumed from the grounds of a certain unnamed temple.

Not long after, it was reported in the newspaper that trials of those suspected of crimes against prisoners of war had started, and that the first guilty verdict had already been delivered on the eighth of January. The man sentenced was a former army lieutenant who had been in charge of Ohmuta Prisoner of War Camp. An American prisoner of war by the name of Hurd had twice attempted to escape and in consequence had been thrown into the guardhouse. When he tried to escape a third time he was severely beaten. The military tribunal judged that the beating constituted serious mistreatment of a prisoner of war and sentenced the accused to death by hanging. Beatings were everyday occurrences in the Japanese army, so Takuya was shocked that merely beating an incorrigible escaper could warrant the death penalty.

Three days later, there were reports of assault charges

filed against a junior officer at the Ohmuta Camp, and charges of burning moxa on a prisoner's arm and slapping him across the face with an open hand against the commandant at another camp. Both officers were sentenced to death by hanging. Numerous similar cases were reported in succeeding days.

Amid all the press coverage, the articles covering the trial of the former commander in chief of Japanese forces in the Philippines, General Yamashita Tomoyuki, stood out to Takuya for their depiction of the stance that should be taken by a commander of an army corps. Yamashita's trial by military tribunal had been held in Manila and he was sentenced to death, but he did not hesitate to accept complete responsibility for the actions of his subordinates.

Takuya had assumed all along that the commander of the Western Region would take a position similar to Yamashita's. As the one who gave the orders in the Western Region, the commander would have been fully aware of what had happened under his command, and Takuya had firmly believed that if the facts of the matter were discovered the commander would take complete responsibility.

"American intelligence knows all your names and addresses. Things being the way they are at the moment, they will doubtless move to arrest you." Shirasaka's speech was free of any trace of the rough language he had used to refer to fellow officers during his time as a lieutenant in the Imperial Army.

"What should I do?" said Takuya dejectedly. He couldn't help but feel indignant at being told that those who had issued the orders in the first place were, only eight months

after the dissolution of the Imperial Army, divorcing themselves from all responsibility for what had happened in that
thicket near Abura-yama. Such things didn't happen in the
army Takuya had known.

Shirasaka fixed his eyes on Takuya. "Run for it. Hide
somewhere," he said in a soft yet compelling voice.

Takuya remained silent.

Shirasaka's eyes glistened as he spoke. "Without a doubt,
they'll hang you if you're caught. You'll die like a dog. Hide.
Lieutenant Hirosaki came this morning. I sent him a postcard worded the same way as the one I sent you. I explained
the situation and told him to lie low. He said he'd do his
best, and now I'm giving you the same advice."

When Takuya remained speechless Shirasaka stood up
and left the room.

Takuya remembered seeing a photograph in the newspaper that showed a former army lieutenant, sentenced to
death for beating a prisoner of war, being led out of the
courtroom by the American military police. If he were to
end up that way, he would have no second chance to escape.
There would only be the wait for the gallows. Takuya
couldn't bear the thought that he, who had served his country so loyally, might be held captive by the Occupation
Forces and forced to die such a humiliating death.

A wave of uneasiness came over him. The warrant for
his arrest might already have been issued, and the Occupation administration would have called upon those winding
up the affairs of the former headquarters. Obviously, just
being in this building was dangerous.

He stood and looked out the window. There were no
people or vehicles moving toward the building, and a dusty

haze shrouded almost half of the wasted terrain. A glint of bright light emanated from somewhere near the station.

The door opened and Shirasaka reentered the room. Sitting down, he produced two pieces of paper from the inside pocket of his jacket and placed them on the desk.

"I gave Hirosaki these too. They're papers for demobilized soldiers back from overseas. With one of these you can get food and other rations wherever you go, and they double as identification. I considered a few options and came to the conclusion that you should make out you're from Okinawa. It's occupied by the Americans, so a demobilized soldier wouldn't be in much of a hurry to get back there now, which would provide a plausible reason for you to keep moving around the main islands. Write in a name that sounds Okinawan. Just in case, I'm giving you a second one to keep as a spare."

Shirasaka pushed the papers toward Takuya. They already bore the official seal of the Western Command's Hakata Office of Demobilized Military Personnel, and the spaces for name and address were left blank. However he had obtained them, the documents appeared very official.

Takuya put the papers in the inside pocket of his army jacket. "I want you to give me my gun back," he said.

Shirasaka stared hard at Takuya, a tinge of surprise spreading across his face. After the surrender, Takuya and the other officers had wrapped their twelve sidearms and a considerable quantity of ammunition in oiled paper and put them all into a waterproof bag, which had then been hidden in a secret compartment in the corridor of the headquarters building. In the bag was a collection of foreign- and Japanese-made pistols purchased with the officers' allowance for personal sidearms. Among them was Takuya's 1939 army pistol.

Takuya had forgotten about the pistol, but Shirasaka's explanation of developments and the words "They'll hang you" had jolted his memory. He felt exposed and vulnerable without his gun, as though the wartime logic that an officer had to have a weapon on him at all times had returned to guide him.

Takuya realized that his war had yet to end. The enemy was close at hand, patrolling with submachine guns slung from their shoulders, driving jeeps and trucks through the streets of the cities and towns.

"Why do you need it?" said Shirasaka, a trace of trepidation in his voice.

"I just want to have it on me," replied Takuya. Being armed was in itself more than reason enough. As long as his own war continued, a weapon would be indispensable.

Shirasaka's fists clenched within his folded arms. Takuya saw the tormented look on the man's face and realized that Shirasaka was afraid he might use the weapon to kill himself. On the twentieth of August, just days after the official document of surrender was signed, a navy lieutenant and a commander from the Kyushu Munitions Depot, distraught at the reality of defeat, had both committed hara-kiri in the woods near the Shoogaku temple, and since then there had been a rash of suicides by men named to stand trial for war crimes. Maybe it wasn't so strange of Shirasaka to interpret Takuya's wanting his gun back as a sign that he planned to kill himself.

"I want it back," Takuya said in a calmer tone, hoping to allay Shirasaka's fears.

Shirasaka fidgeted. Propping his elbows on the desk, he rubbed his clenched fingers against his forehead, pushing his thumbs awkwardly into his cheeks.

"You used to have a Colt, didn't you? I like guns. I was attached to the one I had. I just want it back," said Takuya softly.

His gaze still lowered, Shirasaka nodded several times, then grasped the edge of the desk and rose. Takuya turned to watch him leave the room. Any suspicion he might have harbored had vanished, nullified by the goodwill the man had shown in sending the postcard, providing him with papers and encouraging him to flee. Shirasaka had probably felt unable to stand by and watch a former comrade-in-arms sent to the gallows, but maybe another part of the explanation was that, deep down, he felt an aversion to the "trials" of those accused of war crimes. No doubt, thought Takuya, day-to-day contact with Occupation Forces staff must have left Shirasaka nonplussed by their arrogance, and perhaps this had led him to obstruct their proceedings by encouraging his former comrades to flee. If the Occupation authorities got wind of his actions, the severest of penalties would undoubtedly be meted out to him too. Takuya felt a twinge of conscience knowing that his request would commit Shirasaka to an even greater level of collusion, but it was overwhelmed by his desire to have the weapon back.

There was a faint sound of footsteps, then the door opened and Shirasaka reappeared, his expression strained as he returned to sit opposite Takuya. Glancing toward the door, he reached inside his jacket and offered Takuya the object he had been concealing. It was the same pistol Takuya had carried during the war, but the months it had been out of his grasp made it somehow feel much heavier. The small box of ammunition that Shirasaka placed on the table sat there for several seconds before Takuya stuffed it into his rucksack.

Shirasaka pulled a pack of Lucky Strikes from his pocket and offered one to Takuya, who shook his head in refusal at the idea of smoking an American cigarette.

Takuya felt his composure return. Now that he was armed, he could at least resist his would-be captors, and if necessary, take his own life rather than submit to arrest.

"Well then. I'd better go. Thanks for your help," Takuya said, grasping his service cap and slinging the rucksack over his shoulder as he rose to his feet. Shirasaka stood up, stepped into the corridor and walked ahead of Takuya down the stairs. Outside, Takuya thanked Shirasaka again and started down the cobblestone road.

"Kiyohara!" he heard behind him. Takuya looked back and saw Shirasaka hurrying down the slope, eyes glistening. "Don't go killing yourself," he said imploringly, tears welling up.

Takuya didn't reply. He hadn't thought about how he would use the weapon, and he certainly hadn't made up his mind to end his own life. He would take everything as it came.

"Killing yourself will be meaningless," said Shirasaka in an almost admonitory tone.

Takuya looked away from Shirasaka pensively, then started down the slope.

Maybe it was the reflection from all the burnt pieces of roofing iron, but the temperature down in the ruins of the city seemed higher than up on the hill. Takuya hurried toward the train station, occasionally glancing back over his shoulder. Most of the knoll was hidden behind the remaining walls of the old fire station, and Shirasaka was not in sight. Beyond that, all he could really see was a glimpse of the pink cherry blossoms at the top of the hill.

Chapter Two

The train left Hakata Station.

His arms pinned to his sides in the crush, Takuya was jostled into the space beside the lavatory. There was so little room to stand that two men were crouched precariously on top of the washbasins. The hair of the woman standing in front of him touched his face, a sour smell emanating from her scalp.

Takuya closed his eyes. Suddenly he found himself wondering how his American counterparts would be spending their days. Most of their officers would have been repatriated by now, and were no doubt given a hero's welcome. Throngs of well-wishers would have welcomed them at the station and carried them home on their shoulders. Many would even receive medals for slaying Japanese soldiers in battle. Takuya had killed one American. A tall blond man who had deliberately taken part in incendiary attacks on Japanese cities, sending horrific numbers of non-combatants, old people, women and children to their deaths. If Japan had won, Takuya's act might even have earned him a medal, but now he had only his wits to keep him from the gallows.

There was no option but to get away. The impulse to flee was motivated not by fear of a noose around his neck, but rather by indignation toward the victors. The Allies saw their own soldiers as heroes for killing Japanese and now sought to force a humiliating death upon Takuya and his defeated comrades-in-arms. The irony of it cut Takuya to the quick.

The train moved slowly down the track. By craning his neck, Takuya could just see over the mass of passengers to the outside world beyond the glassless windows. Before he knew it, it was early evening and the sun was setting.

There was a brief twilight, then dusk before the darkness set in and the electric lights came on in the aisles. People got off each time the train stopped, but just as many seemed to get on, so there was no relief from the crush. The man pressed hard against Takuya's back seemed to be falling asleep on his feet. From time to time he gave way at the knees, forcing Takuya to do the same. Takuya could hear a light snoring just behind his head. His rucksack was slung over his shoulder, and through the cloth bag he felt the hard grip of the pistol against the small of his back. The gun was also likely pressing against the stomach of the man standing behind him, as now and then he seemed to pull back as if trying to avoid it.

The train pulled into Kokura Station almost one hour behind schedule. Takuya pushed his way through the mass of bodies and alighted on the platform. There was a two-hour wait before his next train arrived on the Nippoo Line, but Takuya felt almost anchored to the spot. He made no move toward the next platform. He had instinctively boarded the train at Hakata, but now he was having second thoughts about actually going beyond here and returning home. Shirasaka had said that the Allied authorities already knew where Takuya was living, so it was entirely possible that the police would be waiting there to arrest him.

As he stood gazing at the black body of the train slowly recede from the end of the platform, he sensed that he wasn't ready to commit himself to fleeing once and for all. The Occupation would continue virtually indefinitely, so he would have to be prepared to be on the run for the rest of his days. That would mean drawing a line in his current life, and before he could do that there were certain things he must do.

He was carrying very little cash, and to make good his escape he would need at least some money. He would also need to destroy anything at home that might be used to trace him. Besides, unlikely as he was to see his parents and younger brother and sister again, he wanted to say goodbye to them before setting off. He had to make one last visit home. Despite the risk, the pistol in his rucksack fortified the decision to return. If the authorities were waiting for him he could resist, and if escape proved impossible, he could end it all on his own terms.

Takuya walked to the Nippoo Line platform. Under the pale station lights, another sea of people was crammed in from one end of the platform to the other, waiting for the incoming train. Spotting the scantest of spaces, Takuya sat down, placing his rucksack carefully between his knees. Beside him a young mother knelt changing her baby's diaper. As it lay faceup on the patchy concrete, the baby turned its eyes toward Takuya. Tiredness overcame him and he closed his eyes, letting his head drop forward. Perhaps because of the heat from the mass of bodies, the air on the platform was stifling, and in a moment Takuya had nodded off to sleep.

After a while he could sense people around him rising, and he too opened his eyes and got to his feet. The whistle sounded and the train shot steam over the tracks as it pulled in beside the platform. Utter confusion followed, with people trying to get on before any passengers could leave the train. An angry exchange of voices ensued between those trying to climb in through the windows and those who blocked their entry from inside. Pushed from every direction, Takuya just managed to edge his way on board by stepping on the footplate at the end of one car.

The train jolted forward. Before long the bustle of voices and activity gave way to the monotonous beat of the wheels against the joints in the tracks.

A squadron of moths fluttered around the electric light outside the washroom, bashing themselves relentlessly against the misted glass cover protecting the bulb. Just when Takuya thought that at least one moth had decided to sit, wings trembling, on the metal top of the light fitting, it took off again to resume butting against the light, powder from its wings dropping visibly after each assault.

At station after station more passengers jostled their way on board, and by now it was decidedly uncomfortable. The crush was so oppressive that the rucksack on his back was being pushed downward, and he felt himself losing his balance.

The train pulled into Usuki Station just before four in the morning. Takuya passed through the ticket gates and stepped out onto the road in the darkness. Usuki had not fully escaped the ravages of war, but rows of antiquated wooden houses still stood on both sides of the street, as befit the old castle town. The road wound through the town, with different buildings silhouetted around each bend. The moon was on the wane and the heavens teemed with stars. When he reached the outskirts he smelled salt in the air and heard the sound of waves breaking. Before long an expanse of sea opened up in front of him and he could make out a number of small boats moored to a little jetty.

Takuya made his way along the road beside the water. When he got near the ferry terminal he slipped under a canopy and sat down on the ground. Many people were sleeping there, lying or sitting under the eaves of the building. One man stirred and turned to look listlessly at Takuya, who had propped himself up against the wooden wall, pulling his service cap down over his face and shutting his eyes. He was feverish and his joints felt tired and weak. The pistol felt hard yet reassuring through the cloth of the rucksack in his lap. His grip on consciousness loosened and he slipped into a deep sleep.

The sun beat down on his face more and more intensely. Takuya opened his eyes and, still seated, gazed out across the water. His lower back felt cold and his legs were numb.

His sleeping companions were awake now, sitting or lying on the narrow pier.

Takuya pulled a paper bag from his rucksack and dropped a few dry roasted beans into his mouth. He hadn't had anything to eat since the afternoon of the previous day, but he wasn't really hungry.

As he chewed the beans his throat felt dry and he stood up, walked around to the rear of the building, drank some water from a tap and washed his face. He relieved himself on the dirt, and noticed that his urine was a yellowish brown color and frothy.

After a while a long line formed on the pier, and he got on the end. Lice crawled over the scalp of the young girl standing in front of him. As soon as one hid itself in her hair another would appear immediately somewhere else, lift its rear end slightly, then burrow in among the roots of the girl's hair.

After about an hour Takuya followed the others onto the boat bound for Yawatahama. Another forty-five minutes passed before the boat finally chugged laboriously away from the pier. Takuya found himself a corner of the deck near the bow and sat down.

The boat left the bay and passed close by Muku Island on the starboard side before entering Bungo Channel, where the smooth passage ended and a slight pitch and roll began.

Far off to the northwest he could make out Kunisaki Peninsula. The American B-29 bomber squadrons operating out of Saipan would often aim there to enter and leave Kyushu airspace. Aircraft spotters were stationed all over the peninsula, as well as electronic listening devices to detect the approach of incoming aircraft. In the anti-aircraft strategic operations room of the Western Regional Command they would process the information, immediately alert the air defense forces with a precise estimated point of incursion, and then provide them with a specific flight path to intercept the bombers.

As Takuya gazed at the peninsula, his mind returned to an incident involving the people of a fishing village at the tip of the landmass. Six months before the end of the war, a B-29 returning from a bombing mission was hit by fire from an anti-aircraft battery and brought down in the sea just off the fishing village. Three of its crew survived by parachuting into the water. The villagers put their boats out straightaway, found the bomber crewmen and roughly pulled them into the boats before dumping them on shore. One of the three fliers was utterly terrified, running at the nose and convulsing uncontrollably. The villagers—men, women and children—beat the crewmen mercilessly until one old fisherman picked up a harpoon and ran it through one of the Americans. The official report on the incident described the old man's action as motivated by "irrepressible feelings of indignation toward these outlaws who would violate the Imperial realm with the objective of slaughtering innocent old people, women and children."

In all likelihood U.S. military intelligence had already established that some fliers not only had survived their bomber going down, but had then been assaulted, and that one of their number had been killed. At the time, the actions of the villagers met with unquestioning approval, and they doubtless even felt something akin to pride about what had happened. But with the end of the war they too would be leaving for fear of pursuit by the American military.

Takuya stared toward the peninsula, now nothing more than a dim shadow in the distance. He realized that throughout the country countless people must be in the same predicament as he was.

The boat's pitch and roll remained slight, and all he really noticed was the monotonous beat of the engines. Before long Takuya fell asleep.

He was awakened by the sound of the boat's horn. The ferry pulled alongside a pier and a rope was thrown into the waiting arms of a man on shore. Takuya filed off the boat behind the other passengers.

Near the exit from the boat landing there were two policemen in washed-out uniforms watching the passengers disembark nervously. Those carrying luggage tried to pass by the police, but almost all were ordered to enter a holding pen set up to one side. They were confiscating any items, such as food, upon which the authorities had placed trading restrictions. The two policemen hardly glanced at Takuya and his battered rucksack as he walked past.

Takuya made his way to Yawatahama Station, where he again joined a long line to buy a ticket. More than an hour later his turn finally came, and he headed toward the platform, ticket in hand. The train was waiting, a steam engine with four passenger cars and two freight cars. As the passenger cars were already packed, he squeezed into a space on one of the freight cars.

The whistle sounded and the train slowly headed southward. Takuya sat back against the wall and stretched his legs out on the straw-covered floor. The train stopped at each station along the way, sometimes for quite a while at even the smallest of stations. Some of the floorboards in the carriage were missing, and he could see through to tufts of weeds growing among the sleepers and the stones on the tracks.

The sun was sliding down toward the west. Takuya felt the urge to relieve himself, so he grasped the sides of the opening through which he'd boarded, tiptoed clear of the low outer wall, and urinated off the moving train. The sky was a brilliant red and the far-off ridges were tinged with purple.

The sun went down and the freight car was plunged into darkness. That night the stars were out in force, the moon one day further on the wane. Every so often, when the train rushed past electric signals, the freight car was bathed in a blaze of light, providing a split second's respite from the all-encompassing night.

The train pressed along the coast, and just as Takuya thought he glimpsed the black expanse of the sea, the engine and its cars hurtled into a tunnel. From time to time he could make out what must have been lights from clusters of houses and fishing villages along the coast.

Takuya raised his head just enough to read the names on the passing station signs. He figured that the police might be keeping an eye on the station in the town next to his village, so he had made up his mind to leave the train one station short of his destination.

The train slowed and pulled to a halt beside the platform of a small station. He jumped down from the freight car, circled around it, crossed the tracks and walked through the ticket gates and out of the station. Avoiding the densely populated street, he made his way back along the railway line and started walking. The subtle bluish white of the steel tracks stretched before him into the distance, the clearly visible lights ahead reminding him that he had only a short distance to go.

When he was quite close to the town, he stepped down from the railway bed and walked along a path between two paddy fields. Perhaps because his eyes had become used to the dark, the waning moon seemed to illuminate everything around him. There was not a soul in sight.

Having skirted the town by following the paths through the paddy fields, he climbed up the pale white stone steps of the local shrine. Both the inner sanctuary and the shrine office were cloaked in darkness. He remembered coming here to pray with the villagers before joining the Imperial Army, standing among them in his university hat and uniform, the national flag slung over his shoulder. Pausing under the shrine gate, Takuya took off his service cap and bowed toward the inner sanctuary.

Leaving the precincts of the shrine and its conspicuous smell of bark, Takuya followed a narrow, sinuous track carved into the hill behind the shrine. He had walked this path so many times when he was small that he knew it like the back of his hand, so he made steady progress over the protruding roots and potholes.

Takuya stopped under the boughs of a large pine. Below him, by the light of the moon, he could see the cluster of dwellings that made up the village where his family lived. There were about thirty houses, dotted along either side of the winding path, strung out between the hill where he was standing and the low knoll directly opposite. The sun rose from behind the hill overlooking the shrine and set behind the knoll on the other side of the village, so sunrise was late and sunset was early. The village was blessed with soil good enough to offset the shorter sunlight hours, which provided quality crops for those working the land, especially mandarin oranges. The woods around the village were home to countless nightingales whose pleasant warbling filled the air from early spring until autumn. This gave the village its name, Ohshuku.

Takuya's eyes traced the barely visible path through the village down to the area around his family's house at the foot of the hill. No sign of anyone on the path and no movement around the house.

Two dogs appeared on the path, trotting more or less side by side. They passed directly beside the house, then crossed the wooden bridge over the little stream. Takuya relaxed somewhat—clearly the animals were not distracted by anything unusual around the house—but just in case, he pulled the pistol out of his rucksack, loaded it and stuffed it in his belt before making his way down the slope.

Scanning the area, he cut through an open patch of weeds and jumped over the little brook. A light was on inside his house. When he was near the back door he could tell from the sound of running water that either his mother or his younger sister was washing something in the kitchen.

Takuya opened the door. His mother, standing in front of the sink, turned and welcomed him home. In the back room, his father sat hunched forward under an electric lamp, his reading glasses perched on the end of his nose as he read a newspaper. Making haste was Takuya's most pressing concern. Before long the peaceful world his family enjoyed would be shattered by the arrival of those seeking his capture. If they came while Takuya was still at home, the disruption would be all the greater for his family.

His mother asked if he had eaten but Takuya went straight into the living room without answering. His father looked up. Takuya made sure his mother had gone back to her task at the sink before sitting down in front of his father.

In a quiet but deliberate tone, Takuya explained to his father how on August fifteenth of the previous year, after the broadcast of the Imperial rescript announcing Japan's surrender, he had taken part in the execution of American prisoners of war who had parachuted from disabled B-29 bombers. Now American military intelligence was on his trail and his capture was probably only a matter of time.

His father listened aghast.

"I have to go into hiding right away. I'm sorry . . . but can you give me some money please?" he said, fixing his eyes on the old man's face.

For a few seconds his father said nothing. Then, moving his gaze a fraction to the side, he whispered, "So you've killed an American."

"I cut his head off with my sword," replied Takuya.

The old man stayed sitting where he was, not moving a muscle. A mournful look had come over his face.

Takuya stood up and walked over to his own room, switching the light on as he stepped through the doorway. He pulled out his photo album, stripped it of all the photographs taken since he had reached adulthood, and put them and his letters, diaries, and address book in the wastebasket. This in hand, he stepped down onto the earth-floor section of the house and pushed the contents into the kitchen stove, lighting the paper with a match. His mother, not seeming to realize what Takuya was burning, dried her hands on her apron and walked into the living room. He pushed the poker into the fire, checking that the papers were reduced to ashes before stepping back into the living room.

There was a pile of notes on the low table in the middle of the room. To deal with the inflation that followed immediately after the war, the government had restricted the amount of money any householder could withdraw from a bank to three hundred yen per month, and one hundred yen per family member. Takuya knew that without the money on the table his family would inevitably struggle, yet he knelt down, took the notes, and stuffed them into the inside pocket of his jacket. His mother looked on apprehensively as she poured tea for the three of them. His father removed his glasses and sat motionless, staring vacantly into a corner.

Takuya rose to his feet and walked a couple of steps to the chest of drawers. He pulled out some socks and underwear and stuffed them into his rucksack along with a gray army blanket he took from the cupboard. His mother offered cups of green tea to the two men.

"Are you going somewhere?" asked his mother, looking inquisitively at her son.

"I have to go away. I'll be off in a few minutes," he replied as he tied the cord on his rucksack.

"What? Tonight? It's late," said his mother sharply.

"Where are Toshio and Chiyoko?" He thought he should see his brother and sister before he left.

"Chiyoko is in bed. She's coming down with a cold.

Toshio is on the night shift. He won't be home for another hour or so," replied his mother incredulously.

Takuya took a sip of the tea, picked up his rucksack, and got to his feet. He stepped into his shoes on the earth floor of the kitchen area.

"Why can't you go tomorrow?" asked his mother, her tone now slightly angry.

He swung his rucksack over his shoulder, opened the back door and stepped outside. His father slipped on his mother's clogs and followed him out. Takuya turned around to face his father, took off his service cap, and bowed his head.

"If they catch you they'll hang you, won't they?" the old man said hoarsely. Takuya nodded.

His father said, "Go to the Sayama family in Osaka. They'll help you." He handed his son a small parcel. Takuya nodded, then turned and walked away. He jumped over the little stream and headed straight across the grassy patch, onto the slope of the path up the hill. Like an animal trusting its natural instincts of self-preservation, Takuya decided that the safest way to return would be along the same path he had used to come to the village.

He climbed up the track at a brisk pace before pausing under the pine tree halfway up the hill. He looked down over the village, now half shrouded in a rising mist. The houses and the path were barely visible through the pale white murk, with only a few faint strips of light escaping from windows here and there.

Takuya opened up the little package his father had handed him. Under two layers of paper were some two dozen cigarettes. To a father who would cut cigarettes in thirds with a razor and then smoke them stuffed parsimoniously into a pipe, these must have been even more valuable than money.

He sat down on one of the exposed roots of the pine tree, put a cigarette in his mouth and lit it. Having managed to get in and out of the family house safely, he felt somewhat relieved. He'd disposed of his remaining belongings, he had enough money to tide him over for a while, and he had a loaded pistol tucked into his belt. Even if a would-be captor spotted the light from his cigarette and rushed to catch him, Takuya was confident he could escape in the darkness over the track to the shrine and then beyond.

Only the faint gurgling of the little stream below broke the silence. He gazed at the area across the stream where his family house was. It was a small house for five people. Takuya had been born and raised in that house, and had commuted to middle school from there on the advice of his public servant father. He had gone on to high school and then to Kyushu Imperial University, paying what he could of the tuition by tutoring and delivering newspapers. Upon graduation he had gone straight into the Imperial Army. His younger brother, Toshio, had just graduated from a community college. Takuya's father had let him go on to the university despite having to struggle on a meager salary from the town civic office because he expected that Takuya would eventually take over the role of family breadwinner. Never in his wildest dreams could he have imagined his son stealing away from the family home in the middle of the night.

Takuya pondered how his family's position might be affected in the days and months to come. If it became public that his son was suspected of war crimes, Takuya's father could lose the job he'd held for so many years. The police would likely be pitiless in their pursuit, and would no doubt maintain the strictest surveillance over his family. Even the other people in the village might turn cold toward them. Takuya took comfort in the thought that whatever happened, his family would understand that he had done nothing more than his duty as a military man, and that he was in no way a criminal. Surely that would give them the strength to endure the hardships that lay ahead, and he hoped that his brother and sister would look after his parents in his absence.

He stubbed out the remaining embers of the cigarette, took the pistol from his belt, unloaded it, and stuffed it between the folds in the blanket inside his rucksack. As he stood up and took one last look at his birthplace, the thought that he would likely never again set foot in the village, and just as likely never again see his brother and sister or his parents, saddened him.

Breathing in the cool night air, he set off again along the path. Around him in the darkness he could hear the chirps and cries of birds and the flutter of wings as they moved from branch to branch under the forest canopy.

He crossed through the precincts of the shrine and quickened his pace as he made his way along the paths between the paddy fields. The moon had progressed along its arc across the heavens, and by now was much higher in the sky. Takuya looked around as he pressed toward the station. Again, just to be safe, he wanted to board the train at least one stop down the line. A palpable feeling of satisfaction came over Takuya. At last he was on the run and, at least for the moment, in control of his own destiny. It was similar to the feeling of suspense he had felt in the pit of his stomach when he was the officer in charge of the anti-aircraft defense operations room.

The lights of an incoming train came into view as it skirted around a hill and then straightened out alongside the river. Zigzagging through the paddy fields, Takuya drew steadily toward the tracks.

The train rumbled forward, spilling only a modicum of light on the outside world. Takuya stopped and watched as the train turned to the left in a long arc. The engineer was obviously working hard feeding coal into the boiler, as Takuya could clearly see the red-tinged silhouette of a man repeatedly bending and twisting in front of the firebox.

Staring at the taillight of the last car as it moved into the distance, he started off again.

Chapter Three

The first time Takuya set eyes on a crew member of a B-29 Superfortress it made an indelible impression on him.

On June 16, 1944, the bombing attack on Kokura and Yawata by B-29 Superfortresses operating from airfields in China was the first to target mainland Japan.

The first news that long-range heavy American bombers had been seen in China had arrived on April second of that year, in a telegram from the Imperial Army Headquarters in China, and from then on there were continual reports that the U.S. Army Air Force was strengthening its presence around bases in China's Chengdu region. Recognizing that this buildup very likely harbingered attacks on targets in northern Kyushu, Imperial Headquarters followed the recommendation of the Western Regional Command and ordered the Nineteenth Air Force Division, stationed in the northern Kyushu area, to begin preparations for a strategic defense under the direction of Western Regional Headquarters. Comprising two squadrons, the Nineteenth Air Force Division boasted seventy of the latest fighter planes, and could put thirty in the air at any one time, the pilots all veterans with over five hundred hours in the air. They had carried out hours of practice at nighttime interception of heavy bombers, and had rehearsed their angles of attack again and again on a B-17 bomber that had been seized intact and airworthy in the early stages of the war in the Pacific. In conjunction with this preparation, anti-aircraft batteries were deployed in the northern Kyushu area, and joint exercises were carried out with the Air Force under the direction of the Western Command to provide the optimum defensive screen.

At Western Command Headquarters, an air defense intelligence unit was set up, and spotters posted to points all over the Korea Strait and Kyushu region, along with twenty-eight electronic detection stations. In addition, an intelligence network was established involving further spotters, electronic devices and naval vessels outside the defensive perimeter proper.

At 11:31 P.M. on June 15, 1944, a report came in to western headquarters from the electronic detection post on Cheju Island that unidentified aircraft were moving eastward. Forty-five minutes later, it was reported that the aircraft had crossed the line between Izuhara on Tsushima Island and the island of Fukue in the Gotoh Archipelago, and had then crossed the line between Izuhara and Hirado in western Kyushu, meaning that the aircraft were traveling at around four hundred kilometers an hour. At first it was thought that they might be Japanese spotter planes, but none were capable of flying at that speed, and as no friendly aircraft had been reported taking that flight path, it was judged that this intrusion must represent a force of enemy heavy bombers heading for the northern Kyushu area. The tactical operations center reacted by immediately contacting the Nineteenth Air Force Division and the Western Region anti-aircraft batteries on special hotlines, and Takuya, as duty officer, issued a full air-raid alert for the northern Kyushu area in the commander's name.

Forty-seven aircraft attacked Kokura and Yawata that night, but they met with such determined resistance from fighters that the bombing they did manage before heading back to China was virtually ineffective. Seven American bombers were shot down during the attack.

At Western Command Headquarters they had assumed that the intruders were B-17s, but inspections of wreckage of aircraft shot down near the town of Orio in Fukuoka Prefecture and Takasu in Wakamatsu City revealed that the planes had in fact been the latest American bomber, the B-29 Superfortress. A crew member's own film of B-29s during flight, discovered amid the wreckage of one plane, confirmed the appearance of the new aircraft.

Subsequently, raids by U.S. bombers based in China were made on Sasebo on July eighth; on Nagasaki on August eleventh; on Yawata on the twentieth and twenty-first; and on Ohmura on October twenty-fifth, November eleventh and twenty-first, December nineteenth and January sixth of the following year, but after that, the B-29 bases were switched to Saipan, and attacks from mainland China stopped.

During those months, assisted by pinpoint detection of incoming aircraft by electronic detection stations and spotters, the fighters ensured that bombing damage was kept to a minimum, shooting down a total of fifty-one bombers while losing only nine of their own.

Of the American crew members who baled out of their disabled aircraft, seventeen survived to be taken prisoner. These men were escorted by the *kempeitai* to defense headquarters in Tokyo.

Then B-29s operating from bases in Saipan began a concerted bombing campaign on urban targets such as Tokyo, Osaka and Nagoya, and in March 1945 they again turned their attention to the Kyushu region. The Nineteenth Air Force Division defense was so effective that the numbers of American fliers parachuting into captivity increased dramatically. Previously such prisoners of war had been escorted to camps in Tokyo by the *kempeitai*, but in early April the Army Ministry issued a directive to the Western Regional Command, delegating authority by stating that the crew members should be "handled as you see fit."

Six days after that order was received, a *kempeitai* truck carrying twenty-four American fliers pulled up at the rear entrance of the Western Regional Headquarters. The men were unloaded and shepherded in pairs into cells originally designed to hold local soldiers awaiting court-martial.

That evening, together with a staff officer from the tactical operations center, Takuya was assigned to guard the prisoners in the cells. The captive crewmen had just been given their evening meal trays, so when Takuya entered the holding cell area he saw tall, well-built men, some brown-haired and some blond, sitting in their cells eating rice balls flavored with barley, or munching on slices of pickled radish.

Takuya stood in the corridor and stared. The prisoners

behind the bars were the first American fliers he had ever set eyes upon.

As the officer in charge of the air defense tactical operations center, Takuya was among the most knowledgeable of the headquarters staff about the Superfortress bomber. Every time B-29 units intruded into the Kyushu region airspace, his staff painstakingly followed their incoming flight path and then tracked them as they headed off over the sea after completing their missions. Details such as the B-29's total wingspan of 43 meters, its wing surface area of 161.1 square meters, its fully laden weight of 47,000 kilograms, its top speed and altitude of 590 kilometers per hour at 9,500 meters, its maximum range of 8,159 kilometers with a 3-ton load of bombs, its ten 12.7-millimeter machine guns and one 20-millimeter cannon and its maximum bomb load of 8 tons, were etched into Takuya's mind, and he had become very familiar with the appearance of the Superfortress by examining photographs of the aircraft—both in flight and as wreckage on the ground.

Hours of meticulous study of the B-29 enabled Takuya to deduce the likely target by determining the speed and course of the incoming bombers, and then, by calculating the intruders' time spent in Japanese airspace, how much fuel remained, and from that, the probable course and timing of their escape route.

To Takuya and his colleagues who had followed the movements of these aircraft so faithfully since the previous year, the squadron of B-29s were a familiar, almost intimate presence. But now, seeing these American fliers standing and sitting on the other side of the bars, Takuya realized that all along his perception of the enemy had been limited to the airplane itself, and that somehow he had forgotten that there were human beings inside the aircraft.

He was surprised that most of them looked to be around twenty years of age, some as young as seventeen or eighteen. It shocked Takuya to think of the Superfortresses he had tracked so meticulously, constructed with the latest equipment and instruments, being manned by young men scarcely past their teens.

Some of the men were the same height as the average Japanese, but most were around six feet tall, and all were endowed with sturdy frames and well-muscled buttocks. To men used to a diet of meat, the rice balls and pickled radish must have hardly even qualified as food. Nevertheless, they munched away at their portions, licking grains of rice off their fingers and biting noisily into the pickles.

Their facial expressions varied. Most avoided eye contact with their captors, but some, whose face muscles were more relaxed, gazed imploringly toward Takuya and his colleague. Others cast frightened glances at them.

In the end cell a fair-haired man lay on a straw-filled futon on the concrete floor, eating a rice ball. A dark bruise from a blow to the face covered the area from his nose to the point of his right cheekbone, and bandaging on his rib cage was visible through his unbuttoned jacket.

"This one's been shot with a hunting rifle," whispered the slightly built legal officer, appearing suddenly from behind. Takuya looked into the cell as the lieutenant read out the report prepared by the kempeitai on this particular American prisoner. The man had been a crew member of a B-29 involved in a night raid on Yawata and Kokura on the twenty-seventh of March. When his plane was hit, he had parachuted into the woods near Ono in the Oita area. People from a nearby village saw this and ran out to find the man, then clubbed him with sticks before shooting him through the shoulder and right lung with a hunting rifle. Evidently the wounded flier had been handed over to the police by the villagers, and then on to the *kempeitai*, who had arranged for him to receive medical treatment before being transported to Western Regional Headquarters.

The man was obviously aware that people were watching him from the other side of the bars, but he ignored them, staring up at the ceiling as he ate. He seemed to Takuya to have long eyelashes and a remarkably pointed nose.

When he heard how the villagers had beaten and shot this American, Takuya realized that despite his being a military man, bound by duty to clash with the enemy, his own feelings of hostility toward the B-29 crews paled in comparison to the villagers. To this point, his contact with the enemy had been limited to information about aircraft detected by electronic listening devices or seen by spotters. In contrast, inhabitants of the mountain villages no doubt felt intense hatred when they saw B-29s flying over, as the objective of the bombers' mission was nothing less than the mass slaughter of civilians such as themselves. This hatred was the driving force behind their outbursts of violence toward the downed crew members.

It occurred to Takuya that these twenty-four American fliers in front of him were the embodiment of an enemy who had slaughtered untold numbers of his own people. They had come back again and again to devastate Japanese towns and cities, leaving behind countless dead and wounded civilians. The idea that these men were receiving rice balls despite the virtual exhaustion of food supplies for the average Japanese citizen stirred anger in Takuya toward those in headquarters responsible for such decisions.

"Look at the awful shoes they've got on," said the officer, with raw contempt in his eyes.

The prisoners' shoes were all made of cloth, reminiscent of those ordinarily worn when embarking on nothing more adventurous than a casual stroll. Some were torn at the seams. Judging from the obvious inexperience of the young men manning the bombers, and from their cheap footwear, Takuya wondered whether the much-vaunted American affluence was starting to wane.

After that day Takuya was never assigned to watch over the cells, but he took considerable interest in the decision about what to do with the men in them. No doubt the Army Ministry had delegated authority over the fliers because the intensified bombing attacks ruled out the transportation of prisoners to a central destination. This was evident from the concise wording of the order to "handle as you see fit." Even so, the precise meaning of "as you see fit" was unclear.

Takuya thought back to the first raid by North American B-25 medium bombers just four short months after the start of the war. A force of sixteen enemy planes had taken off from an aircraft carrier and flown at low altitude into the Tokyo and Yokohama area to bomb and strafe targets before retreating toward China, where eight crew members from two planes that crash-landed near Nanchang and Ningpo had been captured by the Imperial Army. A university student at the time, Takuya remembered reading in the newspaper how the captured fliers had been tried by a military court on charges of carrying out bombing attacks designed to kill and wound non-combatants in urban areas, and strafing defenseless schoolchildren and fishermen. All had been found guilty as charged and some were sentenced to death, others to terms of imprisonment. Takuya remembered seeing a photograph of the fliers wearing black hoods over their heads as they were led to their execution.

The fact that executions had been carried out after that raid surely left little room for debate over the fate of the twenty-four prisoners now in their custody. Once the B-29s moved their base of operations to Saipan, they began to concentrate their attacks on urban areas in general, as opposed to military installations and munitions factories. The Superfortresses gradually switched their targets, dropping huge quantities of incendiary bombs on medium-sized and even smaller towns outside the Kyushu and Shikoku areas. The extent of the devastation was immense; according to reports from central headquarters, more than one hundred thousand people had already been killed and over nine hundred thousand dwellings razed to the ground, affecting over two and a half million people. These fire raids were serious violations of the rules of war, so surely the handling of B-29 crew members would not be bound by provisions regarding the custody of normal prisoners of war.

Processing these prisoners began with interrogating them to acquire information which might help headquarters staff in their efforts against the bombing raids, and as the officer in charge of anti-aircraft intelligence Takuya observed the interrogations. There were general questions about the number of aircraft at the bases in Saipan, as well as about the runways and hangars, followed by more specific questions about the scale of various kinds of facilities and whether or not there were plans for expansion, and then questions about the capabilities of the B-29, its weak points, and the flight paths used to enter and leave Japanese airspace. The interrogations were carried out both individually and in groups, and the captured crew members replied to the questions posed by the interpreter, Lieutenant Shirasaka, with surprising candor. The content of their answers was consistent and there was no indication whatsoever that they had tried to coordinate their approach to the interrogation. All had some signs of fear in their eyes, but every so often one of them would shrug his shoulders, casually gesture with his hands, and even relax the muscles of his face slightly with the hint of a smile.

One nineteen-year-old crewman looked Shirasaka straight in the face and said he had taken part in twelve raids on cities such as Tokyo, Nagoya and Kobe. There was no mistaking the pride in his expression.

When asked to describe the scene inside the aircraft after dropping the bombs and turning back over the Pacific Ocean toward Saipan, one tall, blond twenty-two- or twenty-three-year-old smiled as he said something in quick reply. Shirasaka seemed momentarily taken aback, but then told the others that the American had said that on the way back the B-29 crew members would listen to jazz on the radio. Other fliers had replied to the same question by saying that crew members would show each other pornographic photos during the flight back to Saipan.

When he heard Shirasaka's translations of these almost nonchalant remarks Takuya felt the urge to lash out at the prisoner. While Takuya and his comrades had been doing their utmost to minimize the damage to their country, these fliers had been treating the bombing raids as sport. He had seen numerous photographs of wrecked B-29s with pictures of naked women painted on the fuselage beside flame-shaped marks indicating the number of bombing raids the aircraft had made, but now he knew that these men felt no remorse at all for having destroyed the lives and property of so many Japanese civilians.

Until that point, Takuya's image of the enemy had been focused upon the aircraft itself, but now the people who flew it, dropped the bombs and manned its weaponry became his enemy. If there were twelve crew per plane and one hundred bombers taking part in a raid, this represented no less than one thousand two hundred of the enemy bent on raining havoc and destruction upon Japanese citizens. Each time he heard that Japanese fighters were engaging the intruders, in his mind's eye he pictured the American machine gunners firing their weapons. When the bombers had reached their target, he imagined the bombardier looking through his sights and pressing the button to open the bomb bay.

With the American landings on Okinawa starting on March twenty-sixth, air raids on the Kyushu region intensified dramatically. The following day and night, there were attacks by over two hundred B-29s on munitions factories in the Kokura and Yawata areas. On the thirty-first approximately one hundred seventy Superfortresses attacked Air Force bases in Tachiarai, Kanoya and Ohmura. And on both the twenty-eighth and the twenty-ninth a force of approximately seven hundred thirty enemy warplanes operating from aircraft carriers attacked Air Force and naval targets on the Kyushu eastern coastline and in the areas of Kanoya, Kagoshima, Miyazaki and Sasebo.

Repeated raids on the Tokyo and Nagoya areas lasted into April, and on the sixteenth, locations in Kyushu were attacked by a combined force of about one hundred bombers and fighters. Raids targeting mainly Air Force installations in Kyushu were carried out on the seventeenth by approximately eighty B-29s, and then from the twenty-first to the twenty-ninth by a total of around eight hundred forty Superfortresses. Takuya was kept frantically busy collecting data and issuing air raid warnings.

During this time Takuya came to think that these twenty-four prisoners would likely all be executed, but on the afternoon of the seventeenth of May, he heard that two of the prisoners had been removed from the holding cells and transported by truck to the Faculty of Medicine at Kyushu Imperial University. The aide to the chief of staff who had told Takuya this said that one of the men was the crewman who had been shot through the lung with a hunting rifle and that the other was a flier who had serious problems with his digestive organs. Both, he said, were going to the University Hospital to receive treatment.

On hearing this, Takuya had thought that surely there was little need to take people to the hospital for medical treatment if they were to be executed soon, but he assumed there was some policy of having the prisoners as physically sound as possible at the time of the execution.

In May the air raids became even more relentless. In the eleven days between the third and the fourteenth around two hundred fifty B-29s and sixteen hundred fifty carrier-borne aircraft attacked targets all over Kyushu.

Just after midnight on the twenty-third, a force of twenty B-29s dropped a large number of mines in Kanmon Strait before heading east back over the ocean at around 1:40 A.M. In the air battle enacted under a canopy of stars the interceptors shot down four bombers and inflicted serious damage on four others. Takuya relieved one of his junior officers that night, taking off only his jacket before slipping into the bed in the rest area just off the operations room.

Awaking at eight the next morning, Takuya ate a simple meal of sorghum with barley rice before heading out to the tactical operations center, a concrete structure half set into the ground behind the headquarters building. On the way he saw two prisoners being led along the corridor and bout the back door. Both wore black cloth covers over their eyes and handcuffs locked in front of their bodies. They were accompanied by a doctor assigned to military duty and five soldiers carrying rifles with bayonets. The prisoners were pushed into an army truck parked in the yard behind the building and the rear flap of the truck's old tattered hood was pulled down and fastened. An army medical officer was with them, and Takuya guessed that these prisoners must also be going to the University Hospital, although there were no obvious signs that they were wounded or ill in any way.

The truck moved slowly out of the yard and down the slope, flicking up pieces of gravel with its rear tires.

By late May, Western Regional Headquarters staff were working frantically to tighten defenses in their region as part of Imperial Army Headquarters' decision to engage the enemy in a final decisive battle on the Japanese mainland.

In the Okinawa area, the American invasion force comprising around fourteen hundred warships and almost two hundred thousand army and navy personnel had already established a bridgehead on the island, but because of tenacious resistance the American advance was much slower than expected. In response to these landings, the Japanese mobilized a special attack force centered on the battleship *Yamato*, with kamikaze suicide units smashing relentlessly into the oncoming American warships. The kamikaze attacks represented a serious menace to the American force, but as their only feasible approach to Okinawa was a course following the line of the Nansei Islands, they were easily detected by radar, allowing the Americans to intercept them with large numbers of fighter planes. As a result, losses were significant and most planes in these units were shot down before they could reach their destination.

The American ground troops, assisted by bombardment from warships and strafing from fighters operating off aircraft carriers, gradually pushed forward, and while the Japanese provided determined opposition, they were eventually forced to retreat to the southwestern corner of the main island of Okinawa, where they were now playing out the final act of their resistance.

With the fall of Okinawa just days away, High Command predicted that the Americans would lose little time in turning their efforts toward a full-scale invasion of the Japanese mainland islands. Based on this assumption, plans were drawn up for the ultimate battle to defend the homeland, which centered on intense analysis of the enemy's situation. Essentially, the Americans' weak point was that they had to rely upon greatly extended supply lines stretching across the Pacific Ocean, and in contrast to previous battles where Japanese troops had little choice but to make desperate banzai charges on far-flung Pacific islands, it was hoped that in a defense of the mainland itself the Japanese would have a decided advantage. Levels of available manpower were still high, and if the local populace was united in its support of the defensive effort, it was thought that there was a significant chance of victory. Public declarations were made that this decisive battle would by no means be a defensive struggle, and that it was indeed nothing less than an all-out offensive against the enemy.

There were numerous opinions as to the specific locations the Americans would target for their invasion, but in the end it was assumed that they would most likely select the southern Kyushu area, as that would allow them to use Okinawan airfields to provide fighter cover for the ground troops. In terms of specific landing points, it was predicted that the invasion would primarily target the Miyazaki coastline, Ariake Bay and points on both the west and south coastlines of the Satsuma Peninsula.

Imperial Headquarters relocated a number of units from Honshu to Kyushu and placed them under the command of the Western Regional Headquarters. In accordance with orders from Tokyo, the extra troops were stationed around the locations judged most likely to bear the brunt of an invasion, and with the cooperation of local authorities and the general public work was begun on the construction of defensive positions. In addition, High Command dispatched a staff officer to Western Headquarters, and other young officers who had completed a course of training at the Imperial Army's Nakano "School" of subterfuge and intelligence activities were chosen to take command of, and begin tactical preparation for, units specifically designed to penetrate and disrupt the invading forces.

At the end of May, operating from repaired airfields in Okinawa, the Americans began a concentrated bombing offensive on the Kyushu area. On the twenty-eighth of May a combined force of around seventy bombers and fighters attacked targets all over southern Kyushu, and subsequently there were raids on both the second and third of June by a total of four hundred twenty carrier-borne aircraft, followed by another combined force of around three hundred bombers and fighters attacking Air Force facilities.

By now the struggle in Okinawa had reached its finale, with the surviving defenders and large numbers of civilian refugees retreating to make a last stand at the southernmost tip of the island. An air of gloom hung over the Western Regional Headquarters as staff listened in on the wireless communications of the defenders in Okinawa.

On the ninth of June, Takuya was told by the staff officer attached to the tactical operations center that eight of the American prisoners were dead. Evidently they were the ones who had been taken in pairs from the holding cells at headquarters to the faculty of medicine at Kyushu Imperial University.

He had been told that the first two captives transported to the University Hospital went to receive treatment, but it now seemed that they had actually been executed by medical staff. The prisoners had been sent to their deaths by staff officer Colonel Tahara and medical officer Haruki, who had decided to use prisoners condemned to death as guinea pigs in experiments for medical research, and so requested that Professor Iwase of the First Department of Surgery use his good offices to facilitate it.

The two prisoners were anesthetized with ether and carried to the anatomy laboratory, where they were laid on separate dissection tables. Professor Iwase operated to remove portions of the lobe of each of their lungs, but both men died from massive hemorrhaging when arteries were severed in the process. Subsequently, another six prisoners were brought to the anatomy laboratory, each undergoing surgery on their stomach, liver, or brain, the complete removal of the gallbladder, or injection of refined seawater into their arteries. All six died on the operating table during this experimental surgery, and evidently both staff officer Colonel Tahara and medical officer Haruki were present on each occasion.

"They were all well anesthetized and in a coma, so maybe it was a painless way to be executed," whispered staff officer Tahara, adding that the bodies had been cremated on Abura-yama and the ashes buried.

The other staff in the tactical operations center learned about the eight prisoners in the course of that day. Colonel Tahara instructed them not to mention what had happened to anyone else, telling them that the official stance was to be that these prisoners had been sent to Imperial Headquarters in Tokyo.

While Takuya felt no particular emotion about their death, it struck him that executing them by means of experimental surgery was rather unusual. Still, regardless of the method used, he did not falter in his belief that it was only natural that they should die for their sins. In fact, more than anything, he felt increasingly indignant that the remaining prisoners were still alive and depleting precious food stocks in the headquarters compound.

That evening, in the Headquarters Judicial Department, the remaining sixteen prisoners were arraigned before a formal military tribunal, and based on a reexamination of the transcripts of their interrogations it was confirmed that every one of the fliers had taken part in the bombing of urban targets. All were found guilty of charges of the murder of non-combatants and, based on the tenets of international law, all were sentenced to death.

The following day, another seventeen fliers who had been captured after parachuting from B-29s shot down over Kyushu were delivered to the rear entrance of the headquarters building in a *kempeitai* truck, then put into holding cells together with the previous batch of prisoners. The cells were too small to handle the influx of prisoners, however, and with four men in each it was almost impossible for all of them to lie down. So the Judicial Department moved immediately to convert the litigants' waiting room in their part of the building into an extra holding cell for some of the newcomers.

Over the next few days, Takuya found himself virtually confined to the tactical operations center. On the eighth of June, reconnaissance photographs taken by a plane flying over U.S. Army Air Force facilities on Okinawa were delivered to headquarters. They showed clearly that the airfields in north and central Okinawa, along with those on Ie Island, were fully operational, and confirmed the existence of at least five hundred twenty-three fighters and bombers. Takuya and his comrades all sensed that an intensification of the attacks on Kyushu was imminent, and that the stage was set for a decisive battle for the homeland.

On the evening of the eighteenth of June, the mood at Western Headquarters grew somber. On the radio they had heard the farewell message from Lieutenant-General Ushijima Mitsuru, commander of the Thirty-second Army in Okinawa, to Imperial Headquarters in Tokyo, informing his superiors that he was about to give his life for the Emperor's cause. "While our forces have fought with supreme heroism over the last two months, the enemy's overwhelming numerical superiority on land, sea and air means that this struggle has entered its closing stages. I most humbly report that the final preparations are in hand to lead those surviving soldiers to a glorious death."

The final battle for Okinawa was a struggle of apocalyptic proportions. According to reports from pilots of reconnaissance planes, the pummeling of the southern tip of the island by concentrated bombardment from warships, ground-based artillery and the air was such that it looked as though there had been a huge volcanic eruption, with streams of tracer bullets, raging fires and plumes of gray and black smoke all adding a macabre effect to the hellish scene. Since the battle for Saipan and the struggles for the islands across the North Pacific, non-combatants had been deeply embroiled in the conflict and had even lost their lives, together with the soldiers of each defending garrison. No doubt this tragedy had been repeated in Okinawa, with scores of old men, women and children losing their lives in the bombardment or choosing to die by their own hands.

That same night, the news came that a force of fifty

B-29s based in Saipan had attacked Hamamatsu and another thirty had raided the city of Yokkaichi, both attacks involving incendiaries and resulting in conflagrations so destructive that the targets were virtually burnt to cinders. To date, the number of aircraft that had been involved in bombing raids on targets in Japan had soared to over twenty thousand, claiming some four hundred thousand lives, destroying one million six hundred thousand homes and producing six million three hundred thousand refugees.

The next morning brought blue skies, with the meteorological office forecasting fine weather all over Kyushu. To those in the tactical operations center, this meant a drastically increased likelihood of large-scale bombing raids, and orders were issued for spotters to be particularly vigilant.

The daylight hours passed uneventfully, and when the sun dipped low in the evening the bright red of the western sky signaled that another fine day would follow. Within minutes of the sunset the sky was a mass of twinkling stars.

That night, at 7:50 P.M., a report came in from an electronic listening post set to cover the Hyuga coastline that a force of aircraft was heading northwest over that quadrant of the Kyushu defensive perimeter. As there was nothing to suggest that this represented friendly aircraft on patrol, Takuya immediately assumed that it was a force of B-29s from Saipan and issued an air raid warning to all areas of northern Kyushu.

Knowing that a lone Superfortress had flown a reconnaissance mission over Fukuoka the previous night, Takuya expected that before long Kyushu's largest city would bear the brunt of an attack. Thousands of tons of incendiaries had already reduced major urban centers such as Tokyo, Na-

goya and Osaka to scorched wastelands, but so far the attacks on Kyushu had mostly been limited to military targets
or munitions factories, and the island had been spared the
saturation raids aimed at razing towns and cities to the
ground. Okinawa was now completely in American hands,
and it was likely that their next move would be to obliterate
the cities of Kyushu before launching an invasion force onto
its beaches.

Red lights lit up on the otherwise darkened map of Kyushu on the wall of the operations room as one report after
another of aircraft intruding into the perimeter came in from
electronic listening points. The sequence of the lights indicated that the enemy bombers were proceeding on a
course toward northern Kyushu.

Processing the incoming data, Takuya realized that this
force, comprising around seventy aircraft, had split into two
separate groups somewhere over Hita City in Oita Prefecture. Around ten planes were continuing straight on their
original course while the other sixty had pulled around
slightly toward the northwest. It was presumed that the ten
aircraft were on what would be the fifth mission to drop
mines in the Kanmon Strait, adding to the total of eighty
planes that had already done so, and that the other, larger
group was heading for Fukuoka. When incoming reports
confirmed beyond a doubt that Fukuoka was indeed the target, the tactical operations center immediately issued an air
raid warning for the city and its environs.

The first word that intruders had entered Fukuoka airspace came from Dazaifu, just southeast of the metropolitan
area, and was soon followed by reports of aircraft sighted
above the city itself. Takuya knew from the data that the

bombers were deploying at a low level over the city, and by now would have started their bombing runs. The intruders appeared to have followed the line of the Nakagawa River into the city and then dropped their load on Shin-Yanagi-Machi and the Higashi-Nakasu area, resulting in a rash of reports of fires raging in those areas.

Those in the tactical operations center, a construction set partially into the ground and cased in reinforced concrete, were removed from the thunderous blasts of exploding bombs and the clamor of a city in the throes of incineration. Takuya and his fellow officers stood staring at the red lamps on the map of Kyushu stretched across one wall. The lights indicating the Fukuoka metropolitan area remained on, as did those positioned to represent Kanmon Strait, confirming that the smaller force of ten aircraft had reached its predicted target.

Takuya sat motionless, staring at the map on the wall in front of his desk. Although the sky above the headquarters building was swarming with enemy planes, and the area around their safe haven was likely engulfed in flames, the atmosphere within the operations room was almost tranquil. As the officer in charge of anti-aircraft intelligence, Takuya focused his attention solely on imparting information about the movements of enemy aircraft, and to him there was no difference between planes directly above and planes attacking some more distant region within the defensive perimeter.

Anti-aircraft batteries and searchlight units along the Kanmon Strait coastline had been reinforced in late May, and reports were now coming in that these units were engaging the Superfortresses dropping mines in shipping channels. Two hours after the initial sightings, these bombers seemed to have finished dropping their mines and had turned back south. Around the same time, reports began to come in that the force which had targeted Fukuoka had started to move in a southerly direction. The Superfortresses had clearly completed their mission and were heading back.

One by one, red lamps went out as the smaller force of intruders headed south from Kanmon Strait, then joined up again over Hita City with the main force which had ravaged Fukuoka, and changed to a course directly southeast. A short time later the aircraft were detected crossing the line between Hosojima in Miyazaki Prefecture and Sukumo in Kochi Prefecture. Similar reports followed from the listening points covering the line between Aojima farther down the Miyazaki coastline and Sukumo over in Shikoku, confirming that the bombers were about to disappear across the Hyuga Sea, heading back toward Saipan.

Orders were issued to give the "all-clear" for all areas of the Kyushu region, and only then was Takuya finally able to leave his desk. The enemy planes were officially recorded as having left Japanese airspace at 3:37 A.M., seven hours and forty minutes after the original intrusion.

Takuya wanted to see for himself what the situation was outside the confines of the operations room, and the lack of incoming reports meant in effect that he was finished for the night, so there was no reason not to slip away for a short time.

Delegating the remaining duties to his subordinates, Takuya hurried out of the room and down the dimly lit corridor. The moment he opened the double steel doors he was consumed by a deafening roar. Each breath of the superheated air seemed to scorch the inside of his lungs. Everything on the outside—the trees, the headquarters building, the ground—was bright red. Powerful gusts of wind lashed the branches of trees, and singed leaves danced across the ground.

Takuya stepped away from the doors and ran a few paces to the edge of the backyard, where he stopped, riveted by the terrifying scene before his eyes. Huge swirling towers of flames reached skyward from a seething conflagration covering an almost endless expanse below him. One thunderous roar followed another, resounding like waves crashing into a cliff, hurling sheets of fire and angry streams of sparks into the night sky. The barracks just to the west of where Takuya stood had been razed, and a frenzied swarm of soldiers were using hoses and buckets to throw water onto the headquarters building. The men were all tinged red, as everything else was in this inferno.

Takuya had heard reports about cities being devastated by incendiaries, but the destruction he was witnessing far surpassed anything he had ever imagined. Like masses of towering whitecaps soaring up from a tempestuous sea, myriad flames pressed upward from the heart of the blaze. His face felt as if it was on fire, and billows of smoke stung his eyes.

The city contained no military installations or munitions factories, so the purpose of the fire raid could only have been to kill and maim civilians and reduce their dwellings to ashes. The thought flashed through his mind that the scene he was witnessing had been repeated time and again in other cities and towns all over Japan, with innumerable non-combatants sent to their deaths.

The strength of interceptor fighter units in Kyushu had been dramatically reduced by U.S. bombing attacks on Air Force facilities in the area, and that night, too, there were no reports of Superfortresses being shot down by fighters, so the anti-aircraft batteries had more or less been left to defend the island's skies themselves.

Takuya blinked in pain as he gazed into the sea of flames.

Dawn came, and reports flooded into the tactical operations center outlining the damage in Fukuoka City. The fires had been extinguished by around 6 A.M., but apart from the Tenjin-machi and Hakozaki-machi areas, the entire city center had been burnt to the ground, with an estimated ten thousand dwellings destroyed in the fires. Early accounts suggested that the death toll would be extremely high.

Subsequent reports described citizens who had fled during the night returning to survey the smoldering embers of what had been their homes that morning. Later several dozen people had gathered around the front gate of the headquarters complex, clamoring for the execution of the captive fliers. There were said to be a large number of women among the crowd, and some of them had been weeping as they screamed out for the crewmen to be killed. No doubt they were infuriated at the thought that the Americans were still alive, safe from the blaze thanks to the firefighting efforts of the garrison. While the prisoners might have been afraid of being burned alive, they also might have felt some kind of satisfaction in knowing that it was their compatriots who were raining death and destruction on the city below.

Takuya had little difficulty understanding the thinking of the people who had gathered in front of the main gate. The prisoners not only had burned to death thousands of defenseless old men, women and children, but were now being kept alive with a steady supply of food that the average person in the street could only dream about. Surely there was no reason to let them live any longer.

"What the hell are they up to in headquarters? They should execute them as soon as possible," muttered Takuya to himself.

Medical officer Haruki's name was on the list of dead. In conjunction with his work as deputy head doctor at the military hospital adjacent to the headquarters building, he had been given the honorary rank of lieutenant, and he was attending a doctors' meeting when the air raid started the previous evening. Evidently he had been unable to make it to safety when their building caught fire. The fatality reports also listed the names of several non-commissioned officers and numerous enlisted men and civilian employees working at headquarters. Word also came in of family members of headquarters staff killed in the firestorms that had ravaged the city's residential areas.

Takuya could hear all this news being reported as he worked at his tasks as anti-aircraft intelligence officer. A deterioration in the weather meant that raids were unlikely from Saipan-based aircraft, but all the same, as the possibility of more short-range attacks by bombers flying up the line of the Nansei Islands from bases in Okinawa could not be ruled out, Takuya was paying particular attention to reports coming in from the southern Kyushu region.

He had just finished eating a late lunch of sorghum with barley rice and a piece of salted salmon when a staff officer from headquarters briskly entered his room, stepped up to Takuya's desk and announced in an impassioned voice, "It's on."

At Takuya's puzzled look, the lieutenant blurted out that eight of the prisoners in the holding cells were to be executed, and that this was to be carried out immediately in the courtyard of what used to be a girls' high school, directly behind the headquarters complex. Takuya was told that the prisoners were to be decapitated, and that headquarters staff with considerable experience in kendo had already been selected. Takuya was to arrange for two of his subordinates to be made available to participate in the executions.

Takuya nodded his understanding and beckoned the two sergeant-majors sitting on the other side of the room to come over to his desk. When he told them they would be taking part in the executions the color drained from their faces and a look of trepidation came to their eyes.

"One good clean blow. Don't let us down," growled Takuya.

The two men stood stiffly at attention as they barked their reply.

They were men with much longer service records than him, including combat experience at the front, and Takuya could not comprehend how they had the gall to show even a trace of apprehension at the mention of the executions. A rumor that one of the men had reputedly succeeded in beheading two Chinese prisoners with successive blows made their attitude all the more enraging to Takuya. Possibly their stint at office work on the home front had dulled the mental hardness they would have honed on the battlefield.

Takuya watched as they put on their service caps, picked up their swords and left the room. By now a weather report that rain had started to fall in southern Kyushu arrived. No sightings of any enemy aircraft were reported. Takuya's subordinates worked away collating the mountain of damage reports received from the city.

Around two o'clock the door opened and the two sergeant-majors walked in, one after the other. Takuya searched their faces for a hint of emotion. They were both pale but there was a strangely radiant look in their eyes. Their brows glistened with sweat as though they had come from vigorous exercise, and a tangible heat emanated from their bodies.

They stepped toward Takuya's desk and in an animated voice one reported, "Duties completed, sir!"

"How was it? Did all go well?" asked Takuya.

"Yes sir, we each executed one prisoner," replied one of the sergeant-majors, exhilaration lingering in his eyes.

"Well done," said Takuya, nodding his approval. The two soldiers returned to their desks and wiped their brows with handkerchiefs.

Takuya heard that four regular officers and three non-commissioned officers had taken part in the executions that day, including Lieutenant Howa Kotaro of the accounting department, the only man who had volunteered. A graduate of Tokyo University, Howa was a mild-mannered man known for writing beautiful tanka poetry. That morning he had hurried down through the smoldering ruins of the Koojiya-machi area of Fukuoka to the house where his mother lived. It had burned to the ground, so he waited for his mother to return from wherever she might have sheltered during the air raid. Casting his eyes over the sheets of roofing iron scattered across the ruins at the end of the little alleyway, he saw a black object resembling a scorched piece of timber. When he looked more closely and saw the gold-capped teeth showing from the gaping burnt hole that had once been a mouth, he realized that this was the charred corpse of his mother. He wrapped her body in a piece of singed straw matting and asked a neighbor to look after it until he could come back to give her a proper funeral. Howa returned to headquarters and began working silently on his mother's coffin. Those attached to the tactical operations center were in charge of organizing the executions, but when Howa heard that the American fliers were to be killed, the request he made to the staff officer in charge of the operations room to be allowed to take part was so compelling that his name was added to the list. A member of the kendo club during his university days, Howa was the only man among the executioners to decapitate two of the prisoners.

While these executions temporarily relieved the frustration Takuya felt, each time he stepped outside the operations room and caught the horrific sight of a city razed to the ground, irrepressible anger and pain welled up inside him. According to reports issued by the municipal office the death toll was over one thousand, with over fifty thousand families losing their homes and untold thousands of people injured in the conflagration. Everywhere there were dazed people sifting through the ashes of the scorched ruins. Here and there groups of men, women and children sat listlessly on the side of the road. Viewing such scenes, and contemplating the fact that these people were destitute because of the B-29 fire raids, he thought it an injustice that the remaining prisoners were still safe inside the headquarters building.

The day after the incendiary attack on Fukuoka City the key members of the headquarters staff moved to caves near Yamae Village in the Tsukushi area, leaving behind only those who worked in anti-aircraft intelligence. After the attack on Fukuoka, the U.S. Army Air Force started saturation bombing raids on other main cities and towns in Kyushu. First, on the twenty-ninth of June, a force of ten B-29s bombed Nobeoka in Miyazaki Prefecture, and then Kanoya in Kagoshima Prefecture. Beginning in July, attacks were made on cities and towns such as Kurume, Yatsushiro, Nagasaki, Kumamoto, Oita, Omuta and Miyazaki.

Among those left to work on anti-aircraft intelligence tension mounted as preparations were accelerated to meet the expected American landings on Kyushu. Defensive earthworks were being constructed everywhere, artillery pieces were placed in caves facing the sea and special kamikaze attack aircraft were hidden in underground shelters.

Plans were also being made to strengthen the mobile

reserve, the Thirty-sixth Army, by redeploying three infan-
try divisions from the Chugoku and Kinki areas, and by
moving the pride of the mainland defensive forces—two
elite armored divisions and six reserve divisions—from the
Kanto region to meet the enemy in Kyushu.

With such crucial forces being readied, Takuya began to
sense that the last decisive moments of the war were close
at hand. If the remaining armies played their part in the
grand defensive strategy prepared by Imperial Headquarters,
it would be possible for Japan to deal the American forces
a body blow. There was no doubting Japan's advantage in
terms of supply lines and the willingness of the ten million
inhabitants of Kyushu to do their utmost to contribute to
the success of the defensive effort. While Takuya did not
doubt that Japan would be victorious in the coming battles,
he now had a premonition that he himself would not live
through the titanic struggle about to unfold. At least, he
hoped, he would succumb knowing that he had inflicted the
greatest damage possible on the enemy.

That summer was much hotter than average. The steel
doors were usually pushed wide open, but because the tactical operations center was encased in a thick layer of reinforced concrete it was oppressively hot inside the building,
the lone fan sending a stream of hot air across the desks.
Sweat dripping from their brows, Takuya and his colleagues
went on processing incoming information and preparing the
anti-aircraft defenses for the next bombing raid.

Toward the end of July there was a dramatic increase in
the number of enemy aircraft participating in each attack.
On the twenty-eighth, a total of 3,210 planes attacked

targets in the Kanto, Tokai and Kinki regions, while around 650 carrier-borne planes made bombing and strafing sorties over Kyushu, some of the latter aircraft even going so far as to attack targets in the Korea Strait and the southern region of the Korean Peninsula. The following day a force of 361 carrier-borne bombers and fighters attacked targets in central and southern Kyushu. The same areas were attacked by 379 aircraft on the thirtieth, 148 planes on the first of August, and another 220 on the fifth of August. The fact that these attacks were concentrated on military and coastal installations was judged to be an indication that the American invasion of Kyushu was imminent, and Western Command Headquarters was on constant alert for news that the invasion fleet had been sighted.

Near-windless days with clear blue skies continued, and the morning temperatures on August sixth presaged another sweltering day. Forecasting another large-scale attack that day, the tactical operations center issued orders for no relaxation of the full-alert conditions in all areas of Kyushu.

Just after eight in the morning Takuya looked up from his desk, his attention caught by something distant, yet quite audible. It was strange, almost rending sound, as if a huge piece of paper had been violently ripped in two. Seconds later a palpable shock wave jolted the air. His subordinates all sat stock-still, looking bewildered. No enemy planes had been reported in Kyushu airspace, and the sound they had just heard was clearly different from anything they had yet experienced. Takuya thought it might have been a distant peal of thunder.

Later that day, as expected, a combined force of 180 bombers and fighters from bases in Okinawa attacked targets in southern Kyushu. Takuya was busy processing incoming reports and issuing orders to anti-aircraft defense units in that region.

That afternoon a communiqué from Imperial Headquarters in Tokyo notified them of the truth about the ominous sound and shock wave they had felt that morning. The message stated that at 8:15 A.M. two B-29s had intruded into Japanese airspace on a flight path over the Bungo Channel before sweeping northeast toward Hiroshima, where one of them had dropped a special new bomb which had caused extensive damage. It went on to advise that on no account was the extreme state of alert to be relaxed.

Western Command staff tried in vain to contact the Central Regional Command Headquarters in Hiroshima by telephone, but before long they received an updated report from Imperial Command in Tokyo to the effect that Hiroshima had been completely devastated, and tens of thousands of people killed or wounded. Considering that the sound and shock wave from the explosion had carried a full two hundred kilometers from Hiroshima to Fukuoka, Takuya and his colleagues realized that this bomb must possess a fearful destructive power far exceeding that of normal bomb technology.

Over the next several hours, a range of reports came in about the new bomb. Evidently, after being dropped it had descended attached to a parachute and had exploded several hundred meters above the ground, unleashing a blinding white flash of light, and punching a turbulent yellowish white mushroom-shaped cloud up to ten or twenty thousand meters into the sky.

On the next day, the seventh, Imperial Command made

a brief announcement on the radio regarding the bombing of Hiroshima. It stated that Hiroshima had been attacked by a small number of enemy B-29 aircraft and had suffered extensive damage, and that surveys were under way to establish the nature of the new weapon that had been used in this attack. While reports from Imperial Command had mentioned nothing that specific, information had now been received to the effect that this new weapon was probably what was being called an "atomic bomb." The term itself was new to Takuya and his staff, but from the incoming reports it was clear that the weapon's destructive power was something completely unprecedented.

That evening Colonel Tahara, the staff officer assigned to the tactical operations center, returned from a visit to Air Force Operational Command. The aircraft he had traveled in had stopped off in Hiroshima en route back to Fukuoka. He described how the city had been reduced to ruins, with corpses lying everywhere.

An air of oblivion hung over the staff in the headquarters building, and no one uttered a word. Each struggled to understand how, in addition to devastating fire raids on towns and cities throughout the country, the American military could unleash a new weapon of such destructive power, expressly designed to kill and maim a city's civilian population. As fresh reports trickled in detailing the situation in Hiroshima, Takuya felt with increasing conviction that the American military had ceased to recognize the Japanese as members of the human race. Evidently all the buildings had been demolished and a large portion of the city's population annihilated in an instant. How, thought Takuya, did the thinking behind this differ from the mass incineration of a nest of vermin?

Two days later, on the ninth of August, news of grave concern was received at headquarters. The Soviet Union not only had unilaterally renounced the Soviet-Japanese Neutrality Pact, but had also declared war on Japan. Red Army forces were already advancing across the border with Manchuria to engage the Kwantung Army. It was clear that the timing of the Soviet offensive was linked to the dropping of the atomic bomb on Hiroshima, and now that the Russians had commenced hostilities, Japan was surrounded by enemies on all sides. Takuya sensed that the day he would be called upon to give his life for his country was near.

That morning at 7:40 A.M. a report came in from electronic detection posts that enemy aircraft had crossed the line between Aoshima in Miyazaki Prefecture and Sukumo in Kochi Prefecture on Shikoku Island. Subsequently they were detected crossing the line between Hosojima in Miyazaki and Sukumo, so an alert was issued, followed by a full air raid warning. But as spotters reported no sightings of intruders in that area of Kyushu, the order to sound the all-clear was issued at 8:30 A.M. The high state of alert was maintained in the tactical operations center, however, and when a report was received from spotters on Kunisaki Peninsula that two Superfortresses had been seen heading westward, the order to sound the air raid sirens was reissued at 10:53 A.M.

The fact that only two B-29s were sighted, as in the attack three days earlier, pointed strongly to the likelihood that one of these intruders was carrying a bomb like the one that had devastated Hiroshima, and the course of the aircraft suggested that their target was a city in the northern Kyushu area.

The two aircraft continued west until they reached the city of Kokura, where they circled for a short time before the dense cloud cover evidently forced them to switch to a contingency target to the southwest. Judging from the aircrafts' flight path, the tactical operations center staff speculated that the target had been switched to the city of Nagasaki, so radio and telex messages were sent to that city straightaway, to warn them of the approaching bombers and advise that everyone should be ordered to evacuate immediately. To avoid panic among the populace, however, no mention was made of the possibility that the bombers were carrying the same type of weapon that had destroyed Hiroshima.

Virtually incapacitated with anxiety, Takuya and his colleagues sat mesmerized by the red lamps on the wall map indicating the movement of the two B-29s. The lamps showed the planes moving inexorably over the Ariake Sea and then down across the northern section of the Shimabara Peninsula, approaching Nagasaki from the northeast and seeming almost to stop for a moment over the city before heading east and then disappearing in the direction of Okinawa.

Queasy with foreboding, Takuya sat at his desk and waited for damage reports from Nagasaki. The only solace was the fact that they heard no sound and felt no shock wave like that experienced when the new bomb was dropped on Hiroshima.

Before long, however, his worst fears were realized. A

report came in from Ohmura Air Force Base that a brilliant white light had been seen a split second before a thunderous explosion had rocked the ground where they stood, and a huge mushroom-shaped cloud had risen skyward above Nagasaki. There was no further communication until, after some time, reports began flooding in that the city had suffered extensive damage. Some information even suggested that the bomb had been dropped on a residential area in the northern part of Nagasaki. The bomb was obviously like the one that had destroyed Hiroshima. The thought that the tragedy visited upon Hiroshima had now been reenacted in Nagasaki made it impossible for Takuya to remain sitting calmly at his desk.

Takuya heard that day that eight prisoners had been executed by headquarters staff who had been relocated to the caves near Yamae Village. Apparently the executions had been carried out in the woods near the municipal crematorium at Higashi-Abura-Yama, to the south of Fukuoka. Among the staff were a number of officers from the Nakano "School" of subterfuge, who were readying themselves to infiltrate enemy lines once the Americans landed. Evidently these men had used the blindfolded prisoners as targets to test the effectiveness of Taiwanese Takasago hunting bows provided by a local archery club, but with such poor results that the idea of using them as weapons was abandoned. After the abortive experiment, the prisoners were taken one by one into a small clearing deeper in the forest, where they were beheaded. The bodies were then wrapped in straw mats and buried in shallow graves.

Distracted by the thought of the devastation inflicted upon Nagasaki, and frantically busy processing data and issuing air raid warnings and all-clear signals following the attacks by a combined force of approximately three hundred bombers and fighters on targets all over Kyushu that day, Takuya registered what had happened to the American prisoners, but had no time to ponder their fate.

The following day, the tenth of August, another combined force of about 210 bombers and fighters darkened the skies of Kyushu, pummeling Kumamoto and Oita cities with incendiaries. In the course of two hours in the morning of the eleventh, over 150 aircraft wreaked havoc on the city of Kurume, destroying 4,500 homes. There was no respite from the raids; around 200 planes attacked Kyushu on the twelfth, followed by another 150 B-29s on the fourteenth. Massive quantities of bombs were dropped on Kyushu, and there were even reports of large numbers of schoolchildren being killed in relentless strafing by American fighter planes.

By now, the urban centers in Kyushu had been reduced to ashes, the munitions factories all but destroyed, and food supplies diminished to such an extent that those living in the vicinity of the main cities and towns were on the verge of starvation. The destruction of most port facilities, the dropping of large numbers of mines into the sea and the lurking menace of enemy submarines made maritime transport virtually impossible, and since late July the frequent sorties by U.S. fighters over southern Kyushu virtually ruled out rail transport during daylight hours.

On the evening of the fourteenth of August Takuya heard some news from a colleague that he could hardly believe. Evidently the man had been told by an officer attached to the headquarters staff in the caves at Yamae that there were indications that some central government officials were prepared to accept the unconditional terms of the Potsdam Declaration, and that at noon of the following day, the fifteenth, the Emperor would be making a radio announcement of momentous importance. Apparently the broadcast would either ratify the acceptance of the Declaration or reject it, with the likelihood of the former being very strong.

Surely this couldn't be true. The deployment of reinforcements, the preparation of weaponry and the strengthening of defenses around anticipated landing points in Kyushu had just been completed. Military installations and munitions factories might have been destroyed and cities razed, but there were still enough forces to repel the Americans. The decisive struggle was yet to come. Before its outcome was clear, it should be unthinkable to even consider surrendering.

This supposedly reliable information from government sources in Tokyo surely represented nothing more than the view of a small group of weak-kneed politicians, thought Takuya. These people should be exterminated immediately for harboring such treasonous thoughts on the eve of the decisive battle for the homeland.

Takuya felt flustered as he attended to his duties. When he heard the seemingly interminable reports of American bombers and fighters attacking targets across the entire country, he couldn't help but think that this talk of surrender must be only a groundless rumor. Enemy aircraft were just as active that day as any other day, with some 250 Superfortresses attacking targets in the Kanto, Fukushima and Niigata areas for several hours before midnight on the fourteenth. Within hours of those raids, a force of around

250 carrier-borne aircraft made yet another wave of strikes on the Kanto area in the two hours after sunrise. Surely, thought Takuya, if the suggestion that the purpose of the Emperor's impending radio broadcast was to accept the Potsdam Declaration carried any credence, this would have already been conveyed to the Allies, who would in turn have ordered the American military to cease hostilities. The fact that as many as 500 aircraft bombed and strafed targets all over the country from the night of the fourteenth into the early hours of the morning of the fifteenth was indeed proof that the war between the United States and Japan was continuing unabated.

After regaining his composure, Takuya slept a few hours before returning to his post at 8 A.M. The weather forecast called for clear skies and high temperatures, so more large-scale air raids were expected in the course of the day.

As noon approached Takuya ordered his staff to assemble in the operations room. The men stood rigidly to attention in two neat rows. As he waited for the broadcast he thought that the Emperor could only be taking this unprecedented step to deliver words of inspiration to his people before the curtain went up on the final decisive battle for the homeland.

The hands of the clock reached noon, and after a recording of the national anthem the Emperor's announcement began. It was delivered in a strange, high-pitched voice, reminding Takuya of the prayers he'd heard recited by Shinto priests. Takuya and his comrades stood stiffly at attention, their heads bowed. The sound quality of the radio in the tactical operations center was excellent, and the transmission of the Imperial rescript was heard clearly by all present.

Takuya listened intently to every word and lifted his head in disbelief on hearing the words, "We have ordered Our Government to communicate to the Governments of the United States, Great Britain, China and the Soviet Union that Our Empire accepts the provisions of their Joint Declaration." This "joint declaration" obviously referred to the Potsdam Declaration, acceptance of which meant nothing less than unconditional surrender.

Takuya felt suffocated. He couldn't believe this was happening. He had known that the war would someday come to an end, but he always thought Japan would be the victor. Beyond a doubt, the current fortunes of war clearly favored the enemy, and it might take months, even years, before the tide could be turned and victory claimed. By this stage, in his mind, the victory he had envisaged had been deferred to the distant future, which Takuya felt less and less confident he himself would see. In any case, it was unthinkable that the war would end in defeat. And to concede defeat in this fashion, before the decisive battle for the homeland, was even more inconceivable.

When the broadcast was finished Takuya felt faint, and he had to concentrate in order to prevent his knees from buckling. The Emperor's words echoed in his head, leaving no room for other thoughts.

Takuya's men all stared in his direction, the bewilderment on their faces revealing that they had failed to comprehend the broadcast. Some even seemed buoyed by the Emperor's words, having interpreted the message as a veiled exhortation to redouble their efforts on the eve of the final struggle. Clearly the men were confused by the absence of the word "defeat," and did not realize that Japan was about to surrender to the Allies.

Takuya turned toward the men, and in an emphatic tone said, "It's all over. We've lost." His strength draining from him, he shuffled back behind his desk and slumped into the chair.

The men remained as they were, staring at Takuya in disbelief. Moments later, muffled sobs could be heard from among the ranks. Propping his elbows on the desk, Takuya fixed his eyes firmly on the knots in its surface.

Eventually the men started to move silently back to their own desks.

Takuya pondered what would happen after the surrender. American warships would likely put U.S. troops ashore all over Japan, and enemy aircraft would swarm onto surviving airfields, delivering loads of soldiers and weapons. No doubt the victors would waste little time in menacing the populace into submission as they went on to occupy all of Japan. Physically sound males would be forcibly relocated to work somewhere as laborers, and young women would most likely become the object of the victors' sexual desires. Those who resisted, he thought, would be thrown into prison or shot.

As if time had stopped, Takuya remained immobilized in his chair, a look of physical and mental exhaustion on his face.

The door opened and staff officer Colonel Tahara came in. When one of the men called the room to attention, Takuya stood up and bowed to his superior.

The colonel walked up to Takuya. "You heard His Majesty's speech. We've had direct word from High Command that the Emperor has agreed to accept the Potsdam Declaration. Orders are to burn all documents at once," he said hurriedly before disappearing out the door.

Takuya turned to the men and barked out the order. "Burn every document in the building. Now go to it!"

That defeat could become a reality with such frightening ease dumbfounded Takuya. His notion of defeat had involved all branches of the Japanese Imperial forces choosing death before dishonor, and his own demise had been a certainty in that scenario. Now he realized that there was nothing left for him to do. By this point, High Command would have already conveyed the news about the cease-fire to the air defense spotters and the electronic aircraft-detection posts, so there would be no more incoming reports to process, no more data to assess, no more air raid alerts to issue. His duties had come to an end.

Unable to watch his men piling documents into boxes, Takuya left his desk and stepped out of the room. The corridor was busy with stern-faced men carrying armfuls of paper to and fro. Takuya walked down the hallway and out the steel doors at the rear of the building.

The sunlight was so brilliant that for a moment he felt dizzy. The trees, ground, and stones all seemed to be parched white. He was overcome by the sense that the air was seething, engulfing him in myriad tiny air bubbles. He squinted as he fought the dizziness. In the rear courtyard, the soldiers had already started a bonfire and were burning piles of the documents that had been carried out through the back door. The fire was burning fiercely now, the flames flickering like red cellophane in the midday sun.

From the rear entrance to the building, among the soldiers carrying bundles of paper, appeared the lieutenant from the legal affairs section, walking straight toward Takuya. His pursed lips were dry and his eyes glistened. Stopping in front of Takuya, he explained that the request he was about to make was an order from the major at High Command.

"The prisoners are to be executed. You are to provide two sergeant-majors to help. If we don't deal with the last of them before the enemy lands, they'll talk about what happened to the others. There are seventeen left. It's to be done straightaway. People from headquarters staff up near Yamae Village are waiting."

Takuya understood that to those at headquarters, the prisoners' execution was as important now as the burning of all the documents. They had already been sentenced to death, and the fact that hostilities had ceased had no bearing whatsoever on their execution.

While his duties collecting data and issuing air raid alerts had finished, Takuya once again sensed that his destiny was linked to that of the captured fliers. He had followed their actions for days and months on end, had busied himself to the very last collecting data about the aircraft that dropped the atomic bomb on Nagasaki, and had personally issued the air raid alert and the order to evacuate the city. Takuya had been in a position to know the full extent of the damage caused by the bombing and strafing attacks carried out by these men. So far his duties had assigned him a passive role, but that was all over now, and the time had come, he thought, to actively show his mettle. Only then would his duties be finished.

At the time of the previous two executions, Takuya's responsibilities as officer in charge of the tactical operations center had kept him at his post, but the Emperor's broadcast released him from all duties. I want to participate in the executions, he thought. Taking the life of one of the prisoners with his own hands would be his final duty. The lieutenant had said that the executions would be carried out in order to dispose of remaining evidence, but for Takuya it was something personal, something he had to do as the officer in charge of air defense intelligence.

"Count me in too," said Takuya.

The lieutenant nodded. "We'll be leaving soon," he said, then hastened back into the building.

Takuya followed him through the steel doors and hurried down the corridor to the air defense operations room, where he called out to one of the two sergeant-majors. He had been removing documents from a filing cabinet, but came quickly over to Takuya when his name was called. His expression did not change in the slightest when he was told that he was to take part in the executions. A firm "Yes sir" was all he said.

Takuya ordered the second of the sergeant-majors to continue burning the documents. Putting on his service cap, he walked out of the room followed by the first one.

The prisoners, blindfolded with black cloth and their hands tied together with twine, were being loaded onto the decks of two trucks outside. Takuya couldn't help being struck again by the physical size of the men in front of him.

A sergeant and a couple of lance corporals jumped up

after them and pulled down the canvas cover. The trucks moved off slowly past the bonfire and down the gentle slope.

Takuya and the sergeant-major stood under a cherry tree watching the hive of activity in the courtyard. Soldiers holding bundles of documents hurried out to throw the papers onto the fire, then scurried inside for more. The air was dead calm and there was no sound other than the snapping of the fire.

The major from High Command and the lieutenant from the legal affairs section stepped out of the rear entrance accompanied by two enlisted men. They joined Takuya watching the bonfire while the soldiers ran over toward the garage. Moments later, there was an engine's roar as a truck rounded the corner of the building and stopped in front of them. The major and the lieutenant jumped up into the cab while Takuya and his sergeant-major clambered onto the deck. A number of soldiers were already sitting on the deck holding shovels, picks and coils of rope.

The truck moved off. Takuya sat down on a coil of rope and looked at the charred ruins of the city from under the rolled-up canvas hood. Reports released in the days that followed would state that nine hundred fifty-three people had been killed in raids on Fukuoka, and over fourteen thousand homes had been destroyed. Over two thousand people had been killed in both Kagoshima and Yawata and more than twenty thousand in Nagasaki, with the estimated death toll from air raids on all eighteen cities in Kyushu close to forty thousand. The execution of a mere seventeen prisoners, he thought, would hardly temper the outrage caused by the deaths of so many defenseless civilians in the fire raids.

The truck moved past piles of rubble and burnt roofing iron that seemed almost to quiver in the hot haze. Takuya stared at the clouds of dust billowing behind the truck as it rumbled forward. The engine raced as the truck began to climb the winding road up the hill. Before long the grassy slopes on either side of the road gave way to forest, with branches of trees brushing noisily against the sides of the canvas hood.

Moments after the truck came out onto a flat stretch of road, it pulled over to one side, close against the face of the hill. Takuya jumped down off the rear deck and saw that another two trucks and a smaller, khaki-colored vehicle had arrived before them. A sergeant standing on the road saluted Takuya and pointed to the left, in the direction of a bamboo grove.

Takuya and the others stepped off the road and down onto the raised walkway between two paddy fields. A battery of frogs launched themselves into the still water as the men thudded down onto the path. Within seconds Takuya and his comrades had left the track and were walking through the dense thicket of bamboo beyond the paddy fields. Mosquitoes buzzed everywhere, and Takuya waved his hand busily from side to side to keep them away from his face.

When they emerged into a small clearing he saw some officers and enlisted men from headquarters. The prisoners, blindfolded with strips of black cloth tied around their heads, were sitting huddled on the grass. Takuya went over to them.

To a man, the prisoners sat dejectedly with their heads hung forward. One was mumbling what might have been prayers, and another, a very large man, was straining so hard against the rope around his wrists that he was almost toppling over.

Takuya noticed a group of officers from headquarters standing off to one side, a purplish-gray plume of cigarette smoke drifting straight up in the still air. When Takuya pulled out one of his cigarettes and lighted it with a match, a few other officers stepped over to him and lit theirs from the flame. Puffing on his cigarette, Takuya stood gazing at the prisoners. The shrill chirring of what seemed like thousands of cicadas in the undergrowth around the small clearing had reached a crescendo, intense as a summer cloudburst. The sickly-sweet smell of wet grass hung in the air and the whirring of insect wings could be heard close by.

"Shall we get it over with?" said the major, throwing his cigarette into the grass and turning toward Takuya.

Almost as if they had been waiting for him to issue the order, two enlisted men stepped forward and pulled a young blond prisoner to his feet. The American dwarfed the soldiers on each side of him.

They pulled him forward, but he moved uncertainly over the grass, his legs obviously weakened from the time in captivity. The major followed, and the four men soon disappeared into the forest.

Takuya stood smoking his cigarette, mesmerized by the noise of the cicadas. The glossy dark-green leaves of the trees glistened in the sunlight. As Takuya stared in the direction where the four men had gone, he felt sweat trickling down the small of his back.

Before long he noticed some movement among the trees. The major appeared, sword in hand, followed by the two enlisted men. The major's face was expressionless except for the faint hint of a smile at the corner of his mouth.

Another prisoner was dragged to his feet, a big, red-bearded man with a remarkably pointed nose. As soon as Takuya laid eyes on the muscular frame he instinctively stepped forward. He'd thought that this man had been executed long ago, but there was no mistaking it, this was one of the fliers who during the interrogations casually replied that the bomber crews relaxed by listening to jazz on the way back to base. The man was held on both sides by the two soldiers and led off toward the path into the woods. Takuya followed close behind. He could almost feel the eyes of the other officers and men burning into his back. It doesn't have to be perfect, he told himself. As long as I end this man's days.

The prisoner was taken along a narrow track through the vegetation. Takuya gazed fixedly at the man's thick neck muscles as he walked into the forest.

Chapter Four

Takuya dozed, slumped against the wooden wall of the freight car.

The previous night he'd walked along the coastal road as far as a town called Yoshida, but as the last train had left two hours earlier he had no choice but to sleep sitting on a bench in the cramped waiting room. Once dawn arrived, he awoke and caught the first train out. It stopped at Yawata-hama, where he would have to change trains, but the only thought in Takuya's mind at this stage was to put as much distance between himself and his hometown as possible.

Awakened by the shrill voice of the stationmaster, Takuya jumped down from the freight car onto the tracks. Afraid that there could be someone amid the throng in the station who might recognize him, Takuya pulled the peak of his service cap down over his eyes and found himself a place to sit down at the end of the platform.

The train that pulled in two hours later was only going as far as Matsuyama, but thirty minutes later, after waiting over two and a half hours on the platform, he boarded a train bound for the port of Takamatsu. On reaching his destination, Takuya left the station, walked over to the dimly lit pier, and joined the long line of people waiting to board the ferry. Moments after he felt himself being pushed down into the crowded hold of the vessel, it started to move away from the pier, and in what seemed a very short time the boat reached the port of Uno, where Takuya then boarded a train bound for Okayama. It was already one in the morning by the time he disembarked. He was exhausted, but at the same time relieved that he had managed to distance himself safely from his hometown and make it to Honshu. Being just one more anonymous body in a sea of strangers must offer some degree of immunity against arrest, he thought.

Following his father's advice, Takuya had decided to pay a visit to his mother's older brother. At the end of the war his uncle had been an army colonel, responsibile for overseeing military training in the country's schools. This uncle was obviously a central figure in his mother's family, and his father had often expressed his respect for the man's integrity, giving pride of place on the wall to a framed piece of his calligraphy. There seemed to be no doubt in his father's mind that the uncle would offer Takuya sanctuary.

Takuya too felt certain that his uncle would help. When he had joined the Imperial Army his uncle had written him a long letter, which, along with the usual congratulatory words and encouragement, seemed to Takuya to have been penned by someone who understood how it must feel to be joining the military without having had the chance to apply the knowledge he had gained at the university. An uncle who could show such understanding, thought Takuya, would surely empathize with his participation in the execution and help him avoid capture.

After a little less than an hour, the Osaka-bound overnight train pulled into the station, so packed that there were even passengers standing on the couplings between the engine and the front car. There was no way Takuya could get on board, and before long the train slowly wrenched itself free from the throng on the platform. Shortly after daybreak another Osaka-bound train arrived, but again every imaginable space was taken. People were even sitting half out of the windows or perched precariously on the steps below the doors. The next two trains, one just before noon and the other in the midafternoon, were just as crowded, and not until early evening did he manage to force himself into the window of a train from Okayama.

Stopping at every station, the train made its way down the line. After sunset, only scattered lights from houses and buildings could be seen from the window. It was after ten o'clock when the train finally reached Osaka.

Takuya followed the crowds through the turnstiles and out of the station. His eyes were met by a dark, overcast sky, without a glimmer of light from either the moon or the stars. Several rows of shacks had been thrown up as temporary housing directly in front of the station, and he could make out the soft glow of an electric light here and there. Beyond that it was pitch-dark.

Takuya knew that his uncle's house, which he had heard

had miraculously survived the incendiary raids, was about thirty minutes away by foot, but as that would involve negotiating his way in the dark through the burnt-out ruins, he decided to spend the night in the relative safety of the station. He walked back in and found the waiting area crammed with people. There were men, women, and even children sitting and lying everywhere, waiting to board a train the next day or simply homeless and seeking shelter.

Finding a space beside a pillar in the concourse, he slipped his rucksack off his shoulder and sat down on the concrete floor. He was feverish, and he felt a creeping numbness in his legs. A warm, sickly smell, not unlike that of urine, hung in the air.

Feeling hungry, Takuya pulled the sweet potato he had bought at Okayama Station out of his bag and took a bite. At first it seemed to have no taste at all, but as he chewed a subtle hint of sweetness reached his taste buds.

Suddenly, in the back of his mind, Takuya could hear a voice, a male voice, barely more audible than a whisper, muttering something like "Lucia" or "Luciana." It was the word the red-bearded man had been saying to himself over and over again as he sat slumped forward in the bamboo grove.

Takuya's mind drifted back to that scene at Abura-yama the previous August. He remembered clearly how anxious he had been about whether he would be able to cut through the man's thick neck. He had concentrated in kendo for martial arts in high school, and had continued training during his days as an officer cadet, but all opportunity for further honing his skills with a sword had ended when he was posted to headquarters in Kyushu. Occasionally he had attended to his army sword, polishing it and then checking and sharpening the blade, but only to the extent necessary to keep it presentable in a ceremonial sense.

He remembered how flies had buzzed around the prisoner's head. There had been a light brown birthmark on the man's neck, with a little tuft of soft red hair in the middle of it. Takuya remembered how he had stood there, imagining in his mind's eye the scene inside the bomber returning to base after a raid. When he pictured the red-haired man moving his head and shoulders to the rhythm of jazz, rage welled up inside him. This man must surrender his own life in return for those of the countless innocent civilians upon whom he had rained death and destruction.

Takuya remembered how the feeling of the sword striking something hard had jarred his palms. For some reason, the man's knees had jerked upward with the first blow, a huge gash opening in the back of his neck as his head drooped forward. Takuya had swung his sword down another two times, but somehow recalled it now as three. He remembered his surprise at the relative ease with which he had severed the man's head, and how he had immediately felt a wave of pride and satisfaction.

Had it been "Lucia" or "Luciana"? Takuya wondered as he sat there against the pillar, rucksack between his knees. Could it have been the man's girlfriend, or was it his mother? Was it "Lucia" or "Luciana"? Takuya whispered to himself. Or then again, maybe it was part of a prayer.

If the major from High Command had given the order, Takuya would have been quite prepared to dispatch another one, maybe even two, of the prisoners. He had stayed there in the clearing and watched as each successive prisoner was led out of the woods, forced to sit down on the grass, and then beheaded. Takuya remembered how high his emotions were running then. Watching, he had felt certain that he would do much better if he were asked to execute a second or even a third prisoner.

Suddenly, as Takuya sat there munching away slowly on the sweet potato, each bite tasting better than the last, a small hand was thrust in front of his face. He looked up to see a little boy, about ten years old, standing in front of him. The boy's shirt was open at the neck, revealing bones protruding from under tightly stretched skin, so thickly caked with grime that it could almost have been burnt-on coal tar. A foul smell drifted from his body.

The boy's face showed no sign of emotion. His cheeks were sunken and his arms and legs astonishingly thin, his distended belly proof that he was suffering from malnutrition. The outstretched hand came nearer to Takuya's face. The boy clearly wanted some of the sweet potato. It was the first time Takuya had seen a homeless waif up close, standing there in filthy bare feet and wearing a shirt with one sleeve ripped open at the shoulder.

As Takuya stared at the child, guilt welled up inside him. His inability to protect this child and others like him had robbed the boy of his family and forced him to beg from adults to stay alive. Important as the remainder of the potato might be to stave off his own hunger, Takuya felt somehow obliged to share with the boy.

As he was about to break the remaining sweet potato in half, the boy reached out and snatched it from his grip. Takuya looked up instantly, but the boy was already running as fast as his legs would carry him toward the exit. That he could find the reserves of energy to propel himself so nimbly and at such speed, around and over the human obstacle course littering the concrete floor and then out into the pitch-darkness beyond the exit, was cause for amazement.

It never crossed Takuya's mind to pursue him. He sat motionless, staring out into the gloom of the night. He could still visualize the glint in the boy's eyes, a look of bold cockiness more fitting for someone twice his age. His eyes bespoke a reserve of worldly cunning and vitality behind his wretched appearance. Neither child nor adult, the boy seemed more like some kind of exotic creature. It disturbed Takuya to think that in just eight short months since the end of the war, the burnt shells of Japan's major towns and cities had become home to such waifs.

His own hunger pangs subsiding somewhat, he imagined the boy crouching down like a wild animal in the darkness of the ruins, casting furtive glances to each side as he wolfed down the remaining sweet potato.

Was it "Lucia" or "Luciana"? Takuya whispered to himself. Leaning back against the pillar, he closed his eyes. Putting his arms through the shoulder straps of his rucksack, he secured the bag firmly on his knees. A deep sleep came over him.

There seemed to be no change in the outward appearance of his uncle's house, or at least what he could see of it over the high wooden fence around the property. A large wooden nameplate was attached to the gatepost, just as there had been the last time he visited. As he opened the gate he heard a bell ring just above his head. The garden was completely different from the way he remembered it. The only trees left standing were those hard up against the fence; the rest of the space had been dug up and turned into a vegetable patch. Buckets and straw mats lay here and there, and the ground was littered with pieces of fine straw. There was no sign of the shelves of bonsai trees that Takuya's uncle had been known to tend so lovingly.

Takuya slid open the front door. "Is anyone home?" he called out as he poked his head through into the entrance. A half dozen slippered footsteps from down the hallway brought his uncle out of the shadows. Takuya stiffened and bowed respectfully to the old man, but he couldn't help being taken aback at the physical change in his uncle. He had lost a great deal of weight and his skin was pale and pasty, as though he had aged years in a very short time. No doubt the want of proper food had taken its toll. There was no sign of the stalwart character he had once been known for. As Takuya followed the old man into the living room, he couldn't help noticing how bare the inside of the house was.

His wife had gone out to buy some food, the old man said. The veins on the back of his wizened hands stood out as he made a pot of green tea.

There was no way, Takuya thought, that he could entrust his life to this feeble-looking old man sitting in front of him. His father's faith that his uncle would provide safe haven had obviously been based on an image of the man before the war was lost, which clearly no longer held true.

But then again, he might be reading too much into his

uncle's physical appearance. Anyone who had spent so many years in the military would surely be stout of heart and mind, and not easily swayed by the vicissitudes of the last few years. Such a person would, he thought, be sympathetic to Takuya's role in the executions at Abura-yama, and therefore would help keep him safe from trial by the Allied authorities.

Takuya quickly came to the point in explaining the reason for his visit. His uncle sat silently, eyes half-closed in concentration, as he listened to his nephew's story. Takuya's description of his own part in the executions immediately prompted an unmistakable expression of surprise on the old man's face.

Explaining how his father had recommended that he seek his uncle's assistance, he finished by saying, "I need a place to hide."

The old man looked at Takuya. A gap must have appeared in the clouds, for a beam of sunlight shone in through the glass door facing onto the garden, highlighting the light brown spots running from his uncle's temple down the line of his cheekbone.

His uncle shifted his gaze from Takuya out to the garden. Takuya sat without moving and waited for his response.

Obviously unsettled, the older man adjusted his position before looking back at his nephew, and for a few seconds his mouth hung slightly open, as though he were at a loss for words. He moved his hands to his knees and straightened his back as he prepared to deliver a reply. Takuya sensed disappointment and a hint of contempt in his uncle's manner, and the reply he was given did nothing to dispel his unease.

"If you were acting on orders from higher-ranking officers, then you've got nothing to fear from the Occupation authorities. You say that they deny giving the order, but a true military man wouldn't lose his nerve and run. Stand up in court and tell your story. Make them see the truth of the matter. That is your only option."

His uncle was obviously putting on an act. His eyes betrayed a lack of conviction in the words he had chosen, and before he finished each sentence the momentum behind it faded away. The newspapers were full of stories about former military men being condemned to death for little more than acts of assault on prisoners of war, so his uncle would have been well aware that "standing up in court" would lead to nothing less than the death penalty. He was obviously afraid of having anything to do with someone on the run from the Allied authorities, and doubtless reluctant to stretch his limited food supply, even for a short time, by taking in another mouth to feed. Given his former position overseeing military education throughout the nation, he may even have feared the prospect of being investigated himself.

Takuya regretted having come all this way to visit his uncle. He had idled away the days since his demobilization, but during that time he had come to resent what he sensed was a growing tendency to denounce every aspect of the defunct Imperial Army. He felt something akin to pride for having been in the military, and was determined to live out the rest of his days without abandoning that feeling. The thought that his uncle could have served for so many years in uniform and then, with the war lost, become a completely different person made Takuya's blood boil.

He stared at his uncle, who had transferred his gaze out toward the garden. Most likely this man was barely justifying his place as the head of the family by working the meager garden plot to help feed his wife and only daughter. The thought that his father had gone so far as to frame and display a piece of the uncle's calligraphy, the words "great achievement" boldly proclaimed in resolute brushstrokes, now seemed rather comical.

Takuya stole a glance at the lintel behind his uncle, remembering how the last time he had visited it had featured a prized piece of calligraphy by an army general from the same village. It was gone, as was the photograph of his uncle resplendent in an army colonel's full-dress uniform. He had evidently chosen to purge himself of all vestiges of his military past, and in the process had been reduced to little more than a helpless old man, concerned solely with self-preservation.

"I'll give it some thought," said Takuya, feigning a pensive expression to avoid injuring what was left of his uncle's dignity.

"That's what you must do. I really think you must go to court and make them understand the truth," said the old man as he turned back to face his nephew.

There was no point in staying any longer, thought Takuya. He wished his uncle well and stood up to leave.

"Sorry I couldn't give you more than just a cup of tea, but with both my wife and daughter out . . . ," said his uncle as he led Takuya back toward the entrance, a hint of relief in his voice.

Takuya bowed once again before stepping out through the gate, and regretted as he did so that coming all this way to Osaka by train and boat and then train again had been such a foolish waste of time. He sighed in annoyance at the thought that this futile exercise had depleted his precious funds.

Fences from the surviving houses defined the road on both sides. Takuya walked back in the direction he had come from. Occasionally, broken sections of fence or low gates afforded him a view into people's gardens, which had all been transformed into vegetable plots. The pungent odor of human excrement reminded him of fields in the country-side.

He came out onto a main road. A tram swayed from side to side as it rattled noisily toward and then past him, men and women perched precariously on the steps at the front and rear of the carriage. The facades of the buildings on either side of the road suggested that they had once been shops, but now they were virtually deserted. Without exception, those who had ventured out into the streets were gaunt and pallid. Some wore suit jackets and trousers, obviously bought in better times to fit fleshier frames; others, equally gaunt, sat beside the road dolefully clutching matchstick knees.

When Takuya turned right at the intersection, a simple bridge slung over a canal drew his attention. Two large trucks were parked one behind the other on the near side of the bridge, and he stopped and stared at what was going on in front of them. A noisy crowd of people, most of them children, stood stretching out their palms toward those in the trucks. Two American soldiers sat in each of the trucks' cabs, and there were more, with submachine guns slung over their shoulders, seated on the flat decks behind. The white star insignia of the American army was clearly visible on the doors of the trucks.

Takuya had never seen U.S. Army vehicles or personnel up this close before. The soldier on the passenger side in the nearer of the two trucks had his back to Takuya and was leaning half out of the window space in the door, apparently talking to those sitting under the furled hood in the back. The soldier in the driver's seat was staring in Takuya's direction.

While Takuya knew that these trucks surely had nothing to do with his being on the same street, the thought that they could very well be making random checks on passersby made him want to turn back in the direction he had come from. Unnerved by the gaze of the soldier behind the wheel, Takuya shuffled to the side of the road as nonchalantly as he could and sat down on the dry ground, as though he were merely stopping to rest along his way. He wiped the sweat from his neck with a cloth from his pocket, then pulled out the bag of roasted beans he'd bought at a stall in front of the station and dropped a few into his mouth.

Takuya could hear the crowd of urchins still calling out to the soldiers, "Haroo, Haroo!" He could not understand what on earth these children, and the adults standing behind them, could be doing milling around American military trucks.

As he sat contemplating the scene, he saw something quite astounding. The children had stopped calling out, and were now bent over, frantically scrambling to grab something off the ground. The adults who had been bystanders seconds earlier were also racing helter-skelter among the children, picking things up off the road. The soldiers in the trucks were throwing small objects out from under the furled canvas hoods. A black soldier in one of the trucks purposefully threw them as far as he could, and one of his white comrades in the other truck watched in fits of laughter as adults and children responded to his feigned throws. Takuya sat there aghast, transfixed by what he saw.

The slamming of truck doors was followed by the roaring of engines. The two vehicles edged slowly forward one after the other, and the crowd of people moved with them, adults and children breaking into a run as the trucks accelerated off down the road. The adults gave up after a few paces, but many of the children tore past Takuya in hot pursuit.

The trucks swung left around the first corner, leaving the young pursuers in a cloud of dust. The children stopped chasing and gathered at the corner of the intersection, and others who had not run after the trucks hurried past Takuya to join them and wait for the next truckload of Americans to appear. Some of them were holding their booty: pieces of chewing gum, chocolate bars and even cigarettes.

Takuya gazed at the crowd of children squatting and standing on the street corner and mused that while the newspapers never mentioned this, it must occur every day, not just here but in all the towns and cities where the Occupation Forces were stationed.

Takuya got to his feet and started walking. Since the reduction of the cities of Japan to scorched wastelands was the work of the American military, Takuya reasoned that the representatives of those who had committed such heinous acts should be the object of nothing less than revulsion. The sight of adults grasping at candy in front of laughing Americans made Takuya feel sick to his stomach.

He crossed a bridge and faced an expanse of burnt ruins, a few makeshift shacks standing here and there to one side and a row of concrete buildings behind them. A cart pulled by an emaciated horse went past, soon to be overtaken by a man on a rickety old bicycle. There were potholes everywhere, and the cart and the bicycle bounced up and down as they moved along the road.

Takuya followed the road as far as the station. He couldn't shake the image of adults and children milling around the American army trucks. It was hard to believe that those people had lived through the same war he had.

Suddenly he was jolted by the unexpected sight of his brother, Toshio, walking toward him. Even though he was wearing his service cap pulled down low, there was no mistaking that tall, lean frame and distinctive gait. His brother had obviously noticed Takuya too, as he quickened his pace toward him. Takuya felt the energy draining from his body and a wave of foreboding struck him. His brother worked in their hometown post office and there was no chance that his work had brought him to Osaka, so he must have come to intercept Takuya at their uncle's house.

Takuya's brother stopped in front of him. His eyes were bloodshot from a sleepness night on the train and the pallor of his face betrayed weariness.

"The police came," he blurted out. "At five in the morning the day after you left. Two detectives and one constable." Takuya felt himself flinch. Obviously his brother had followed him all the way to Osaka to alert him to the danger.

"What did they say?" Takuya asked timidly.

"They said that they had an order from the Occupation authorities for you to report for questioning and that they'd come to take you in. They came inside and searched everywhere. Father told them you'd gone to visit a friend in Fukuoka and hadn't been back since. They told us to let them know if we heard from you or if you came home, but I reckon they'll have people watching the house," said the younger brother. His face was now ashen gray.

"Did the old man ask you to come and tell me?"

"Your mother and sister wanted me to as well. I got Mother to tell the people at work that I was sick and jumped on the train straightaway. They all said you should make sure you stay away from home," said his brother, in a voice barely more audible than a whisper.

"OK. Don't worry, I won't let them find me," replied Takuya, thinking of his good fortune in deciding to flee from his parents' house the night before the police turned up. His instincts had saved him then; if he stayed focused and alert, he should be able to keep one step ahead of the authorities.

"So you've been to Uncle's house, then?" said his brother, a hint of doubt in his tone.

"That was a waste of time. He said a military man should come forward and straighten things out. It is ridiculous. He's just scared to get involved. He won't take me in because he's too worried about himself," said Takuya, making a wry face.

"Really? Father told me to give him this sack of rice, since he was supposed to be looking after you and all," said Toshio disappointedly.

"He'll never let me stay there. All I got was a cup of

tea. You can leave the rice with me," said Takuya. The expression on his face was almost defiant.

Toshio put down his shoulder bag, pulled out a small cloth bag from inside, and put it into his older brother's rucksack.

"What will you do now?" asked Toshio as he began walking beside Takuya.

"I just remembered there's a fellow from Osaka University working in a steel company here. We were in the same officer training company. I may look him up while I'm here. He took part in executing the American airmen too," said Takuya without turning to look at his brother.

He felt an almost primordial instinct for self-preservation welling up inside him. Just as he had thought, the Occupation authorities had instructed the police to arrest him on suspicion of involvement in war crimes. Unable to return home, he would have to stay one step ahead of those who wanted to put him behind bars.

"You'd better get straight back home. If the police catch on to the fact that you're away, they'll realize you've gone to get in touch with me. You don't seem to have been followed, but you shouldn't be with me too long. Each of us should be on our way," said Takuya, stopping to face his brother.

Toshio nodded reluctantly.

"Give the folks my regards. I won't be in touch again. Just know that I'm lying low somewhere in Japan. Well, take care of yourself," said Takuya, squeezing his brother's arm affectionately before he turned away and crossed the road.

He strode along the path through the scorched ruins,

not once pausing to look back. Since the end of the war, he had received just one postcard from this man Himuro, who worked at a steel company, and in it he had suggested that Takuya visit his company if he should ever be in Osaka. The company would be located among the buildings in front of him, which had somehow escaped the ravages of the bombing. He couldn't come this close without letting his friend know how serious his situation had become.

All the same, visiting Himuro's company could be as dangerous as returning home. No doubt Himuro had also been cited as a suspected war criminal, and so he may have already been taken into custody. Or maybe he had gone into hiding. The police might even have the company under surveillance, which could put Takuya at risk if he were to visit the premises.

He paused for a few seconds on the road leading to the steel company, then resumed walking, his gait more decisive than before. A moment's thought had brought Takuya to the conclusion that if his friend had not yet been arrested, he could not allow himself to get this close and then leave without alerting Himuro to the impending danger. While Takuya had learned from Shirasaka about the arrests of those directly below the commander in chief, and that the search had already begun for those who had carried out the executions of B-29 crew members, it was unlikely indeed that his friend, distanced as he was in Osaka, would be aware of such developments, and there was no doubt that for Himuro too, capture could only mean the gallows. Takuya remembered how Himuro had married while still at the university, and how his friend carried a photograph of his young wife in the inside pocket of his uniform. Himuro had always been the archetypal outgoing student, a gregarious man known for his raucous laugh. He had beheaded the oldest of the American fliers, a well-built thirty-two-year-old man with deep-set, melancholy eyes.

Quite a number of people seemed to be moving in and out of the buildings here, considering the fact that virtually all factories had been destroyed and that the companies represented here would have long since lost all their production capacity. Maybe they were involved in buying and selling what was left of the factories and their contents.

Himuro's company office was housed in a relatively unscathed four-story building. Takuya paused on the footpath and peered inside. On the wall just past the entranceway he could see a piece of paper with the word "Reception" written on it, and a wizened old man sitting at a desk on the other side of a little window.

Takuya steeled himself and took a couple steps past the doorway, slid the glass window to one side at the reception desk and told the man he had come to see Himuro. When asked "What's your name?" he thought for a second before blurting out the name of his form master at primary school, "Masuoka Shigetaro." The grizzled old receptionist looked over his shoulder and grunted a couple of words to the young woman sitting behind him. She rose and walked out into the hallway and up the stairs. Himuro must still be around, thought Takuya.

People who were probably employees of Himuro's company came and went in the corridor. The range of the men's clothing was quite striking, from suits to army uniforms and overalls. One man even wore his spectacles held in place with black string looped around his ear to replace a missing sidepiece.

Before long Himuro appeared, looking skeptical as he walked down the stairs behind the young woman. He was wearing a baggy gray suit and had grown his hair quite long, parted neatly on the side.

When he recognized Takuya, his expression changed from suspicion to bewilderment.

"I've got to talk to you," said Takuya, leading his friend out the door and down the footpath. They turned past the bank at the corner and stopped on the other side of a telegraph pole. Himuro stood facing Takuya, waiting to be told the news.

"Things have taken a very serious turn," said Takuya, going on to explain what Shirasaka had told him.

Himuro's jaw dropped. Maybe it was the weight he had lost, but he looked a mere shadow of the man Takuya remembered from their army days.

"I was sure it would be all right. We didn't leave anything that could be used against us," said Himuro in a hollow voice.

"They worked out the number of prisoners that were handed over to headquarters from their investigations into the *kempeitai*. It seems the senior officers couldn't blow them off and ended up telling them everything. No doubt the authorities will even know about the prisoners sent to the university medical school. By now they'll know everything," said Takuya, watching Himuro's expression harden.

"I actually came here to Osaka hoping my uncle would give me a place to hide in the meantime, but my brother came after me and told me that before dawn yesterday the police came to my parents' house looking for me. When I heard that, I thought they'd have already arrested you, being here in a big city like this. They won't be far away. For all you know they could be waiting for you at home right now. If we're caught we'll go straight to the gallows, I assure you," said Takuya emphatically.

Himuro pressed his right hand hard against his forehead. "They could come looking for me at work," he said, glancing furtively over his shoulder.

"That's right. Who knows when they'll come. You know it's too risky to go back there. You've got to run for it now while you can," said Takuya. Himuro nodded in agreement, a look of utter consternation in his eyes.

"Where will you go?" asked Himuro.

"I don't know. Even if I did, I wouldn't tell you. It's best if we don't know where the other's going. If one of us is caught and ends up being tortured, the other could be found. Neither of us needs that. I'm not trusting anyone from here on out. There's no way I'll let them put a noose around my neck," said Takuya in a clear, determined tone. Himuro nodded again without replying.

"One thing, though, you'll need to get some money and food before you make your move away from here. This will help," said Takuya, pulling the carefully folded identification papers out of the inside pocket of his jacket.

"If you show this you can get a ration book. Shirasaka gave me two, so you can have one of them. He said to pretend to be from Okinawa and to say that going back there isn't an option. Just choose an Okinawan name and write it on the identification paper and you'll have a new identity."

Takuya handed the form to Himuro. The square, red ink seal of the Western Region's Hakata administration office for demobilized servicemen validated it as identification for the bearer.

"Well, I'd best be on my way. Don't get caught," said Takuya, squeezing Himuro's bony arm before he moved from behind the telegraph pole. He took half a dozen hurried steps across the road before stealing a glance back over his shoulder. Himuro had already gone.

Takuya headed back toward the scorched ruins. The area around the myriad makeshift huts in front of him was now teeming with people. To get to the station Takuya would have to make his way through the crowd, so he pulled his cap down over his eyes to hide as much of his face as possible. He had last shaved when he left home to go to Fukuoka, so he was now sporting a considerable beard.

As Takuya moved into the throng he heard a steady drone of hoarse male voices coming from shacks on both sides of the path. Once he had worked himself comfortably into the flow of the foot traffic, he craned his neck past the people walking alongside him to peer into the huts on each side of the road. He was taken aback at what he saw. There were people ladling curry from large pots into steaming bowls of rice and others selling steamed dumplings. People were handing over money in exchange for bowls of soup, vegetable porridge, and noodles, and between these food stalls others hawked mud-brown-colored cakes of soap or little open boxes of cigarettes. The pungent smells wafting from the stalls and the bustling air of the market left Takuya dazed as he arrived in front of the station.

There were men and women sitting everywhere on the cracked concrete floor inside the station hallway, some curled up sound asleep.

Takuya found space to sit on the concrete floor near the waiting room and started to think about where he should go. Maybe he should go north. If he headed up to Hokkaido he should be able to find work in a mine without too much trouble, but the thought of heading in that direction and having to go through Tokyo, where SCAP headquarters were, weighed on him heavily.

On the other hand, maybe he should go south. One of his juniors in the anti-aircraft tactical operations room had gone back to Tanegashima, and Takuya thought there was a good chance that this man would give him shelter. But getting there would involve passing through Kyushu, where the majority of those involved in the executions of the American fliers were living. Since investigations were likely to be centered in that region, it was difficult for Takuya to bring himself to head that way.

He tried to visualize the faces of comrades who hadn't taken part in the executions, searching his mind for someone who would still treat him the same way as during the war, despite the collapse of the military and the scarcity of food and other essentials.

The face of one man came to mind, a corporal named Nemoto Kosaku. He had been attached to the tactical operations room and had always gone out of his way for Takuya, ordering the soldiers on duty to change his bedding and make tea for him. Takuya remembered that Nemoto was from a little fishing village on Shoodo-shima in the eastern Inland Sea. An anti-aircraft observation post had been located there during the war, but as there had been no other military facilities to speak of, the Occupation Forces were unlikely to station troops there. The fact that it was a fishing village also meant that they would probably not want for food.

Takuya also recalled that Nemoto had said that he could get from his village to Kobe or Osaka by ferry, an option much more appealing to Takuya than another ride on a jam-packed train.

He stood up, walked over to the ticket window, and asked the way to the Osaka harbor ferry terminal.

"The pier?" muttered an old station worker sitting on a stool beside the entrance to the platforms, who then grudgingly told him the way.

Takuya started walking.

Chapter Five

The ferry left Osaka that afternoon and arrived in Kobe in the early evening. For some reason it didn't depart that night on schedule, but stayed in port until early the next morning. The boat was jammed with passengers, but Takuya managed to find a spot on the deck to curl up and close his eyes. Shutting out the light focused his mind on himself.

An itchy sensation spread slowly down his back and he felt as if tiny creatures were crawling over his skin. In the crush on the train from his hometown to Fukuoka his clothes must have become infested with lice.

The ferry trip was long. The boat steadily threaded its way past islands of all sizes and shapes, but Takuya paid little heed to the view beyond the bulwarks, lying on his side munching on a sweet potato.

He recalled the look of panic on Himuro's face and wondered whether his friend had taken his advice and fled straightaway rather than risking going back to work.

Maybe he had first tried to reach his wife to say goodbye. Either way, in very little time the authorities would move to make an arrest, and whatever happened from now on, Takuya felt good knowing he had at least been able to warn his friend and give him the identification papers to help him on his way.

Takuya was as bewildered as Himuro that they could have been found out despite their having left nothing that could be used against them. Colonel Tahara had called a meeting of all those involved in the executions to stress the importance of ensuring that not one scrap of evidence be left behind.

While none of the POWs were alive to testify, there remained the problem of what would happen if the Occupation Authorities found out that forty-one American fliers had been transferred from the *kempeitai* to the Western Command. Obviously, their first question then would be what had happened to these men. One suggestion was that they say the fliers had all burned to death when the camp in Fukuoka was destroyed in the incendiary raids. The problem with this, someone pointed out, was that they had no plausible explanation as to why the burnt bodies could not be exhumed for inspection.

After some debate, they had agreed that their story had to involve the bodies disappearing altogether. Colonel Tahara had already sworn to silence all those who participated in the executions, and had told them that if questioned, they were to say that the POWs had been sent to Tokyo. It was decided that the story should be an extension of that, namely that the prisoners had all died in transit; that given the already desperate situation in mid-July, and with no military aircraft available, two large fishing boats had been requisitioned to transport the men. They were all told to say that both fishing boats had sunk in the Kanmon Strait after striking American mines. If questioned further, they were to say that American aircraft and submarine activity had forced the two vessels to leave Hakata port under cover of darkness, and that no sooner had they entered Kanmon Strait than both boats hit mines and sank without a trace. That area of water had been literally peppered with mines and such incidents had become an everyday occurrence, so this story had the ring of plausibility.

The only thing left was the actual disposal of the bodies. While almost half had already been cremated and the rest buried in a nearby graveyard, it was decided that they should all be reduced to ashes and then disposed of at sea. The bodies were exhumed, hurriedly cremated and the ashes placed in urns before being loaded onto a truck, together with the ashes of those cremated earlier. Takuya rode in the front cab as the vehicle wound its way down to Hakata port. His charges sat on the wooden benches in the back of the truck, staring blankly anywhere but at the forty-one urns in front of them, now in bundles of threes and fours. A large fishing boat moored beside the pier was ready to take Takuya and his men far enough offshore to dispose of what the boat's crew had been told were boxes of military documents. About four kilometers east of Nokonoshima, Takuya ordered the forty-one urns dropped overboard.

By this time a wave of panic had struck northern Kyushu. Alarming rumors were circulating that within hours of the Emperor's radio broadcast announcing defeat, U.S.

troops had begun landing in Hakata Bay, that black American soldiers had ravaged large numbers of local women, and that the Soviet Pacific fleet was steaming ominously toward Kyushu. The hysteria was fanned when many local government offices instructed their female staff to evacuate immediately. Crowds of frantic people carrying their belongings swarmed the railway station in hopes of escaping to somewhere safe. The Moji Railway Company went so far as to bring in extra engineers and organize special train service to evacuate as many people as possible. Even on government-run lines, passengers were encouraged to board the trains without paying to save time, and instead were given tickets requiring payment when they got off at their destination. These trains headed inland from northern Kyushu several times each day. Those who couldn't force their way inside the cars through doors or windows clambered onto the roofs, sat amid the coal in the engine tender, or even stood precariously on the cowcatcher at the very front of the engine.

This confusion had reigned for a number of days, but Takuya and his comrades felt secure in the knowledge that they had disposed of all evidence linking them to the executions. Even if the American military did come and occupy the burnt ruins of Fukuoka, he thought, how on earth could they ever discover that forty-one fliers had actually been taken prisoner?

Such confidence meant that Shirasaka's revelation that the Americans knew everything about what had gone on came as a tremendous shock, of course, and the realization that they had seriously underestimated the Americans' investigation had filled Takuya with fear. At the same time, he felt ashamed that his lilly-livered superiors had been so quick to break down under interrogation and tell all about the experimental surgery and the beheading of the surviving POWs.

The Americans obviously were not an enemy to be taken lightly, thought Takuya. They certainly would have ordered the Japanese police to move to arrest those suspected of war crimes, and would surely be carrying out independent investigations as well.

The boat sounded its steam horn and its progress through the water slowed as the engine was eased back. Takuya sat up and turned his gaze in the direction of the prow. The shore was not far away now, and he could make out a number of houses nestled below the low hills behind the village. Lines of small boats were moored at the shoreline on both sides of a short jetty sticking out at a right angle into the water.

Slowly edging forward, the ferryboat drew up alongside the little pier. Crewmen threw ropes to others waiting on the jetty, and in a moment the boat had stopped moving altogether. Takuya stood up and looked toward the little village. Houses dotted both sides of the narrow, winding road that ran parallel to the shoreline. Almost all were of a single story. The slopes behind the village were covered with terraced fields.

Takuya thought this looked like an ideal place to hide. There was no chance of American trucks or jeeps appearing on the road, and a police station was highly improbable in a village this size. There would be very few people coming and going, so there was little chance of his being spotted by someone who might recognize him. Once familiar with the villagers, he thought, he should be able to get a job and stay here for quite some time.

Takuya followed the other passengers off the boat and onto the wooden pier. A group of old people were squatting on their haunches in one corner of the open area in front of the jetty, enjoying a chat with their friends in the sun. Takuya sauntered over in their direction and asked where he might find Nemoto Kosaku's house. Without moving to stand up, and almost in unison, two of the old men pointed down the road and explained how far to go and where to turn. Takuya followed their directions, walking up the road until he came to a small wooden bridge, which he crossed before turning right onto a narrow path up a slight slope. There were a number of houses along the path, but the old men had told Takuya that Nemoto's was the one on the left at the corner where this lane met the next. The house was quite small, but it had obviously originally been built to also serve as a shop, as just inside the door, on the lower concrete floor section of the house, was what seemed to be an old counter. There were no goods for sale.

Takuya hesitated. The outward appearance of Nemoto's house suggested that the family was not likely to be able to put him up and feed him. Having been turned away by his own uncle, Takuya thought he should not expect too much from Nemoto. Defeat had swept away the obligations required of a subordinate toward his superior.

But then again, he'd come not because he wanted to impose upon Nemoto's hospitality, but to ask for assistance in finding a job. Reminding himself that all he wanted to do was start a new life here, and that there was no way he would allow himself to become a burden on Nemoto, Takuya stepped across to the entranceway, slid the glass door to one side and called out to those inside.

A man's face appeared from behind the sliding door dividing the shop area from the rest of the house. It was Nemoto. His hair was cropped almost to his scalp, and he wore a vaguely suspicious look. The contrast between the bright sun outside and the shade inside seemed to make it difficult for him to identify who had arrived.

"It's Kiyohara," said Takuya, removing his service cap.

"Lieutenant!" said Nemoto, jumping to his feet. He was clearly taken aback, but his face was the same picture of loyalty it had always been during his days as a corporal under Takuya's command.

Stepping down from the raised tatami mats onto the concrete floor of what had once been the shop, Nemoto apologized for the poor state of the place, but invited Takuya to come through into the living area. When they were both inside, Nemoto knelt on the mats, placed his hands in front of him and bowed low in front of Takuya, thanking him for his kind guidance during their time together at headquarters. While this polite reception embarrassed Takuya, fond memories of Nemoto's devoted service during the war made him feel slightly more at ease.

As Nemoto moved to prepare a pot of green tea, his expression betrayed a growing suspicion as to the reason behind his guest's sudden appearance. When Nemoto knelt down again on the faded tatami mats, Takuya explained himself in a very calm, matter-of-fact manner. Nemoto, having known about Takuya's involvement in the executions, quickly grasped the seriousness of this being found out by the Occupation authorities.

Takuya went on to explain that he wanted to take refuge on this island and asked if Nemoto would help him find work.

Nemoto nodded and said, "I understand. You're welcome to stay here with us in the meantime. As you can see, it's not the poshest place in the world, but what little we have is yours to use as your own."

Takuya told him about the situation in Fukuoka and the other cities and towns he had seen from the trains in the last few days. As he described the bustle of the black market in Osaka, the village merchant in Nemoto seemed to rekindle and he keenly quizzed Takuya about the things being sold in the market. During the war his family had opened up a general store, but shortages of salable goods had eventually put them out of business.

"Do you think it will be long before we can start buying things to sell again?" asked Nemoto earnestly.

"I have no idea," replied Takuya. "Everybody seems to be stretched just getting enough food to feed themselves these days."

The rattle of the sliding glass door being pulled across was followed by the high-pitched voice of a small child. Nemoto got to his feet, stepped down onto the concrete floor and whispered something to those who had just come in. A little girl, five or six years old, peeped around the door at Takuya.

Nemoto stepped back into the room, followed first by a woman of about thirty and then by an elderly lady. He introduced the older woman as his mother and the younger as his wife. Both women bowed politely, the mother affording her guest a friendly smile as she thanked Takuya for the guidance and kindness he had shown her son during the war. It struck Takuya as somewhat unusual that despite the fact that Nemoto was no more than twenty-four or twenty-five years old, he was already married with a daughter not too far from primary-school age.

As the two women led the little girl through the door into the next room, Takuya leaned toward Nemoto and whispered that he did not want his part in the executions known to either of the women. Nemoto nodded without saying a word.

That evening, Takuya sat with Nemoto's family at the low table in the living room. The meal was rice gruel flavored with pieces of potato, along with a little pile of tiny dried fish on a separate plate. In front of Takuya there was also one egg. Despite Nemoto's protestations, Takuya moved the egg across beside the little girl's chopsticks.

After the meal Takuya pulled the bag of rice out of his rucksack and gave it to the younger of the two women. Nemoto tried to refuse this contribution also, but Takuya, insisting, pushed the bag back into the woman's hands and pulled the cords closed on his rucksack. Seemingly resigned to accepting the gift, Nemoto guided Takuya to the third room, at the back of the house. Laying himself down on a futon for the first time in longer than he cared to remember, and soothed by the sound of the waves on the shore, Takuya soon fell into a deep sleep.

The next morning Takuya awoke just after nine. Nemoto's wife was nowhere to be seen, and the grandmother was looking after the little girl. After eating a late breakfast he shut himself away again in his room at the back of the house. It was one thing to give them a bag of rice, but he knew there would likely be a limit to how long they would be prepared to share their food with him. While the older lady seemed quite happy with his presence, it was clear from the wife's expression that such feelings of generosity were not shared by all the family.

Occasionally Nemoto went out on an errand of one sort or another, but he seemed to spend most of his time sitting in the living room next to the old shop part of the house. Whenever Takuya came through to see him, he quickly placed an extra cushion on the tatami mat and poured him a cup of green tea. On one such occasion, ill at ease about having mistakenly assumed that Nemoto's being unmarried would make it easier to impose upon him, Takuya asked about the man's family.

"I didn't know you had a wife and child."

Nemoto looked down at the floor. "She's my older brother's wife. He was killed during the war, so when I came back it fell to me to look after his wife and child. His daughter being so young . . . I felt sorry for her," he said almost in a whisper.

The man's sincerity impressed Takuya, but more important, he now realized that the unusual situation the wife found herself in, losing her first husband and then being married to her brother-in-law, likely explained the hard, unfeeling look in her eyes.

"Any sort of work is fine, but can you help me get a job? I want to be able to look after myself, to rent my own place," said Takuya. While Nemoto didn't seem too concerned about putting Takuya up a little longer, his wife gave the impression that their guest was quickly outliving his welcome.

"Finding a place to live shouldn't be a problem, but work is another story. My wife has a job at a new salt refinery, built just a few months ago, but she's one of the lucky ones. There's just no work here. The fishermen don't have fuel to get their boats out onto the water, and you can see how I spend my time, twiddling my thumbs because I have nothing to sell. Some people loaded themselves up with dried fish and kelp and headed to Kobe to sell it, but most of them had it confiscated by the police when they arrived at the port, so no one goes anymore," explained Nemoto mournfully.

Takuya realized that he'd miscalculated the prospects of setting himself up in this village. There might be massive schools of fish in the sea, but that counted for nothing if the fishermen lacked the means to get out on the water. It probably wasn't only a problem of fuel, either. They were just as likely to be short of the tools of their trade as everyone else around them.

"This is a fishing village, so it's as good as dead if the fishermen can't get their boats out. All that's keeping their hopes up is the rumor that special fuel rationing might be on the way. During the war hardly any fishing was done, so the fishing beds around here are full of fish waiting to be caught. If the fishermen can get their boats out, the number of jobs will start to increase. I doubt there'll be anything where you could use your university training, but something will come up to get you by. You've just got to wait a little while," said Nemoto, trying to reassure his guest.

Nemoto was right; surely it couldn't be too long before fuel got through to the fishermen. With agriculture obviously going to take more time to recover, stimulating the fishing industry was the quickest way to relieve the food shortages. So the government must be endeavoring to get fuel to the fishermen to help them feed the nation. Once fuel reached the village, Takuya thought, it would surely come back to life, and Nemoto's cash register would start to ring once again.

The request that he wait until then obviously implied an invitation to accept their hospitality for a little while longer, and this thought gave Takuya the fortitude he needed to endure the unwelcoming looks Nemoto's wife would doubtless cast in his direction. With gruel served at virtually every meal, the sack of rice he had given to Nemoto's wife should cover his food needs for at least a month. Takuya remembered that during their time in the army he had often shared his sake or rice crackers with Nemoto, so it was only natural that the man should help him out now. As someone facing the prospect of death on the gallows, he must steel himself, he thought, and ignore the needs of others.

Takuya spent his days quietly in his room in the back of the house. Nemoto's wife was working on rotation with the other women of the village, two days on, then one day off. On her days off she either went down to the shore to look for kelp or shellfish, or went up into the woods behind the village to look for wild vegetables.

Soon Takuya noticed that Nemoto's family's attitude toward him seemed to be hardening from one day to the next. The wife avoided eye contact, and the grandmother's affable expression had disappeared altogether. Before he knew it, even Nemoto had less and less to say, and was clearly giving Takuya a wide berth by spending more time out of the house.

When eight days had passed since his arrival on the island, though he realized he was probably wasting his time, he asked Nemoto about his chances of finding a job. The family were finding it increasingly difficult to hide their annoyance at his presence, and this would obviously get worse the longer he stayed. He had to find his own place to live, he thought.

"Well, there isn't . . . ," said Nemoto, looking down to avoid Takuya's keen gaze.

"If there are no jobs at the moment, can you find me a place to live, then? I don't want to be a burden on your family," said Takuya, hearing the hint of sarcasm in his own voice.

"A burden?" Nemoto's reply was barely audible, as though the thought had never entered his mind. But there was no doubt, thought Takuya, that Nemoto had been scolded by his wife for taking Takuya into their house, and was starting to regret making the decision.

"It's a very small village," said Nemoto, still looking at the floor.

Takuya stared at the man's face, not quite understanding what he meant. Maybe this was a ploy to get the now unwelcome fugitive to leave his house.

"There are hardly ever any visitors in the village, so word spreads pretty quickly when someone does come. Everyone here knows that you're staying with us, and they're starting to ask me and my family a lot of questions. I've said that you're an officer from the same unit during the war, but . . ." Nemoto lifted his gaze. There was a glint in his eye as he plucked up the courage to speak his mind.

"I haven't said a word to my wife or my mother about you being on the run, but it's almost impossible to keep a secret on this island. I really don't think this is the best place for you to hide. I'm honored that you thought to come here, but I'm starting to worry about the risk involved for you," said Nemoto, his voice faltering at the end.

Obviously he wanted Takuya to leave, but at the same time the genuine concern in Nemoto's voice was unnerving. Takuya had not set foot outside Nemoto's house since the day he stepped off the ferry, but apparently the whole village was aware of his presence. He had thought a remote fishing village would be an ideal place to hide, but now he realized that in fact the opposite was the case. Obviously he would be a fool not to take Nemoto's comments seriously.

Takuya pictured the heaving throng at the black market stalls in Osaka. He remembered shouldering his way through the crowd as hawkers on both sides of the narrow lane plied their wares in rough, husky voices. With each step he'd been jostled and pushed by those around him, but he recalled how losing himself in the crowd produced a feeling of respite from the relentless tension of being on the run. Maybe he should seek refuge not in a quiet backwater, but in a big city where he could more easily conceal himself.

"When's the next boat out? I want to leave," said Takuya in an emphatic tone.

Nemoto looked taken aback, obviously worried that he had offended his guest. "So soon? Please stay a little longer," he said, a look of dismay in his eyes.

"No, you're right. It's not a good idea to stay here," replied Takuya.

Nemoto implored him not to leave in such a hurry, but soon he gave in to Takuya's persistence about the ferry, and got to his feet and left the house to check the departure details.

A wave of apprehension came over Takuya at the thought of what might have been a fatal error in judgment in coming to this village. No doubt the police search would be both wide-ranging and focused on places where Takuya would likely seek refuge, so the addresses of his relatives, friends, and those close to him during the war would become targets of investigation. Nemoto's place would almost certainly come up eventually as a possible point of refuge for the police to check out. What on earth had made him come to such a dangerous place?

Now completely unnerved, Takuya looked furtively out the window of the shop. A glum-looking old woman walked past with a young child clinging to her back. The sun beat down oppressively in the windless sky.

A few minutes later the glass door slid open and Nemoto stepped back into the house.

"There's a boat leaving for Kobe in thirty minutes. The next one after that is the day after tomorrow," he said kneeling down on the raised tatami mat.

"Good. I'll leave today," said Takuya, and walked through to the room at the back, where he grabbed his laundry off a piece of string drawn across the room and stuffed it into his rucksack. Nemoto looked anxious as Takuya stepped back into the living room, ready to go.

"Why don't you go on the next boat, two days from now? This is a bit sudden, isn't it?" said Nemoto frantically.

"No, I'll go now. Thanks for putting me up. Give your family my regards," said Takuya, sitting down to put on his shoes.

Nemoto went to the kitchen for a moment and returned with the bag of rice Takuya had brought. He placed it beside Takuya's rucksack, saying, "Please take this with you. It's unopened."

Takuya turned to look at Nemoto. "I really am indebted to you. Keep it," he said pushing the bag back into Nemoto's hands.

"No, I can't take it from you," said Nemoto, looking embarrassed.

Takuya started lacing up his shoes. He knew he would need the rice to keep himself going on the run, so he did want to take it with him if he could. Nemoto was prepared to give it back, and there was no good reason not to go along with that. Takuya stood up, knowing Nemoto had just stuffed the bag of rice into his rucksack.

"You're too kind, you know," he said, taking the rucksack from Nemoto and slinging it over his shoulder. He stepped outside and Nemoto followed, a couple of paces behind.

They walked down the road beside the river and crossed the bridge at the bottom of the slope. The water was running high so the tide must have come in. Half a dozen villagers standing on the jetty watched the two men approach. They smiled at Nemoto as he walked up to them. Takuya paid the fare to the man nearest the ferry and in return was given a piece of paper with the date and destination stamped on it in black ink. Holding the ticket, he turned and thanked Nemoto quietly for his kindness, and in response Nemoto stiffened to attention and bowed in military style.

The boat was brimming to the gunnels with passengers, many of them women and children. As Takuya threaded his way across the crowded deck to an empty spot near the prow, he wondered why so many of these people were carrying such large loads of luggage.

The boat's engine rumbled to life and the rope was pulled free from the wooden bollard on the jetty. Takuya stood and looked to where Nemoto was standing with the other men. He waved briefly and Nemoto responded with a less exaggerated bow. The boat's horn sounded as the ferry moved away from the shore, and in moments Takuya had a clear view of the village and the hills behind it.

As he sat down again the reality of being a fugitive sank in once more. His uncle had wanted nothing to do with him, and his friend Nemoto had been able to offer safe haven for barely a week. Nemoto had been as honest and genuine as he was during their army days together, but an unemployed man with a family couldn't be expected to feed another mouth. The fact that he'd returned Takuya's rice unopened was a measure of his sincerity.

The thought of having taken back the bag of rice unopened made Takuya feel ashamed. They might only have served him rice gruel, but the knowledge that he had eaten their food for almost ten days and then come away with his own rice still untouched made him cringe with embarrassment. As he gazed out over the sea, his conscience troubling him, he caught sight of something glistening on the surface of the water. Almost instantly he realized that it was a school of flying fish, just like the ones he'd seen so often in the Uwa Sea offshore from his home in Shikoku. The noise of the boat's engine had probably sent the frightened fish jumping out of the water, skimming the surface before disappearing again with a tiny splash. Once the boat rounded the cape the shimmering fish were no longer in sight.

Takuya pondered his destination. He now felt sure that it would be dangerous to rely on any of his army friends, so obviously he should seek refuge with someone the police would never connect with him.

Recalling the names of those who had sent him New Year cards, he remembered Fujisaki Masahito, a friend living in Kobe. Fujisaki had been one year behind him at the university, and the fact that his father was originally from Takuya's village had provided the two young men with something in common. The younger man had been exempted from military service on account of a bad limp, the result of a broken leg suffered in a fall down some stairs in his childhood. The New Year's message had said that their house had survived the bombing and that Fujisaki was helping to get the family business running again.

A police investigation would never trace him there, and as it was a big city he would have the advantage of being able to lose himself in the crowds. Takuya was inclined to pin his hopes of finding safe haven on Fujisaki, but having been turned away by his uncle and then having to leave Nemoto's house made him cautious. Wherever he went, it would be a struggle for people to ensure their own survival, let alone take on an outsider. And needless to say, being a fugitive was not going to help.

Gripped with anxiety, Takuya gazed out over the water until the glare off the sea made him squint and look away.

As his New Year card had suggested, Fujisaki's house was located in a residential pocket of Kobe which had largely survived the ravages of the fire raids. Takuya had visited him twice during his university days, and the house looked just as it had in those days. He approached the house but continued walking past, then stopped to lean on a lamppost at the next street corner. After standing there nonchalantly for some time he turned back, but walked past once again without lifting a hand to open the lattice door.

He crossed the street and paused under a lamppost, this time turning casually to look toward the Fujisaki house. He could see strands of light leaking out from the edges of the blinds covering the windows. Because of his friendship with Fujisaki at the university, Takuya felt sure that as long as he made the right approach and offered his bag of rice he could get them to put him up for at least a fortnight. But he wasn't so confident of Fujisaki's reaction if he told the full story about executing POWs and being on the run from the Occupation authorities.

Memories of his time at Nemoto's house flooded back. Even with such a sincere former subordinate he only managed to last eight days. Takuya tried hard to prepare himself first for astonishment and then for consternation at his unexpected appearance, feeling a foreboding he hadn't experienced when he'd left home for Osaka and then Shoodoshima. At first the prospect of being tried by a victors' kangaroo court had made him determined to elude detection at any cost, but now, after a mere ten days, he was starting to flinch at the thought of relying on others. He felt preyed on by a mental weakness that would have been unthinkable in his army days.

Fighting back the anxiety, Takuya remembered the pride he had felt in being a lieutenant in the Imperial Army, and shuddered to think of the pathetic figure he cut standing there under the lamppost. He stepped off the footpath and walked across the road toward the house, stopping in front of the latticed door to the entranceway before reaching to open it. Obviously it was locked from the inside, as it wouldn't budge.

He knocked lightly on the door frame. There was no reaction from within the house. When he knocked once more, a little louder, a light switched on inside the glass door of the entranceway.

"Who's there?" came a voice which Takuya recognized straightaway as Fujisaki's.

"It's Kiyohara. Remember me from the university?" said Takuya timidly.

He heard the scuffing of shoes over the concrete floor inside the entranceway before the latticed door opened in front of him.

"Kiyohara san!" said Fujisaki, astonishment coming over his bespectacled face as he stood silhouetted by the electric light behind him. Takuya felt himself wavering as to what to do next. Obviously he would be invited inside, but he knew in his heart that he must explain himself before imposing any further.

"Can we talk out here? I want to tell you something," said Takuya.

An incredulous look on his face, his friend stepped out beyond the latticed door and followed Takuya down the road. Takuya stopped and waited under the lamppost for Fujisaki, who stared speechlessly at his unheralded guest. Takuya looked earnestly into Fujisaki's eyes and explained that he had fled from his own home after being cited as a war criminal, and that he had gone to Shoodo-shima but had to leave for Kobe to escape the little fishing village's prying eyes.

"Can you put me up for four or five days, just until I find somewhere to hide? I've got some rice so I can feed myself," said Takuya. But deep down he wanted to say a couple of weeks, or even a couple of months.

"You executed Americans? They'll hang you for that, won't they?" said Fujisaki with a hint of fear in his eyes.

Takuya nodded, thinking that Fujisaki must be unnerved at the idea of harboring a fugitive.

"Anyway, come inside," said Fujisaki, grasping Takuya by the arm.

"No, not yet," he replied. "Even if you say it's all right, what's your family going to say? Your father in particular, he has to agree."

Fujisaki stood thinking for a moment, then nodded, let go of his friend's arm, and turned to walk back to his house. Takuya watched him push open the latticed door and disappear inside. Glancing furtively both ways down the dark street, Takuya hid himself in the shadows to one side of the lamppost. The streets were deserted and dead quiet. The stars in the sky above were pale specks of light.

Takuya waited, staring at the latticed door. After a while he started to visualize Fujisaki sitting in front of his father, deep in conversation.

Suddenly the lattice door opened and the two men seemed to step straight out of Takuya's dream onto the road. Fujisaki came out first, followed by his father, who was slightly balding on top but roughly the same height and physique as the son.

Takuya took off his army cap and bowed to the older man.

Fujisaki's father walked over to the lighted area under the lamppost. "Come inside," he said, grasping Takuya by the arm. He ushered him toward the house and gestured for Takuya to step through the latticed door ahead of him. Inside the entranceway, they took off their shoes and Takuya followed the other two down the narrow hallway to a three-tatami-mat-size room at the back of the house.

"It's not very big, but you're welcome to stay here until you decide on your next move," said Fujisaki's father amicably before disappearing down the hallway.

Takuya set his rucksack in a corner and sat down after Fujisaki had swung out his bad leg to lower himself to the tatami floor. Takuya leaned over and reached for his bag, from which he pulled out his sack of rice.

"I want you to take this," he said, offering it to Fujisaki.

"You don't have to do that," said his friend, fixing his eyes on the sack of rice.

"Take it, please, you couldn't put me up otherwise," said Takuya.

Fujisaki nodded and got to his feet in the same awkward fashion, then carried the bag of rice out of the room and down the hallway.

As Takuya pulled the cords tight on his rucksack he thought that he had done the right thing in taking the rice back from Nemoto. Without the rice he could never have brought himself to ask Fujisaki for shelter. Who knows, he thought, maybe the fact that he had his own supply of food had made the difference.

For the first time in days, he felt almost relaxed. He had given Fujisaki the equivalent of almost twenty-five days of government rice rations, which could always be blended with millet and other less nourishing grains.

The next morning Fujisaki asked Takuya to come through to the living room and meet the rest of the family. He was married, and by the look of his wife—a frail-looking, pale young woman twenty-one or twenty-two years of age—she was not far away from giving birth. Fujisaki's mother was as friendly and welcoming as she had been when Takuya visited them as a student. She was now a little thinner, and the wrinkles on her face revealed how much she had aged over the past five or six years. Her questions about Takuya's hometown and her description of the night air raids on Kobe lacked none of the lively spirit Takuya remembered her for. As he answered her questions, it occurred to him that maybe she had not been told the full story about his situation.

For breakfast they each had a bowl half full of rice gruel flavored with a couple of thin slices of radish. Takuya joined the others around the table, the silence broken only by the occasional clicking of chopsticks. As he ate, Takuya looked across to Fujisaki and his young wife. There was certainly nothing out of the ordinary for a man of twenty-five, one year Takuya's junior, to be married and about to become a father, and as a couple they certainly gave the impression of being contented with their lot. Nevertheless, Takuya couldn't help being surprised that this delicate young woman, surviving on rations barely sufficient to keep herself going, was expecting a child. How much nourishment would rice gruel and radish provide for the baby? he thought. The fact that she was about to have a baby was testimony not only to her toughness but also to the strength of the family for not seeing this as anything out of the ordinary.

Takuya whiled away the hours in his room from morning till night from that day on. He borrowed a razor from Fujisaki and shaved each morning, washing himself in the cold tap water. The area behind the house was part of the workshop grounds, and he could hear the noise of the machines from his room. Power outages were an everyday occurrence, and if he stood up, from the little window he could see the workers taking a rest, seated on wooden boxes.

Takuya felt quite uncomfortable at mealtimes. The usual fare was a combination of barley noodles, gruel and steamed bread flavored with the odd piece of sweet potato, but occasionally they would each have a whole sweet potato to themselves. Unlike other times, the atmosphere around the dining room table was decidedly gloomy, with no one speaking a word. Though he had handed over his bag of rice, each time he sat down for a meal Takuya felt guilty that he was depriving them of part of their rations.

There's no way I'll be able to stay here long, he thought. In a fortnight Fujisaki's family will end up thinking the same way as Nemoto's. If it was just a matter of time, he mused, he must do everything in his power to at least delay the inevitable.

He took the demobilized soldier certificate out of his inside pocket, recalling how Shirasaka had said that if he presented this to the local authorities he'd be able to get his share of rations. The false name he had written on it meant that it doubled as the papers he needed as a fugitive, and by using it to claim rations he could lessen the debt he owed the Fujisaki family.

Handing over the rice and giving them his ration allowance should at least help convince them of his goodwill on the food front, but spending every day in the little room at the back of the house doing nothing was undoubtedly a cause of annoyance to them. He was desperate to find a way to earn an income. But the country was overflowing with demobilized servicemen and residents returned from Japan's former colonial empire, and with virtually all of the country's industrial and commercial sector destroyed, there were very few potential employers. However much he might pound the pavement, there was little chance of finding work. Getting a job in Fujisaki's workshop would obviously be the best option by far.

That evening, Takuya asked Fujisaki if he could look at their university yearbook. Flipping through the pages, he found the name of a student from Okinawa, one year his senior, and began copying that man's name, Higa Seiichi, and Fujisaki's address, onto the demobilized soldier's card. When he had finished he called Fujisaki into his room and handed him the card, saying, "If you show this to the people at the ward office they'll issue you a ration book. It's a false name, but you can claim the rations and use them for your family."

Fujisaki looked down at the card and nodded.

"Then there's the matter of a job," said Takuya. He explained to his friend that if at all possible, he wanted to avoid being a freeloader, and so until he decided his next move, he wondered if there might be a job for him at Fujisaki's workshop.

Fujisaki seemed taken aback at the question, as his first reaction was to tilt his head to one side and knit his brow. But after a few moments he said, "That isn't something I can decide by myself, but I'll speak to my father and see what he says." With that he awkwardly got to his feet and left the room.

By now Takuya had come to realize that Fujisaki was a very different man from when he had been a student. At the university he had been lively and extroverted, offsetting the fact that he had one bad leg. He'd been a broad-minded young man, not overly carried away by issues, and not at all afraid to laugh out loud on occasion. There was little sign of those traits in Fujisaki anymore. Working in the family business obviously had brought about some change in the man, but his reaction to Takuya's request suggested that his heart wasn't in it and that he was just going through the motions. Even more worrisome was his increasingly brusque manner toward Takuya.

There was the sound of slippered footsteps in the hallway, and the door to Takuya's room slid open.

"I've talked with my father, and he says orders are so low that we already have too many staff in the workshop.

The only thing we might have for you to do would be making deliveries," Fujisaki said, standing in the doorway.

"That's fine," said Takuya, "as long as I've got something to do." He was a little uneasy, because it would of course take him out into the streets, but he could no longer bear the thought of doing nothing.

"I really feel bad having you do that sort of work," replied Fujisaki, with an embarrassed frown.

The next morning Takuya left the house with his demobilized soldier's card in his hand. Following Fujisaki's directions through the ruins, he soon came to the building being used as temporary municipal offices.

There was a hint of doubt in his mind as to whether the paper Shirasaka had given him would be safe to use, but the stamp of the Hakata office of the Western Region Demobilization Bureau looked real, and the middle-aged man at the desk did not hesitate as he filled in the name "Higa Seiichi" on the ration book.

Relieved at having passed the first hurdle, Takuya whispered his adopted name to himself. It sounded fine, almost suited him, he thought. From now on he would lead his life as Higa Seiichi. The name Kiyohara Takuya was a relic from his previous life and must play no part in his future.

When he got back to the house he handed the new ration book to Fujisaki, who was busy doing the company accounts in the living room.

"I have a favor to ask of you," Takuya said. "Since I'll be walking around the streets making deliveries, I want to change the way I look. I'm a bit nearsighted, so I think maybe I should start wearing glasses. Do you know of anywhere around here I can find them?" he asked.

Fujisaki tilted his head to one side for a few moments, looking thoughtful. "The glasses I wore when I was in junior high school should still be in the drawer. In those days I didn't wear strong lenses, so they might actually be about right for you. I'll have a look," he said, getting to his feet. He went up the narrow staircase across the hallway.

When he handed the glasses to Takuya, he said, "Well, they were there all right, but one sidepiece is missing." They were basic black-rimmed glasses, just the sort junior high school children would wear. The left sidepiece was missing and the lenses were covered in a thin layer of whitish-gray dust.

Takuya blew on the glasses and wiped them with the cloth he had tucked into his belt. They seemed a little strong, he thought, but probably wouldn't put any strain on his eyes. He attached some dark string to the left lens and hooked that over his ear. Everything looked a little blurred, almost as though he were looking at the outside world through a film of water.

Fujisaki led Takuya out the back door to the factory area. In the corrugated-iron workshop a middle-aged man was pushing a foot pedal on the cutting press, each movement of the machine producing a complete cardboard box ready to be folded into shape. A few meters away a man was brushing the company name in black ink through a thin metal stencil onto the cardboard, and beside him two women were working deftly to fold the boxes into shape and stack them to one side.

Takuya followed Fujisaki into the workshop, casually

greeting each of the workers as they looked up from their tasks. Fujisaki introduced him to the man working the press as being from Okinawa, adding that he would be handling deliveries from now on. The cart he would be using was standing to one side. It had obviously seen better days, the wheels leaning inward and rust creeping along the handle frame, but it looked as though it could carry a decent load.

The next morning Takuya piled the cart high with boxes and pulled it out through the back gate. After passing several rows of houses that had survived the bombing, he walked down a road through the ruins, the sea now visible on his right, with a number of what looked to be freighters anchored just offshore. The low range of hills straight ahead of him was covered in a thick blanket of green.

The cart creaked as it moved forward. Takuya slowly wound his way downhill, straining against the handle with every step to keep it from getting away from him. The effort required him to stop more and more often. Sweat poured down his brow and clouded the lenses of his glasses.

He finally reached his destination, an improvised warehouse owned by a box wholesaler, hastily constructed down on the reclaimed land along the wharves. A surly-looking old man sitting in a shack marked "Reception" took the delivery documents without saying a word. Then he got to his feet and waved his approval for the cart to be taken into the warehouse. After a quick check to see if the load matched the documents, the old man grunted that Takuya should unload his cargo and take it to the back of the big shed, where boxes and bags of all shapes and sizes were stacked neatly in rows.

After getting the man to stamp "Received" on the job

sheet, Takuya picked up the handle of his cart and started
to retrace his steps back to Fujisaki's factory. People seemed
to have already begun building shelters here and there
among the charred ruins. Men and women walked along the
road, others rode past him on bicycles. Determined to avoid
the gaze of passersby, Takuya fixed his eyes on the ground
ahead of him whenever someone approached.

No one around him could be trusted anymore, he
thought. Since the surrender, the newspapers had been full
of articles espousing the tenets of democracy, renouncing in
no uncertain terms anything to do with the politics or military of wartime Japan. The Imperial Army came in for the
strongest criticism. Without fail, the thrust of the commentary was that Japanese militarists had started the war and
that the Allied powers had no choice but to respond in kind.
Those charged with war crimes were cited as symbolizing
the outrages committed by the defunct Imperial Army, and
without exception those writing the articles supported the
measures being taken to rid the earth of such reprehensible
criminals. On the radio, too, there were broadcasts exposing
atrocities committed by the Imperial Army and denouncing
those charged with war crimes. Average Japanese citizens
were nothing less than victims of the war, with the blame
laid fairly and squarely on the military.

It seemed that in keeping with such media coverage, the
people in the streets would be falling into line with the intended message. Among the commentary of prominent leaders of public opinion there had even been drastic statements
to the effect that exacting the ultimate penalty upon war
criminals was a requisite for establishing democracy in Japan.

Assuming this represented the new rationale for society,

every passerby was potentially as much an enemy for Takuya as the Occupation authorities or the police. Any one of them who found out that he was charged with war crimes would likely go straight to the authorities. SCAP must know that he was on the run, so pictures of him would be on the walls of police stations all over the country. Each moment he spent in the public eye was fraught with danger. The only solace, he thought, was that confusion still reigned in Japan's cities. But that too might be false, for while the increase in crime involving vagrants and prostitutes must be keeping the police occupied, instructions from SCAP would surely give efforts to find and arrest war crimes suspects priority.

When he reached the factory Takuya sat down wearily on a straw mat inside the workshop door. He was exhausted from his labors, and the mental strain of cringing each time a passerby cast more than a glance in his direction had taken its toll. Still, he was pleased that the day's work had at least slightly lessened the weight of his debt to the Fujisakis.

Looking over that day's newspaper, he saw that eleven Allied nations, headed by the United States, had charged twenty-eight military and political leaders, including former prime minister Tojo Hideki, as class A war criminals. The acts in question were said to have been committed between 1928 and 1945, and fell into three major categories: conspiracy to commit aggression, aggression, and conventional war crimes, these being further broken down into fifty-five separate counts. The article went on to state that the International Military Tribunal would first be considering charges against the class A war criminals, and that the arrest and trial of the class B and C suspects would soon follow. It closed with the comment that "War criminals are the enemies of mankind, utterly repulsive beasts of violence."

As he read the list of the twenty-eight men charged as class A war criminals, he imagined that they would all end their days on the gallows. If this article was a reflection of current public opinion, the average Japanese citizen would agree with the Allied position, and therefore would no doubt call for the execution of all those implicated in such crimes. Who knows, he thought, maybe even Fujisaki and his family saw him as a "beast of violence" for his part in killing the American fliers. He felt uneasy at the thought that he might not be safe where he was after all.

Power shortages were still happening every day, and production in the workshop languished far short of that required to generate any sort of profit. In one sense, the lack of electricity was a blessing in disguise, as without sufficient paper the workshop could never run to full capacity anyway. Takuya's delivery duties were limited to once every three days, and he spent the rest of his time picking up cardboard offcuts and bundling them for fuel, or sweeping the workshop and the open space behind the house.

Fujisaki's mother's attitude toward Takuya had changed discernibly. She would often mutter, "Getting rations is all very well, but stretching what we get to feed us all isn't so easy." The amount and quality of the rations were now even worse than during the war. The designated staple, rice, was more often than not substituted with corn flour, potatoes or wheat bran, and the vegetable allocation was down to one giant radish per week, to be thinly sliced and divided up among several households. She would often head out to the countryside with her son, looking to barter a few articles of clothing for anything to help supplement the food rations.

The family's only entertainment was listening to the radio. Takuya sometimes joined them in the living room to listen to the day's broadcast. There were programs providing details about soldiers returning from overseas, and others for people seeking information on the whereabouts of family members in the armed forces. One interview with an economist made Takuya feel quite uncomfortable sitting in the living room with Fujisaki and his family.

The economist forecasted that Japan was on the verge of a food crisis of cataclysmic proportions, stating that the official current allocation of rice to each individual was barely enough to avoid starvation, and that when this absolute minimum requirement was calculated for the total population, the amount was almost twice the size of the previous year's total rice harvest. From this he deduced that at least ten million people would starve to death, and that most of these would be living in urban areas. He went on to say that no rice had reached Tokyo and other big cities for the last twenty days, and closed by saying that city residents must be prepared to eat grass to avoid starvation.

From around that time on, Fujisaki and his father both became increasingly taciturn. After dinner they would either play games or sit silently reading the newspaper, neither one looking at Takuya. Takuya had no choice but to excuse himself as soon as the family had finished eating dinner.

More often than not, Takuya would spend his evenings

sitting in the little room at the back, squashing the fleas crawling over his clothes. Most of those he dispatched were a pinkish color, gorged with blood which would spill out onto his fingernails as he crushed them. Occasionally he would hold a piece of underwear up to the electric light and find lines of delicately formed eggs, like tiny rosary beads, sitting neatly inside the stitching. He would pierce each of them individually with a needle before going on to check the next piece of clothing. Other times, after he had got under the covers in his futon, he would take the pistol out of his rucksack and caress it in the semidarkness. He would wipe the barrel with a cloth and test the tension of the trigger with his index finger. When he held it up to his nose, he could just detect the faint smell of gun oil.

In May, the opening of the International Military Tribunal for the Far East proceedings against class A war criminals received daily coverage in the newspapers.

The attitude of the Fujisaki family toward Takuya grew colder with each passing day. He had asked them to put him up for four or five days when he first arrived on their doorstep, but that was now more than three weeks ago. Though he was supposedly working to earn his keep, pulling the cart to the warehouse three times a week would hardly make the Fujisakis regard him as anything other than a freeloader. Almost certainly they would be reading the newspaper coverage of the war crimes trials, and by now could only see Takuya as an increasingly unwelcome guest.

On his way to the box wholesaler's warehouse one day in mid-May, as he guided his cart down a gentle slope in the middle of the ruins Takuya noticed two policemen walking up the road toward him. He regretted having pushed up the peak of his service cap so he could wipe the sweat off his brow, but he could hardly pull it down over his eyes now, so he simply tramped forward looking at the ground as though he were tired out.

He edged the cart farther over to the other side of the road, away from the approaching policemen, his heart pounding furiously as cold sweat poured down his neck.

The two policemen approached Takuya and his cart and then passed by, but just as he thought he was in the clear he heard one of the men say, "You there. Stop!"

Takuya felt the blood drain from his face, leaving him as white as a sheet. His first thought was to drop his cart and run for his life, but his feet were anchored to the spot. He turned half around sheepishly.

The closer of the two policemen stepped over to the cart and put one hand on the folded cardboard boxes. Bending over slightly, he lifted up each box in turn to look in the gaps between them.

"Where are these going?" he said, moving around in front of the cart. Takuya pulled the job slip from the inside pocket of his jacket, which was stuffed down in the load of cardboard boxes. He realized that the policeman was only checking to see if the load included any controlled goods, but all the same he was afraid that he might get a clear look at his face. The scar on his left cheek from where he'd gashed himself on a branch as he fell from a tree as a child was still clearly visible, and the thought that this might give him away started a wave of panic which threatened to overcome him.

"Anything other than boxes on the cart?" asked the policeman, casting only a cursory glance at the paper before switching his gaze back to Takuya's face.

"No, nothing else," said Takuya in a muffled voice.

The other policeman had by now moved around to the front of the cart. "You're as white as a sheet, and the sweat's streaming off you. Something wrong with you?" he said with a suspicious look in his eyes.

"Yeah . . . I came back from China with tuberculosis, but I have to work to buy food," said Takuya, pursing his parched lips.

"Tuberculosis?"

"Yeah."

"What's your name?"

"Higa Seiichi."

"Higa?" said the policeman in a skeptical tone.

"Hi-ga," said Takuya, tracing the characters out on top of the cardboard boxes. "From Okinawa. It's a common name there."

"Okinawa?" replied the policeman, apparently happy to leave it at that. The stern look had melted from his face as he ran his eyes once more over the cart and its load.

Satisfied that all was in order, he turned back to Takuya. "You went white as a sheet when you saw us coming. So we thought something was amiss. If you're just sick then we won't hold you up any longer. On your way," he said, and nodded to his colleague that they too should be off.

Takuya picked up the bar at the front of the cart and stepped off down the slope, feeling another deluge of sweat stream down his face. The policemen had probably mellowed at the mention of Okinawa, the only part of the Japanese homeland where combat had taken place. Shirasaka's advice had paid off in an unexpected way.

As Takuya maneuvered the cart down the gentle incline, he chastised himself for the stupidity of his behavior with the police. It was pathetic that losing his composure had obviously made them suspicious and led to their interrogating him. Since being warned by Shirasaka in Fukuoka that he should flee, he had been back to his hometown and then on to Shoodo-shima after traveling through Osaka, and had caught sight of policemen on any number of occasions, but never had he been as intimidated as today. The incident with these two policemen brought home how much his nerve had weakened in this last month on the run. If he panicked every time he came across the police, it wouldn't be long before he gave himself away and was arrested. He longed to somehow instill in himself the backbone he had before the war ended.

Takuya recalled the policeman's intent gaze as he asked the questions. While the glasses he'd borrowed from Fujisaki might have helped obscure it from view, the officer must have caught at least a fleeting glimpse of the scar on Takuya's cheek. Slipping the net this time didn't necessarily mean he'd be so lucky next time around, as the policemen could surely match what they had seen of his face today with the "Wanted" posters they no doubt had on the wall back at the police station. If one of them did happen to see a resemblance, it wouldn't be difficult to go one step further and trace Takuya to Fujisaki's place through the box wholesalers. Suddenly the idea of Kobe as a safe haven was eclipsed by that of its being a trap ready to snap shut.

On the way back to the factory after dropping off his cartload of boxes at the warehouse, Takuya observed something that made him uncomfortable. To avoid the spot where he'd been questioned by the police, he took a detour through the busy streets near a bustling black market, where he saw a young American soldier with a Japanese girlfriend. The American was very tall, well over six feet, but the lithe young woman with him was also of impressive stature for a Japanese.

She would have been twenty-one or twenty-two years of age, had attractive, clearly defined features and a figure that suited the western clothes she was wearing. Her conservative makeup suggested that she was no streetwalker. On the contrary, she was probably from a good family. The two approached at a leisurely pace, her fingers entwined in his.

Forgetting his fear of American soldiers, Takuya watched the young woman, mesmerized. There was no mistaking the fact that she was delighted to be out walking with an American military man. To Takuya, who had never seen Japanese couples holding hands like this in public, there was something lewd and untoward about the way the American and the young woman were carrying themselves. But her relaxed smile made it clear that she paid no heed to the disapproving eyes turned their way.

Takuya struggled to understand how a young woman of her obvious pedigree could have become familiar with an American soldier in the first place. It was inconceivable to him that someone who could surely manage an admirable match among her own should want to be seen walking hand in hand with a low-ranking American soldier. The couple walked past Takuya, the young woman leaning against her suitor.

Disheartened with the world, Takuya pulled his cart along the road between two lines of buildings that had been spared the ravages of the fire bombing. There seemed to be an increasing number of people walking out on the streets.

Upon taking half a dozen more steps, he caught sight of another American soldier and his Japanese date. This couple was approaching on the footpath on the other side of the street, both laughing out loud at some private joke. Her showy clothes and garish makeup pointed clearly to her being a prostitute. The tall American had his arm around her shoulder, while his much shorter girlfriend hung hers around his waist.

Takuya picked up his pace as he left the city center and came back out onto the road between two broad expanses of burnt-out ruins.

That night he told Fujisaki that he wanted to move on to another city and asked if he would help him find a job. Fujisaki nodded, the relief in his expression unmistakable.

Takuya took the following day off from work, saying he had a fever. He lay in his room, visualizing over and over again the American soldier walking with his tall Japanese girlfriend. He struggled to understand how this woman could walk hand in hand so jovially with someone who just nine short months ago had been the enemy. Had she forgotten that the Americans had destroyed Kobe and most other cities of any size in Japan? Had her anger toward the American military for dropping atomic bombs on Japan and killing and maiming countless civilians already disappeared? It was to be expected that such bitterness would diminish with the passage of time, but surely the degree of fraternization she displayed was unnaturally premature. But then again, the U.S. military wanted for nothing, so associating with them would likely be beneficial in more ways than one. Maybe this explained her intimacy with the American, but somehow it had seemed more innocent than that, free of any ulterior motives. The faint, portentous rumble he had heard from the blast of the atomic bomb on Hiroshima. The horrific damage report from Ohmura air base after he had tracked the flight path of the two B-29s headed for Nagasaki. Obviously, the young woman had already stopped thinking about the tens of thousands who had died in those two attacks.

The thought of staying in Kobe and seeing many more scenes of such fraternization was too much to bear. He wasn't just on the run, he thought, he was still at war. The feeling of the sword in his hand as its blade cut into the American flier's neck was still fresh in his mind, and the woman's name that the man had repeated over and over as he sat there waiting in the bamboo grove still rang in his ears. That in the context of the same conflict there could be such a difference between himself and this woman baffled him. It was almost as though she had purged herself of all recollection of the war as she walked holding hands with the tall American.

Takuya had skipped breakfast and lunch that day, but his hunger pangs were so strong by late afternoon that he joined the family in the living room for the evening meal of rice gruel.

Fujisaki's father asked if Takuya would be interested in

going to Himeji. He explained that the owner of a company making matchboxes had set up a temporary office in Kobe to arrange the purchase of building materials needed to re-build his burnt-out factory in Himeji. He went on to say that when he had telephoned this man about a job, he had been told that if Takuya was a good, reliable worker, he'd be prepared to take him on.

"What did you say about me?" asked Takuya.

"I told him that your name is Higa, and that you're a returned serviceman originally from Okinawa. I said that I'd given you some work as a favor to a friend."

Takuya thanked Fujisaki's father and asked him to go ahead with the introduction. The chance to leave Kobe could not have come at a better time, he thought.

It was raining the next day.

Takuya left the house with the simple map that Fuji-saki's father had drawn for him. Rain dripped steadily off the peak of his cap, and he could feel the collar of his shirt becoming uncomfortably damp from the water trickling down his neck. His glasses kept clouding over, but he felt exposed without them, so there was no way he would take them off just for the sake of being able to see properly.

Fujisaki's father had mentioned a temporary office, but the factory chief was obviously just renting the premises of a vacant shop, whose old wooden sign above the door, paint flaking off at the edges, proclaimed it to be a fish shop. A desk was placed squarely in the middle of the concrete floor.

When Takuya stepped inside and announced himself, the glass door at the back of the room slid open and a diminutive man with close-cropped gray hair poked his head out to peer at Takuya. When he explained that he had come on the introduction of Fujisaki's father, the man, maybe fifty-five or fifty-six years old, stepped down onto the concrete floor and sat at the desk, pointing to a low stool for Takuya to sit on.

When asked about his background, Takuya said that he was born in Okinawa and that after finishing high school he had joined the army, first being posted to Manchuria and then moving on to Kyushu as part of an air defense unit. He said he had finished the war as a lance corporal and was twenty-six years old.

"Where are your parents?" the man asked.

Takuya replied that they were still living in northern Okinawa. The central and southern areas of Okinawa had been the scene of intense fighting, so he thought that saying his parents were alive, but in the north, seemed a more natural response.

The man explained that the preparations for rebuilding his factory in Himeji were all but complete. "I'll give you a job. We're taking all the stuff I've collected here back to Himeji tonight by truck. Might be a bit rushed, but there's space for you on the truck. Can you go with us?" he asked.

"Yes, I can," replied Takuya, without a second's hesitation.

"OK. Then be back here by late this afternoon. Regarding your wage, we'll feed you, so how does six yen a day sound?" he asked.

"That's fine," said Takuya. It was more than enough, he thought to himself. His younger brother was getting almost four hundred yen a month, but had said that he was doing pretty well if he had more than one hundred fifty yen left after food costs were covered.

Takuya expressed his gratitude, bowed and left the "office." The man seemed likable. He might be running a factory, but he seemed quite down-to-earth, much more humble than Takuya had expected for a man in his position. The fact that Himeji wasn't as big a city as Kobe meant that food would likely be more readily available, and being able to leave that very day was a stroke of luck. The rain began to ease off, with only an odd drop disturbing the puddles here and there.

The promise of a steady income eased Takuya's mind, and he thought that this might be an opportune time to do some shopping with the money he'd been given by his father. If possible he wanted to buy some new clothes and rid himself of the army issue he'd been wearing since leaving his parents' house in Shikoku.

Takuya trudged off toward the station. He knew clothes weren't cheap, but he thought he could at least get a new hat. Coming out onto a crowded street, he turned right and followed the flow of foot traffic until he found himself in the middle of the black market, a collection of shacks reinforced with old pieces of corrugated iron. Most of the stalls were selling food, tobacco or soap, and there seemed to be no sign of any clothing for sale.

After searching about ten minutes, he found a stall selling shoes. There were leather boots of the kind worn by officers, Air Force pilots' shoes and infantrymen's shoes lined up in rows on sheets of newspaper, along with what looked like virtually worn-out low-cut civilian shoes. In one corner of the display there were a number of hats piled one on top of the other. Takuya stepped over to that part of the table and began looking through the hats. Most of them were military caps of one kind or another, but there was one that was a bit different, the sort of hat mountaineers would wear. He picked it up and tried it on. It seemed to be quite a good fit.

"How much is this?" he asked the young hawker who was sitting, legs splayed, on an apple box behind the display table. Takuya almost fell over when the young man replied, "Eighty yen." How could one hat be worth the equivalent of two weeks' wages at the job he was about to start? "You can't make that a bit cheaper, can you?" he said to the hawker.

"It's almost new. This isn't cheap synthetic fiber, it's one hundred percent cotton. OK, I'll do you a favor and knock the price down ten yen. That's the best I can do. Look how thick the material is. This is a quality product here," he said, still perched self-assuredly on his apple box. The manner of this well-built young man reminded Takuya of the haughtiness of pilots just out of cadet training, known for carrying themselves as though they were a cut above everyone else.

Takuya stood and thought for a moment. He wouldn't have another chance to buy a hat, and if for seventy yen he could change his appearance and thereby make himself a little safer, maybe it wasn't so expensive after all.

He took seven ten-yen notes from the inside pocket of his jacket and handed them to the hawker in return for the hat. The young man counted the notes without saying a word, before stuffing them into his trouser pocket and looking past Takuya for the next customer.

As he walked away from the stall, Takuya took off his old service cap and put on the mountaineer's hat. A satisfied smile came to his face as he realized not only that the size was just right, but also that the peak of the hat would cover part of his face, just as his army cap had done.

The smell of food whetted his appetite. Sure that he had long overstayed his welcome at the Fujisakis', Takuya felt decidedly uncomfortable whenever he joined them for a meal. The idea of getting something to eat here in the market was appealing, and it would save him having to impose on them at mealtime again. Crowds were milling around in front of the men and women hawking plates of boiled *oden*, curry and rice, fried fish and bowls of rice gruel. He threaded his way across the flow to a little tin shack with a notice in front advertising bowl-size servings of tempura on rice. He placed his order and the middle-aged woman on the other side of the table scooped two helpings of rice into a bowl and passed it to the man standing next to her, her husband evidently, to put some pieces of vegetable tempura on top and pour on some broth before handing it to Takuya as he sat down at the table.

The deep-fried vegetables were more batter than anything else, but the rice and the broth poured on top were both piping hot and delicious. Takuya savored each grain of rice and each sip of broth, reluctant to swallow them and cut short the ecstasy. Finishing every last scrap in the bowl, he pulled out two ten-yen notes from his pocket and handed them to the woman. It was somewhat ironic, he thought as he moved away from the tin shack, that there was so much food here in the black market when not far away the talk was of ten million people facing death by starvation.

When he got back to the Fujisakis' that day, the father told him that he had just spoken on the telephone to the factory owner who had offered Takuya the job earlier. Evidently the man from Himeji had been so impressed with Takuya's courteous and well-spoken manner that he was very keen to take him on.

"Everything he has now he has earned by the sweat of his brow, so if you work hard it won't go unnoticed," said Fujisaki's father in an unusually cheerful tone.

Going to his room, Takuya took his clean loincloths and shirts down off the improvised washing line and stuffed them into his rucksack before retracing his steps down the corridor to the living room, where Fujisaki, in his mother's absence, handed over the ration book Takuya had lent them.

Kneeling on the tatami mats in front of Fujisaki and his father, Takuya expressed his gratitude for their hospitality, bowing so low that his forehead almost touched the floor. He repeated the performance for Fujisaki's wife when she came out of the kitchen. The slowness of her movements suggested that she was not too far from giving birth.

He went out to the factory and politely said goodbye to each of the workers before stepping out through the door at the back onto the road. The rain had stopped and the sun was trying to force its way out from behind the clouds.

Chapter Six

After dark the rain started falling again, lightly at first, but soon it turned into a veritable downpour.

On the rear deck of the truck there was a stack of corrugated iron, obviously salvaged from one or more bomb sites, a large box of nails and a collection of carpenter's tools. Terasawa, the man who had hired him, stepped under the truck's hood with a pile of bedding in his arms and sat down directly behind the driver, a young man by the name of Kameya. Takuya sat down on the precariously small seat to the left of Kameya.

The engine roared to life and off they went into the rain. The hood stretched far enough forward to protect the driver from the elements, but the left side of Takuya's body was fully exposed to the rain. Soon his left trouser leg was so wet that spray came up from the saturated cloth, and in no time at all his left shoe felt as though it was filling up with the water running down his leg. His glasses were covered with drops of water, so he put them away in the inside pocket of his jacket.

Kameya did his best to avoid the potholes along the way, but once they came out onto the main road the ride was so bumpy that Takuya had to hold on tightly for fear of being bucked right out of the vehicle.

Occasionally a powerful beam of light would approach from behind. Each time Kameya would pull over to the left and slow to a crawl as the light closed on them. There would be a tremendous blast from a horn and a U.S. Army truck or jeep would rumble past them.

"The Ame-chan scare me something wicked," said Kameya, his eyes fixed on the road ahead. "The other day I saw a truck driven by a Japanese overtake an American jeep. The jeep sped up and forced the truck off the road. They dragged the driver out of the cab and beat the living daylights out of him."

After another hour of driving through the rain they pulled over and parked in an open space beside the road. The strain of trying to avoid the deeper-looking puddles and keeping a grip on the steering wheel as the truck bounced in and out of big potholes had obviously taken its toll on Kameya.

When they came to a complete stop, Terasawa asked where they were. "Just past Suma," was Kameya's reply.

After a short break they were back on the move. The going seemed a little easier once the rain eased off somewhat, but the truck's engine was straining so much that it sounded as though it might blow up any moment. After crossing a long bridge, they turned right and followed the road running along the embankment on one side of a river.

"This is Himeji," said Kameya. Before long the neat row of houses came to an end, and wide, empty spaces opened up on both sides. The truck's headlights illuminated the area in front of them, and Takuya realized straightaway that they were driving through another vast tract of bombed urban wasteland.

The truck turned into a narrow lane before stopping in front of some ramshackle houses.

Takuya stepped out of his side of the cab after Kameya had alighted from the right. His jacket and trousers were wet and heavy from the rain, and he felt chilled to the bone. Not far away he could see a train, the line of dim lights from its cars chugging off to the right through the red-tinted smoke belching out from its smokestack. Takuya followed Terasawa and Kameya into the house.

Terasawa disappeared off to the other end of the house as Kameya pulled a couple of futons from a pile of bedding in a corner of the room next to the entrance. After helping to set them out, Takuya stripped off his wet clothes, put on a dry shirt and loincloth he'd kept in his rucksack and lay down on the futon.

As he closed his eyes, Takuya could hear the train whistle in the distance.

He awoke to the sound of Terasawa's voice. Kameya pushed aside his bedcovers and sat up, rubbing his eyes. The rain had stopped and the morning sun shone brightly.

The clothes he had been wearing the previous day were still wet, but carrying his towel, Takuya followed Kameya outside dressed in his shirt and loincloth. Terasawa was standing with his hands cupped under the end of a broken water pipe sticking out of the ground, washing his face.

Takuya stood beside the lead pipe and surveyed the area around them. In every direction scorched ruins stretched endlessly toward the horizon.

His gaze settled on a point off to the north. Takuya had been on Sanyo Line trains through this area before, but as it had always been at night he had never actually set eyes upon what was left of Himeji City. He knew that Himeji's White Egret Castle was one of the most famous of its kind in the country, but seeing it there in the distance, towering majestically above this desolate wasteland, anchored him to the spot in awe. The main donjon and a smaller one nestled into its side seemed to soar above the castle's steep white walls. Maybe it was because the air was so clear after the rain, but the whiteness of the donjon and turret walls seemed unusually bright in the morning sun, in vivid contrast to the green of the trees on the slopes surrounding the castle.

The sight of the castle, untouched in the middle of this scorched wilderness littered with rubble and burnt roofing iron, seemed bizarre. It must have been caught in the same conflagration that consumed the town, but as far as Takuya could tell, there was no trace of damage.

"The town was burnt beyond recognition. The Kawanishi Aircraft Works were just off to the east of the castle, so they pummeled that whole strip on the twenty-second of June, and then a really big fire raid on the night of the third of July burnt most of what was left. This area was hit on the same night," said Terasawa, wiping his face and neck as he gazed out over the ruins.

"The castle did well to survive all that," said Takuya, staring at its white walls off in the distance.

"The night of the big fire raid, we fled up into the hills. When we came back the next day the castle was standing there, untouched. Everything around it had been burnt to ashes. Some of the pine trees just outside the castle walls caught fire and burned, but the castle itself was unscathed. I can't tell you how happy I was when I saw it," said Terasawa, keeping his eyes on the White Egret Castle as he went on to explain how most of the white plaster walls and the outlines of the moats had been camouflaged with netting because of concern that the castle would provide a perfect landmark for enemy bombers.

"The netting made her look really drab during the war, but when they took it off she was just as beautiful as she's ever been," said Terasawa, obviously entranced by the sight of the castle and its towering white donjons.

Takuya's first job was to clear the burnt remnants of the previous setup from the factory grounds. He and Kameya lived on site and two other men came in each day to work.

Terasawa's only son had been killed in the war in China, so he now lived alone with his wife.

The Himeji-Kobe area had boasted the highest number of factories manufacturing matches in Japan, and in contrast to the complete destruction of the factories within metropolitan Kobe, those concentrated along the coastline near the town of Shirahama had somehow escaped the conflagration, and were continuing production with what poor materials were at hand. With matches already being produced, Terasawa was desperate to get his factory running again to make the boxes needed for them.

Terasawa's wife went out shopping virtually every day, coming back in the evenings with her rucksack full of food bought from acquaintances in farming villages in the countryside or fishing hamlets along the coast. She was a good-natured person who did her best to look after her husband's workers, sometimes even making shirts for them out of pieces of cloth she'd found along the way.

Trying to be as casual as he could, Takuya scrutinized the newspapers every day. He was most interested in anything concerning the investigations into the Western Regional Command. Any information he could gather, he thought, must help him get a clearer picture of how safe, or indeed how dangerous, his situation was.

While he found no coverage of matters concerning the Western Regional Command, there was a sudden spate of articles about the class A war criminals, as well as details of those being tried overseas and in Japan for crimes in the B and C classes. He couldn't help but notice that the words "death by hanging" and "death penalty" appeared frequently in all this writing. Both were used in an article about the verdict in a case against men found guilty of executing American airmen in Honshu. He read the article over and over to himself.

One day toward the end of May, Takuya was poring over that morning's newspaper when he spotted an announcement made by a SCAP press secretary. It read: "The Supreme Commander of Allied Powers in Japan has instructed the Japanese Government to move immediately to freeze or confiscate any or all personal property or real estate owned by those people already arrested and incarcerated, or by those criminals yet to be arrested and incarcerated. In particular the possession of precious metals such as gold, platinum or coins, as well as stocks and bonds or bank deposit books will be subject to direct control."

A harsh step indeed, thought Takuya. Not only would SCAP punish those found guilty of war crimes, but now they would go so far as to seize their property as well. If the individual had owned a house, the house and all its contents could be confiscated and the family turned out onto the street if the authorities saw fit. Surely this was no different from the laws of the feudal Edo period, which had punished a criminal's family for "complicity by association."

His mind drifted to his family back in Shikoku. His only property at his parents' house was his post office savings book and some government bonds, and his family wouldn't suffer in the least if these items were confiscated. Even so, if the police decided to make a thorough search of the house, in the course of their investigation they would no doubt put considerable pressure on his parents and brother and sister to reveal what they might be hiding. Maybe they were even shunned by those around them for having spawned a war criminal.

Noticing that Takuya seemed to be preoccupied with one particular article, Terasawa's wife called out to him, her expression quite different than usual.

"Are you worried about your family back home? Is there something in there about Okinawa?" she asked sympathetically.

Takuya breathed a sigh of relief, reminded again that assuming an Okinawan identity had been a wise choice. If he could relegate Takuya Kiyohara to the past and become

Higa Seiichi, maybe he would be able to lead a safe life from now on. In the short time since he chose it he had grown used to his new name. Maybe he was finally on the right track after all.

Despite long periods of heavy rain they made good progress clearing the factory grounds, and by the middle of June the task was complete. Terasawa had Kameya use the truck to bring in stacks of old boards, coils of wire and sheets of metal framing that he'd somehow acquired from merchants in town. Takuya and the other three men toiled away between downpours, following Terasawa's instructions as they laid the foundation for the new workshop.

The food supply situation in Himeji was just as bad as it had been in Kobe. Regulations governing the economy were still in place, and foodstuffs were subject to particularly strict control. The newspaper was full of articles about passengers at railway stations in the Himeji area being ordered off trains to have food they had bought or bartered at farms and fishing villages confiscated. According to the newspaper, those caught transporting food more than once were charged under the economic control regulations, and all forms of black market activities were frowned on by the authorities.

In these circumstances, the food served in Terasawa's house became increasingly bland with each passing day. Most meals consisted of biscuits made from cornflower, salt and water, or bread baked with little pieces of sweet potato in it, and the only time rice appeared was in a thin soup or rice porridge. The Terasawas ate the same food as their live-in workers, and sometimes, as a special treat, Mrs. Terasawa would give them some potato sweets or tobacco she had managed to buy on the black market.

The rainy season ended and summer came.

Prices continued to rise at a frightening pace. Postcards jumped from five sen to ten and then to fifteen in the space of a week. The monthly subscription rate for newspapers went from one yen and sixty sen to eight yen, and prices of goods on the black market seemed to virtually double overnight. Terasawa grumbled every day that he could barely keep up with the price hikes on the building materials he needed to start up his factory again.

Takuya knew how fortunate he was to have found a job with Terasawa. In contrast to when he had to sponge off Nemoto, his old army subordinate, and Fujisaki, his younger friend from university days, here he had a job, and the food on the table was part of the remuneration for his labor. Everyone, including the Terasawas, was friendly to him, all were quite happy calling him "Higa" and obviously saw nothing suspicious about his claim to be from Okinawa. He was also completely used to wearing glasses, and by now was feeling a good deal more secure about his situation.

Occasionally, and quite unexpectedly, Takuya would imagine that he heard something like the woman's name uttered over and over again by the American flier before he was killed. At other times, quite suddenly, he would recall the moment when his sword cut into the back of the man's neck, and the strange sight of the flier's knees jerking up violently would come back to him. Each time this happened he felt unnerved, and more often than not he tried to calm himself down by furtively taking his pistol out of his ruck-sack and cleaning it behind the large pile of burnt iron and debris on the factory grounds.

If captured, he would be made to stand in the dock, told that he was to receive the death penalty, and then dragged to the gallows. When he imagined the agonizing wait for that moment of truth, he thought it would be much better to take his own life. The American he had executed had managed to keep his composure to the end, but Takuya was not at all confident that he would be able to do the same.

There was still no word in the newspaper about the investigation of those in the Western Regional Command. Shirasaka had already explained to him that high-ranking staff officers, including the commander himself, had been interrogated, and his younger brother had told him that the police had been to their house. But even so, it made him uneasy to think that there had been nothing in the newspaper about the executions despite the fact that a good number of arrests must have been made by now.

When Takuya opened the newspaper after work on the twentieth of July, his eyes were drawn to a short article at the bottom of the front page. As he read it, his last vestiges of hope that the full truth about the executions would evade the investigators slipped away. Takuya could almost feel the color drain from his face as he lifted his eyes from the newspaper. Under the headline "Professor Iwase Commits Suicide" it read "War crime suspect Professor Kotaro Iwase of the faculty of medicine of Kyushu University hanged himself in the afternoon of the seventeenth in his cell at Fukuoka Prison. He was fifty-four years old."

Takuya remembered how he had observed an operation

Iwase had performed on one of his subordinates who'd slipped and fallen from a truck, breaking a hip. The fact that the professor was being held at Fukuoka Prison as a suspected war criminal was proof that the authorities had found out about the vivisections carried out on the eight prisoners of war, making Takuya think that the others who had been involved must also have been apprehended. Army surgeon Haruki, who had suggested performing the dissections of live POWs, had been killed in the fire raids on Fukuoka, but Colonel Tahara, who had witnessed the operations as a representative of the tactical operations staff, would no doubt have been arrested with the others. Tahara had been involved in organizing the executions of the other thirty-three fliers. Obviously he would have been grilled by his interrogators as to their whereabouts, so by now warrants for the arrest of all those who had taken part would have been issued, and it was highly likely that many were already in custody. The fact that Iwase had chosen to take his own life was probably an indication of the severity of the interrogations, and doubtless the prospect of dying on the gallows had been too much for him to bear.

Clearly, by now the Occupation authorities would know all there was to know about the fate of the forty-one captured airmen.

Takuya looked up from the newspaper. A wave of apprehension came over him, as though suddenly he were cowering naked in the middle of a vast expanse with nowhere to hide. He felt as though he wanted to crawl into a cave deep in the mountains and hide there for the rest of his life.

That day Takuya struggled to keep his mind on the job, and two or three times Terasawa and his co-workers laughed at him for giving odd replies to their questions. He was suddenly on tenterhooks again, and these men seemed to represent nothing less than a threat to his life.

The summer heat intensified with each passing day.

When Terasawa had gathered all the building materials he needed, he got a man who had been a carpenter's apprentice before joining the army to come in and start the construction.

Kameya invited Takuya to accompany him on his trips to the black market, but the risk of being spotted in the crowd made him turn down every invitation.

Since the end of the war, the American forces had taken over the Suyari munitions works, and U.S. Army jeeps and trucks were everywhere on the streets of Himeji. New brothels, bars and shops catering to their needs sprung up virtually every week in the areas frequented by the Americans.

Kameya told him all sorts of stories about what he saw on his trips into town. He talked about the time he saw a young couple waiting for a train on the platform at Himeji Station. An American soldier had swaggered over, grabbed the young woman by the arm and tried to drag her off, knocking her husband to the ground when he tried to intervene. He talked about the tawdry women he had seen brazenly consorting with American soldiers in the streets, and how some of them had even set up a hut near the U.S. military camp, where they would solicit customers. Kameya said he had even seen these women shamelessly copulating with their American customers out in the open. He also told Takuya about the number of times he had witnessed innocent young women being accosted and dragged off to be raped by American troops. Evidently soldiers threw things from their vehicles for the locals to scramble after all the time, and he even described unscrupulous dealers who collected food scraps from outside the Americans' tents and boiled them up to sell as broth on the black market.

No way, thought Takuya, would he venture into the town center if that was what he was going to find.

As he worked during the day, every few minutes Takuya would steal a glance down each of the approach roads to the factory. The number of people throwing up shacks made from burnt roofing iron was gradually increasing, and there were even some out there living in what were for all intents and purposes crude mud huts. Whenever people approached the workshop grounds, Takuya would scrutinize them to see if they posed any threat. Takuya had decided that if someone did come with the intention of arresting him, he would first rush into the house to get his pistol before dashing down to the embankment by the river, where he'd fire some warning shots if followed. He had resolved to blow his brains out rather than be taken alive.

Deep inside, Takuya recognized that his feelings of outrage toward the American military for devastating his country were gradually mellowing, but that his fear was intensifying with each passing day. His reason for staying on the run was fear of the gallows.

On the thirteenth of August, Takuya found an article in the newspaper which raised his vigilance to yet another level. The headline read "Kempeitai Chief Flees, Female Companion Arrested."

"When a warrant was issued for his arrest this April on charges of war crimes, former Imperial Army colonel and commander of the Tokyo Kempeitai Oishi Kojiro (forty years of age) of 1–16, Kaga-Cho, Ushigome-Ku, Tokyo, mysteriously disappeared with his maid, Hirakawa Fumiko. However, Hirakawa was recently apprehended after being spotted by a policeman at Ueno Station while she was in the city to buy food supplies. She told police that Oishi was living in a village in the Nishi-Tama district, but when the agents moved to arrest him they discovered that he had already fled. According to Hirakawa, they had left suicide notes at their residence in Tokyo before absconding to Kawaji with what money and food they could lay their hands on. They had moved from one farmer's shed to another before finally managing to rent a four-tatami-mat storeroom in a private house in Hikawa."

Takuya tried to calm himself with a cigarette. It was strange to think there was another fugitive out there in exactly the same predicament as himself. He could almost sense the fear in Oishi, driving him to stay one step ahead of the police.

At the first opportunity, Takuya stepped behind a pile of building materials and scanned the article one more time. The arrest warrant for Oishi, chief of the Tokyo Kempeitai, had been issued in April, about the same time the police had turned up at his parents' house in Shikoku. Obviously the SCAP authorities had issued a blanket order for the arrest of all suspects wanted on charges of war crimes. That Hirakawa's maid could have been apprehended on her way through Ueno Station was proof that their photographs must be in circulation, and also that police agents were watching passersby even in places as crowded as railway stations. This must be the case all over the country, so there would undoubtedly be police agents standing watch in and around Himeji Station, holding photographs of war crimes suspects.

Obviously, when the maid confessed Oishi's whereabouts to the police, they would have rushed there only to find that he had slipped away from them once again. Oishi must have been constantly on the lookout, somehow sensing their approach and skillfully evading arrest.

This article taught Takuya a valuable lesson. Oishi had been lying low up in the mountains, but had kept sufficiently alert to recognize the impending danger and avoid capture by pursuers who no doubt had taken great care to approach as stealthily as possible. Takuya realized that no lesser degree of vigilance would be needed to keep himself safe from the gallows. His impulse was to cut the article out and save it as a reminder, but the risk of drawing attention to himself made him reject the idea.

After the corner supports of the warehouse were erected the men started attaching the crossbeams. Perched precariously on lengths of wooden scaffolding, Takuya and the others toiled under the summer sun. The sweat from his brow had already stained the front of his mountaineering hat, and his face was so tanned that the skin was peeling from the bridge of his nose.

The clear view of the White Egret Castle gave Takuya the solace he needed to get through the day. Sitting majestically amid the desolation that once had been Himeji City, the castle seemed to project a feeling of stability, like a lead paperweight sitting on a sheet of rice paper. Its indomitable presence somehow buoyed and comforted him. It changed color with the weather, light brown under an overcast sky, purplish in the evening sunlight.

The area around where the workshop was being constructed was known for the profusion of fireflies. They were so concentrated that at night the air above the river a short distance away would glow in the dark, and the luminescence seemed to spill over beyond the stream as thousands of the little insects flew out over the devastated land. Depending on the direction of the wind, there were also days when the house would be enveloped by myriad tiny beads of light, while out in the desolate expanse pieces of twisted roofing iron and the rubble from white stone walls would be illuminated, fading into and then out of sight.

Toward the end of August, three iron girders were stolen one night.

Incidents of theft were reaching epidemic proportions. Crops in the fields were plundered and stories about cattle being stolen and butchered for their meat were not uncommon. A spinning mill which had survived the fire raids had the glass taken from almost two hundred windows. Even lead water pipes were dug up and carried away. If people let their guard down for a moment, their bicycles, handcarts or even their shoes disappeared in a flash, and instances of luggage being stolen at the station were rife. Concerned about the materials he had to store outdoors, Terasawa made sure that at night everything was tied up with rope, but this had not deterred the thieves.

Judging from the number of girders taken, this seemed to be the handiwork of one person. If the thief had been a man of considerable physical strength, he certainly could have carried three of them at one time.

Knowing how hard Terasawa had worked to obtain these girders, Takuya was incensed by the theft. The man was probably an incorrigible thief, whiling away his hours in the black market rather than working, and feeding himself with the proceeds from his criminal activities. The girders were to be used for building the warehouse, and without them construction was not possible.

Terasawa seemed disillusioned with everything, and spent his time walking mutely around the property.

That evening, he announced that the property would have to be guarded through the night. He seemed to think that, like a mouse that has found a source of food, the thief would definitely be back for more. The only way to stop him was to keep watch for the whole night, so it was decided that Kameya and Takuya would alternate shifts watching the yard. Terasawa said that he would do a shift as well, but Takuya insisted that it was the employees' duty and he should leave it to them. Beginning that night then, Kameya kept watch from ten o'clock at night until one in the morning, when Takuya would take over until daybreak.

While Kameya seemed to struggle on less than a full night's sleep, Takuya took it in stride. Working through the night in the tactical operations center had hardened him to the extent that if he awoke some time before beginning his shift, he wouldn't hesitate to let Kameya go back to bed. Keeping watch until dawn with only an hour's catnap hardly affected him at all. Fatigue wasn't a problem, but the swarms of mosquitoes that appeared during the night certainly were. Together with Kameya he fashioned some bags out of cloth to cover their hands, and stitched together two hoods with small holes cut for their eyes. Their vantage point was the spot behind the metal drum used by the workers to bathe in.

Just before dawn on the fifth day after they started their vigil, from his position crouched behind the drum, resting a piece of timber on his knees, Takuya noticed that someone appeared to be walking along the road in his direction.

Tiny bulbs of incandescence from the fireflies glimmered in the still night air as the person stopped in front of the yard, presumably to survey the scene before making his next move. Takuya remained motionless, only his eyes moving to follow the man as he stepped off again toward the pile of building materials, just close enough now for Takuya to make out that this was no small individual. In the faint light from the stars in the clear night sky he was able to see that the man was maneuvering a couple of steel girders onto his shoulder.

Takuya jumped to his feet and moved quickly from his spot behind the steel drum toward the thief. The man obviously heard Takuya, for no sooner had he taken a couple of steps toward the road than he swung around and dropped the girders to the ground with a clatter. Before the thief could make another move, Takuya swung his makeshift truncheon down onto the man's shoulder with all the force he could muster. After staggering three or four steps back toward the road, the man dropped to one knee, giving Takuya the chance to push him over, twist his arm up behind him and thrust a knee into the small of his back. The man was certainly well built. Takuya turned his head toward the house and yelled for those inside to come out and help. The man groaned slightly as he lay pressed to the ground, but showed no other signs of resistance.

A light flicked on inside the house, then the door burst open and Terasawa ran out into the yard. As Takuya held the man's legs, Terasawa shouted back to his wife, who stood silhouetted in the doorway, to wake up Kameya and get him to bring some rope. In no time the younger man was by their side, dressed in his underwear, holding a coil of rope.

As Takuya held the thief down, Terasawa and Kameya bound the man's hands behind his back and tied his legs together with the same length of rope.

"Go get the police," said Terasawa, panting from exertion. Kameya ran inside, put on his trousers and rushed back out again to the truck. He jumped into the cab, started up the engine and the vehicle rumbled out onto the road.

Takuya watched the truck move off down the road and a frown came over his face at the stupidity of what he had just done. Apprehending the thief meant of course that the police would become involved. The police would come to ask questions, and as the person who had caught the thief in the act Takuya would be obliged to make a statement for their records. Giving a false name wasn't much of a concern, but the prospect of being recognized by someone at the police station terrified him. He was not at all confident that he could stay calm, and if he reacted the way he had before being questioned on the road that time, he might very well arouse the suspicions of the police.

Maybe he should make a run for it now, he thought. The article about Colonel Oishi returned to his mind. Kameya had already been gone for a few minutes, but he still had plenty of time to escape before the police arrived. Maybe he should just stroll into the house, grab his rucksack and slip out the back door. But then again, disappearing like that would alert the police to his real situation, and it wouldn't be difficult for them to trace his real name in their files on suspected war criminals. With the police stepping up surveillance at railway stations and street corners, it was obvious that they were doubling their efforts to close the net on the last fugitives. Maybe it wouldn't be wise to tempt fate by bolting at this stage.

Takuya considered his options. If he went to the police station, his chances of walking out again without attracting the police's suspicions were not good. Indeed, in the worst-case scenario he could very well be arrested and thrown behind bars.

He asked himself what Colonel Oishi would do in this situation, but the question merely reminded him of his own stupidity. The answer was simple: Oishi wouldn't have put himself at risk by catching the thief in the first place. During his training as an officer cadet, Takuya had done his best to memorize the sections of the field service code that covered engaging the enemy. He remembered how the instructions had stressed that for a commander of men in the field, hesitation or inaction was even worse than choosing the wrong course of action. In the present situation, with the police being the enemy, maybe boldly facing them was best after all.

"He's a big fellow, Higa. You certainly did well to catch him," Terasawa said, looking down at the man lying trussed up in front of them. The thief had a prominent nose, set amid clear-cut features, and the service cap lying by his side suggested that he was a demobilized soldier.

Takuya brooded over his foolishness. If he had just

moved out from behind the steel drum and yelled, the man would have dropped the girders and run away. Once the thief knew that someone was guarding the building materials during the night, surely he wouldn't risk coming back. Takuya's task had simply been to prevent any further theft until the warehouse was built. That didn't necessarily mean apprehending the man to bring him to justice.

The stars faded and the sky took on a bluish tint.

Takuya vacillated between the two options open to him. Fleeing seemed like a good idea, but he realized that if he ran now his pursuers would be much closer than ever before. Maybe trying to feign composure in front of the police was worth the risk after all.

The noise of an engine was soon followed by two faint beams of light rising and dipping as the truck approached along the bumpy road. Takuya pulled the peak of his mountaineering cap down lower and pushed his glasses further up the bridge of his nose.

There were two policemen sitting on the flat deck behind Kameya. When the truck stopped they jumped down and rushed over to the thief lying facedown on the ground. While the younger police officer placed his knee in the small of the man's back, the older one checked the thief's pockets, then untied the rope and snapped a set of handcuffs on him. They made the man kneel on the ground with his legs folded under him.

The older policeman appeared to know Terasawa, engaging him in what seemed to be friendly conversation. The part Takuya had played must have been mentioned, as the officer nodded and turned to walk in his direction.

Takuya told himself to stay calm, but a slight grimace

came over his face and he looked down at the ground while the policeman approached. A furtive glance toward the house allowed him to measure the distance between himself and his gun. If the officer's expression betrayed the slightest hint of suspicion, the moment they moved to arrest him he would dash into the house, grab his rucksack and flee out the back door.

The sun was starting to rise, the earthen bank along the river coming faintly into view through the morning mist.

The policeman stopped in front of Takuya, pulled out a notebook and asked his name and age. Takuya replied that his name was Higa and that he was from Okinawa, which the officer quickly jotted down, his face the picture of concentration as he asked for details of the time and nature of the incident.

Each time Takuya sensed the policeman's eyes turning in his direction, fear welled up inside him. He was struggling to avoid the gaze of his questioner without being too obvious, but he could see nothing but goodwill in the policeman's expression.

Terasawa sauntered over. "Good job to have dropped this guy with one blow. These army men are terrific, aren't they," he said with a hint of triumph in his voice.

The policeman nodded and smiled at Takuya as he put away his notebook. Terasawa instructed Kameya to take the police back to the station, and the handcuffed thief was pushed up onto the rear deck. As the truck's engine revved, the senior policeman saluted Terasawa and stepped up onto the deck himself. The truck pulled out of the yard and off down the road.

Watching the vehicle move away, Takuya thought that

he didn't seem to have attracted any undue suspicion during the questioning.

The scene was now bathed in morning sunlight and a plume of smoke rose into the air from the chimney above the kitchen.

Before long Kameya returned, and they all went inside to have the morning meal of rice gruel with thin slices of seaweed.

Obviously in fine spirits, Terasawa excitedly described how his heart had raced as he dashed outside to answer Takuya's call for assistance. Terasawa's wife and Kameya gave enthusiastic accounts of their own parts in the episode, Kameya explaining that the man hadn't said a word during the trip into town, and that he'd walked passively into the police station with his head hung forward.

After finishing his meal, Terasawa got to his feet and stepped over to a cabinet in the corner of the room, where he opened the lid of a small wooden box and took out two packs of Lucky Strike cigarettes. "Well done," he said, handing each of the men a pack.

Kameya looked curiously at the packaging before breaking the seal.

"Try one," said Terasawa. Takuya opened his pack and pulled out a cigarette. The paper was of good quality and the pleasant smell of tobacco wafted out of the box. Holding it between his fingers, Takuya noticed how much thicker it was than the Japanese ration cigarettes, and that the tobacco was packed in much more evenly. To Takuya, these cigarettes symbolized all he had heard about the material wealth and affluence of America.

He lit it and inhaled. It certainly smelled nice, and tasted as though it must have been made from good-quality tobacco, but it was far too pungent for his uninitiated palate and he coughed as soon as he inhaled the smoke. Terasawa laughed happily at the scene in front of him.

They completed the "workshop" that evening. At least it was called a workshop, but in actual fact it was only a square structure with sheets of roofing iron nailed onto the top and sides. Most of the floor was just bare ground, with only a small section covered with recycled wooden boards.

The next morning, the carpenter turned his attention to the construction of the warehouse. Terasawa and Kameya went out in the morning in the truck and returned in the afternoon with the rear deck loaded with a jumble of machines, motors, belts, and shafts, which the men hauled straightaway into the workshop. Takuya played his part in assembling the machinery, but as he worked he stood in such a way as to keep a clear line of sight down the road in the direction of the police station. He still couldn't shake his lingering uneasy sense that the police might have recognized his face from wanted posters and at that very moment might be on their way back to arrest him.

In the evening of the fifth day after the thief's capture, Terasawa returned from town saying he had stopped at the police station and found out some details about the man. Evidently he was a known criminal, a specialist in the theft of metal goods, which he then sold through a broker. When the broker was arrested, he in turn had spilled the beans about the full extent of his betrayer's activities. The man was a demobilized soldier, as Takuya had guessed, and had moved to Himeji by himself to start his life of crime after losing his family in the fire raids on Osaka.

"The police were really pleased about this one. They figure he'll probably admit to still more crimes," said Terasawa, cutting a cigarette in half and stuffing the tobacco into a clay pipe he held in his hand. Putting the pipe in the corner of his mouth, he turned to Takuya and said, "I didn't think of this till after I left the police station, but I think I'll get them to give you some sort of award for this. I know all the top brass down there, so if I say something they'll move on it. That was some criminal you nabbed here, and you should get something for it."

Takuya was flabbergasted. Getting an award would require him to go to the police station and give more details of his personal history. He would have to meet all sorts of police officials, and in the process they would most likely work out his real identity.

"I can't have you doing that," said Takuya in a strained, high-pitched voice.

The faintest of smiles appeared on Terasawa's face before he replied. "I won't have to stand up and shout about it. You really caught a big one here. The police will be more than happy to give you an award for your efforts," he said as he picked out the last bits of tobacco from his pipe.

Takuya's mind raced as he tried to think of a way to get out of this predicament.

"He's a demobilized soldier just like me. I couldn't accept an award for putting a fellow soldier behind bars. And remember, he lost his whole family in the war, so he must have been beside himself. I couldn't accept an award for capturing someone like that," he said, raising his voice.

"I see," said Terasawa, obviously recognizing that there was no point in pressing the matter further. His wife smiled warmly across the table at Takuya.

After that there was no more mention of awards, and no policemen turned up to discuss Takuya's capture of the thief.

The machinery had all been installed in the workshop and test runs had gone without a hitch. Terasawa obviously still had considerable funds left, as he purchased a large handcart and had a telephone put into his house.

One day the owner of the match factory turned up on his bicycle and had a long talk with Terasawa. By all accounts the quantity of matches being produced was steadily increasing and with it the demand for matchboxes.

Even into September, the late summer heat showed no signs of abating.

Takuya spent his days pulling the cart to get materials from a timber processing yard at a little town down near the coast. There was a press there which would cut out the shapes for large and small matchboxes from pine boards.

He felt uneasy about walking around on the streets, but with the construction of the warehouse complete the only job left for him was pulling the handcart. Using a splitter machine, the men in Terasawa's workshop cut the boxes out. Two recently hired middle-aged women then stuck the striking paper onto the outside of the boxes. They were obviously experienced, and kept up a steady pace with no problem at all.

With Kameya now also working on the striking paper, Takuya found himself in charge of carrying all goods and materials in and out of the factory. He wrapped a hand towel around his head and wore his mountaineering hat on top of that to avoid being burnt by the late summer sun as he traipsed through the ruins to pick up materials at the timber processing yard or the paper wholesalers. He always made a point of choosing the less crowded paths.

On the morning of the twenty-fifth of September, Takuya opened the newspaper and found the article he had been fearing all along. The name of the commander at the regional headquarters was printed boldly under the headline "Jailed in Sugamo Prison."

"The Judiciary Division of SCAP has announced that the following seven high-ranking officers of the Japanese Imperial Army have been arrested and are being held in Sugamo Prison in relation to the unlawful execution in Fukuoka of thirty-three crew members from B-29 bombers," it read. Those arrested were the lieutenant-generals in command of the Western Regional Forces and the Sixteenth Army, and of the southern Kyushu–based Fifty-seventh Army; the chief of staff of the Sixteenth Army; a major-general who had been second in command in the Western Region; a colonel in charge of the Western Region Air Defense Tactical Operations Center; a major; and finally, Lieutenant Howa Kotaro, listed as a company officer attached to headquarters.

Although this was the first article about the POWs since the coverage of Professor Iwase's suicide, Takuya knew instantly that this meant the SCAP authorities would now know every last detail about what happened to the fliers. Like Professor Iwase, these officers would have undergone relentless interrogation in Fukuoka Prison, and only after they had told all they knew would they have been transported to Sugamo Prison in Tokyo, where class A war criminals were incarcerated.

Most of those listed were elite, high-ranking officers bearing ultimate responsibility for what happened under their command, but seeing Howa Kotaro's name unnerved Takuya. Distraught and incensed by his mother's death in the fire raids on Fukuoka the previous night, Howa had volunteered to take part in that day's execution and had decapitated two of the fliers. Of the seven men imprisoned at Sugamo, only Howa had actually been involved in carrying out the executions rather than giving the orders to do so. His arrest must mean that by now Takuya had also been designated a war criminal. He stared fixedly at the name Howa Kotaro in the last line of the newspaper article.

In a column further down the page, in fine print, he read that ninety-three war criminals had been put to death in Rabaul, and another one hundred twenty-three in Australia. Many more were probably meeting the same fate all around the Pacific, thought Takuya.

The mornings and nights grew cooler as autumn approached. The trial of the class A war criminals was approaching a climax, and articles covering each day's developments in court filled the newspapers.

One afternoon, on a day one of the regular power outages occurred, a local government officer came and sprayed DDT around Terasawa's house, sprinkling some of the white powder in the hair of all the workers, and even shoving the funnel down into their jacket sleeves and trousers. The officer explained that lice had been identified as the cause of the spread of typhus through the country, and that three thousand people had died. He went on to say that there had already been outbreaks of the disease in the Himeji area.

"This spraying is ordered by the Occupation Forces, who have supplied us with the DDT and the spraying equipment," the man reported in an official tone before climbing back into the truck and driving away.

Takuya and the other men followed the orders and left the white powder on their bodies for the rest of the day. The effect of the pesticide was startling. The itchiness and the sensation of tiny creatures crawling over his skin disappeared in no time, and the number of flies and mosquitoes in the house dropped away dramatically.

"The Americans certainly don't do anything halfway," muttered Terasawa as he ran his fingers through his powder-covered hair.

Takuya hauled ever-increasing loads of materials into the workshop, and matchbox production was soon in full swing. The men and the machines seemed to be in almost perpetual motion, and on the wooden floor of the workshop the women, sitting on old, worn-out cushions, toiled away tirelessly, sticking paper covers onto the completed boxes. Terasawa racked his brain thinking of ways to keep a supply of glue ready for his workers, and when flour, a key ingredient, wasn't available, he bought scraps of cheap wheat-gluten bread, which was then boiled to produce a substitute. It worked just as well as flour and water, so from that point on Terasawa's wife got up early every morning and boiled up the day's supply of glue.

Before long, the system changed so that Kameya used the little truck to bring in the materials while Takuya devoted his energies solely to delivering the completed boxes to the match factory.

He loaded the handcart as high as he could and trudged out along the street to the match factory. It was a real struggle to get the cart up the slope to the bridge, and when he made it up onto the long wooden structure he always paused to get his breath. The bridge was showing signs of age and disrepair, with long sections of the handrail rotted away and gaping holes visible in the upright supports, where ornamental iron fittings had been removed to be melted down during the war.

There was a magnificent view of Himeji Castle from up on top of the bridge. The whiteness of the walls of the donjons and turrets was truly spectacular. One of the workers at Terasawa's factory said that many people believed the castle had survived the inferno only because the Americans had recognized its historical value, and had therefore ordered the B-29s to leave it standing. But Takuya gave this theory little credence. He thought the suggestion that an air force which had incinerated cities and towns all over Japan, and then dropped two atomic bombs, would be concerned with sparing historic buildings was nothing more than disinformation.

After crossing the bridge he came out in front of a row of old houses which had somehow escaped the conflagration. There was a gradual incline off to the left, and a line of hills on the right. The road threaded its way through the little valley in a way that reminded him of his own village back in Shikoku.

At this point Takuya always stopped to rest and cast his eyes over the gentle slopes on both sides. Every time he paused there the line of the road and the low hills to the east and west caused memories of home to come flooding back. Often he would stand there gazing at the hills and think of his father. With SCAP ordering all assets of war crimes suspects frozen or confiscated, there was a very real chance that his father would have lost his job in the public service. Each time Takuya stopped, he visualized his father standing by the back door to the family house, ready to hand over the package of cigarettes.

The match factory was in a place called Shirahama, amid a cluster of several dozen factories. It was a good five-kilometer haul from Terasawa's workshop. A large operation, it bustled with more than a hundred workers.

Takuya announced his arrival to a young man in the office who led him around to the warehouse beside the rear entrance of the factory, where he unloaded his cargo. In the warehouse there were stacks of small and large matchboxes and men were busy loading these onto horse-drawn carts.

While he waited for his receipt to be stamped, he peered into the factory. It was the first time he saw how matches were actually made, and he watched the workers and machines with interest. The young office worker explained the names of the machines, the manufacturing process and the materials used.

Sometimes while he was waiting, horse-drawn carts would deliver bales of matchsticks. The workers would arrange these on trays, where they would be painted with paraffin before the head was dipped in potassium chlorate mixed with fish glue. The matches would then be dried and taken out to the area where the women workers packed them into boxes. They sat on both sides of a long table grabbing the matches and putting them neatly into boxes at a dizzying pace. From years of experience, each one of these women could virtually guarantee that any box would contain the required eighty-five matchsticks. Red phosphorus striking paper was attached and stamped with the company's trademark, and finally the boxes were wrapped, ready to be dispatched.

Restrictions of everyday commodities had been lifted when the war came to an end, but the unregulated sale of daily essentials such as matches and food was prohibited. The "Match Supply Regulations" of 1940 were still in place, so the government would buy up all the matches produced and distribute them to organizations running the disbursement of rations. Every match manufacturer was plagued with a shortage of materials, and as matchbox supply could not keep up with demand, matches were often shipped loose in bags rather than in boxes.

No wonder the match manufacturer was happy that Terasawa had started making boxes for them. Every time Takuya arrived with a load of boxes they would bring him out a steamed potato or a little bowl of potato starch soup.

The best wood for making matches was white willow from Hokkaido, but as this was almost entirely unavailable, they had to make do with local pine. The problem with pine was its lack of strength when cut into match size, which led to waste during the manufacturing process. Apart from this, the paraffin, red phosphorus and the fish glue were all of inferior quality, and the supply was inadequate, forcing manufacturers to thin their materials to get by, resulting in a much less effective product.

Takuya delivered matchboxes to the factory day after

day. The leaves of the trees on the surrounding hills took on autumn colors, and before long Takuya was hauling his load through swirling eddies of yellow and brown leaves.

Terasawa, Kameya and the others went to a barbershop in an enclave of town which had more or less survived the bombing, but because he was wary of being recognized, Takuya got Kameya to cut his hair with some electric shears.

Occasionally Takuya would look into the long, narrow mirror hanging on a post in the house and see a completely different face from that of his days as an army officer. The outline of his face had completely changed. He was gaunt, and his skin was deeply tanned from hours of labor under the sun. The change in his eyes was particularly striking. The piercing look had disappeared, replaced by an unsettled look of apprehension. When he tried to force an angry glare, he couldn't produce anything beyond a weak and unconvincing grimace.

But that's all right, he thought. The transformation was certainly dramatic, considering that only six months had passed since he had begun his life as a fugitive, but for someone in his position the change was hardly undesirable. If the photographs being used now by the authorities were from his days in the army there was a good chance, he thought, that even if he was stopped no one would be able to make the connection. The glasses were now part of his normal appearance, and it was almost as though the months of hard work had sculpted the features of his face anew.

The temperature dropped, and there was frost in the morning. The food shortages worsened. While the government had announced that staple rations of rice were to be increased, more often than not only potatoes and the like were available, and even they were increasingly slow coming through. The newspapers reported an increase in the number of unemployed every day, and there were often stories about people dying of starvation in the big cities.

Takuya reminded himself once again how fortunate he had been to find a job with Terasawa. Having a ration book didn't guarantee enough food to survive, and the only place anyone could get proper sustenance was still the black market. To be blessed with a job where his employer provided food and shelter must be extremely unusual. Takuya counted his lucky stars that he had come across someone as decent as Terasawa.

Nineteen forty-six came to a close and a new year began. On New Year's Day they had rice cakes delivered, and ate them in traditional *zooni* soup. The rice cakes weren't as sticky as they should be, and felt rough on the tongue. The first snow fell, and when Takuya awoke the next morning the mountains in the distance were covered in a white blanket.

When work started again after New Year's, a twenty-seven-year-old man called Kimijima was taken on to manage the procurement of materials in the match factory. Takuya often conversed with him in the course of his work. Kimijima was a thin man with penetrating eyes, and the way he wore his naval service cap suggested that he had actually served in the Imperial Navy. He told Takuya he had been a petty officer on a destroyer which had been sunk in the Pacific. He had drifted in the sea for five hours before being picked up. He explained that the scar on his neck was a burn mark from when the ship burst into flames when it was hit.

When Kimijima asked Takuya about his background, he told him that he had been a lance corporal in the army. The younger man still had the air of someone whose character had been forged in an atmosphere of harsh discipline. Takuya couldn't help but think that there was little left in his own nature to remind him that he too had once been a military man.

Occasionally he would pass a policeman approaching from the opposite direction. Other times American soldiers in jeeps would thread their way through the foot traffic, leaving clouds of dust in their wake. Each time Takuya would lower his already well-concealed face toward the ground as he pulled the cart down the road.

One day, as the snow was disappearing from the surrounding hills, Takuya was on the way back from delivering a load of boxes to the match factory when he heard someone call to him from behind. When he looked around he saw two men approaching, one about thirty-five or thirty-six and the other not much over twenty. For a second he felt the color drain from his face at the thought that they might be plainclothesmen, but a closer look put his mind at ease. The older man was wearing a jacket and leather boots, and the younger an Air Force flight suit. Both looked unusually healthy and strong.

Still wary, Takuya turned slowly to face them.

The younger man sidled up to him and offered him an American military cigarette. Takuya declined, saying he didn't smoke.

The older man started talking, at first beating around

the bush but eventually explaining that they had seen Takuya delivering boxes to the match factory and followed him on his way back.

"Anyway, can you help us get some matches? We'd really appreciate it," he said, familiarly placing his hand on the cart.

Takuya replied that his job was to deliver boxes and that he wasn't in a position to get matches for them. He did not let on that he knew very well they were suggesting he steal from the match factory.

"So you can't get some for us. We'll pay whatever price you say," said the man irritably.

Takuya shook his head. "I can't do that. Not my line, I'm afraid," he said, shaking his head as he pushed the cart forward down the road.

"Not your line, eh?" said the man with a chuckle as he walked alongside Takuya. After a few paces, looking intently at Takuya's face from the side as though to try to decide whether or not he should give up, he grabbed the handle and stopped the cart. He pulled out a pencil and scribbled a name and address on a piece of paper.

"You can find me here. Remember, I'll pay good money whenever you have matches to sell," he said, stuffing the piece of paper in Takuya's jacket pocket as he let go of the handle.

Takuya trudged along the road back toward the workshop.

Eager to demonstrate his honesty, that night he showed Terasawa the paper and told him what the man had said.

"It's a dangerous world we live in, isn't it," muttered Terasawa as he stared at the piece of paper in his hand. He told Takuya that controlled goods such as matches were sold on the black market, and that while some of them were probably stolen, a sizable number of match manufacturers were illicitly selling their products to dealers in black market goods. Evidently these matches were made of better-quality materials than those supplied for rationing, so the sticks hardly ever broke and were far easier to light.

The blossoms came and went on the cherry trees. Takuya recalled the belt of cherry trees in full bloom around the headquarters building. Shirasaka had undoubtedly finished winding up the affairs of the Western Regional Command and returned to his hometown. Takuya had been on the run for twelve months now, although it felt much longer.

The two men who wanted him to purloin matches did not approach him again. The trees and bushes on both sides of the road were flush with the green of spring, and the air around the road through the hills was alive with birdsong.

Prices ran wild on the black market. The same large bottle of sake that had cost thirteen yen in February was now, two months later, selling for one hundred nine yen. In the same time span, a monthly newspaper subscription went from eight yen to twelve yen fifty sen, and a postcard costing fifteen sen had shot up to fifty sen.

By this stage, it was a struggle to keep up the production of matchboxes with the gradually increasing output of the match factories. Materials were scarce, wood more and more difficult to come by. Often only half the amount of timber ordered was available.

Terasawa made the rounds of the timber dealers, but soon concluded that the supply situation would get worse before it got better, and struck upon the idea of producing his own wooden sheet. He instructed his workers to erect a makeshift work area beside the warehouse and bought a secondhand sawing machine. No one knew how he managed to get it, but before long, loads of rough-sawn pine started to come in by rail.

Near the end of the rainy season, production started on the timber sheet. The saws whirred and rumbled and pine boards were stacked up one after another, wet and pressed thin to make the material which would then be dried out in the sun. Soon this new source of materials increased production in the workshop dramatically.

Chapter Seven

Not a day went by that the trials of class A war criminals didn't dominate the newspapers. There were also excerpts from Tojo Hideki's response to the prosecutor's questions about the execution of some of Major Doolittle's fliers who had taken part in the first air raid on Tokyo in 1942. Tojo maintained that this raid had been a clear violation of international law because its specific objective had been to slaughter defenseless civilians, including women and children. For this reason, he stated, he had not hesitated to grant his chief of staff, former field marshal Sugimoto, permission to execute the captured crewmen. At the same time he insisted that complete responsibility for this action lay with himself and no one else. Tojo went on to say that executions of POWs by subordinates on the instructions of their commanding officers had been accepted practice in the Imperial Army, and that holding these men to account was unjust. However, the reality of the situation was that many officers and lower-ranking soldiers had already been hanged. Tojo's testimony would undoubtedly have no bearing whatsoever on the destiny of someone, such as Takuya himself, who had beheaded an American POW.

The articles about the war crimes trials left Takuya depressed, but those about food were equally disheartening. By now food shortages far exceeded what could be safely endured; supplies of rations were an average of twenty days late across the country, and nothing had reached Hokkaido for three months. The economist's prediction of ten million people dying was obviously no exaggeration, and dramatic increases in deaths from starvation were reported in big cities such as Tokyo and Osaka, with truckloads of bodies collected every day.

There were no stories of people starving to death in Himeji, but increasing numbers of women and children were going out to the rural areas to barter for food. They would take articles of clothing and the like to farming villages and exchange them for pitiful amounts of produce.

Amid all this hardship and privation, Terasawa's timber sheet operation led to some unforeseen good fortune for Takuya and the other workers. The scraps and sawdust produced in the process of making the wooden sheets were highly sought after by salt manufacturers, to use as fuel when boiling seawater to distill salt. After dark, in exchange for the timber scraps, they would secretly deliver bags of salt, a controlled item, to the workshop. Merchants would in turn come offering foodstuffs in exchange for salt, and occasionally farmers living nearby brought in vegetables or beans to barter. Small though the quantities were, Terasawa would then pass on to his workers some of the food or salt he had acquired.

There were times, as Takuya worked away hauling matchboxes, when he thought that maybe he could live the rest of his life like this, without anyone ever discovering his true identity. During the eight months he had pushed the handcart between Terasawa's workshop and the match factory in Shirahama, never venturing beyond that five-kilometer stretch of road, the only people who had ever called out to him had been black market dealers, and he had never once felt in any danger.

As summer came, the sun's rays became more intense. Day by day Takuya plodded along the road in front of the handcart, breathing heavily as beads of sweat formed on his brow and trickled down his neck. On rainy days he covered his cargo with a canvas tarpaulin, put on a raincoat and trudged off toward Shirahama. By now the precise location of every pothole and exposed stone in the road was so clear in his mind that he unconsciously avoided the obstacles on his way to and from the match factory.

One drizzly, hot day, just after Takuya had finished making his delivery of boxes, the young worker in charge of the stores led Takuya to a desk at the back of the warehouse. Something about the man's expression was out of the ordinary. When they reached the desk the man stepped out a side door for a moment before coming back in with the factory manager and Kimijima, the former naval petty officer in charge of materials procurement.

When he saw the looks on their faces, Takuya felt himself flinch. The normally affable factory manager wore a particularly stern expression, his eyes betraying pent-up anger. A feeling of foreboding came over Takuya. His first thought was that somehow the men in the match factory had discovered his real identity, and now the manager was going to question him about his past. The blackness of his hairline stood out in stark relief against his deeply furrowed brow.

The manager sat down and began to explain the situation. On Sunday, two days earlier, Takuya had made a delivery of matchboxes to the factory, and on Monday, when stock was taken, it was discovered that ten packs, each holding ten boxes, were missing. He said that the old caretaker had opened the warehouse door to let Takuya in to unload his boxes on Sunday, but other than that no one had access to the storage area, which naturally made Takuya the prime suspect.

Relieved to know that his identity was not at issue, Takuya protested vehemently against the unfairness of the manager's allegations. Obviously, it was because he was just another shabbily dressed laborer that he was the object of this ridiculous accusation.

The manager ignored Takuya's protestations of innocence, repeating that if he owned up to the crime nothing would be done. The young clerk glared at Takuya as if he were a criminal.

Continuing to shake his head in denial, Takuya had a sinking feeling that this would end up in the hands of the police. If he were to be questioned as a suspected thief, there would be an investigation into whether or not he had any prior convictions, and the police would no doubt go through their wanted posters as part of that process. The next step inevitably would be identification and arrest. To have the police involved was obviously the last thing he wanted, but Takuya couldn't bear the thought of being suspected of stealing from anyone.

The factory manager was unshaken in his insistence that Takuya must have done it. Takuya shook his head vigorously in denial.

An uncomfortable silence followed, then the factory manager glared at Takuya and walked out of the warehouse.

Takuya too stepped outside. He didn't want to leave knowing that they still thought that he was the culprit. Thinking of the look in the eyes of the manager and the clerk made him feel so humiliated and incensed that he trembled with emotion.

"Don't worry about it," said Kimijima from behind.

Takuya turned around to face him. He felt a sudden desire to tell this man everything about his past. Of all people, Kimijima would surely understand his situation, he would know that he wasn't the sort of man who would commit such a stupid crime.

"These days I might be pushing a handcart, but . . . ," was as far as Takuya went before clamming up.

"I know what you're saying. I know you're no laborer. You've got a family and a proper job back in Okinawa. Not that those things count for much these days. At least pulling a cart is a job, and brings in money to buy food," said Kimijima, trying his best to be comforting.

If only he could open up to Kimijima and at least have this man understand both his innocence and the desperate nature of his situation, thought Takuya.

He took a couple of steps toward Kimijima and tried to bring himself to say something to him, but his lips wouldn't move. Kimijima certainly wasn't the sort to blab to the police, but he might tell people close to him, who might in

turn tell others, and before long the police would be bound
to pick up on the story.

Deep down he still wanted to confide in Kimijima, but
he was relieved that he had held his tongue, at least on this
occasion. Looking to Kimijima for support made him feel
pathetic.

"Suspecting you this way without a shred of evidence . . .
it's just ridiculous," said Kimijima with a trace of anger in
his voice.

Takuya stopped in front of the office and bowed his head
to Kimijima, then wrapped the hand towel around his face
and put on his mountaineering hat.

He stepped behind the handle of the cart and started to
push it out of the yard. Before he had gone half a dozen
steps he felt tears rolling down his cheeks. He asked himself
why he was crying. He hadn't done anything to justify being
suspected of this theft and had done his best to deny it, so
there was nothing for him to regret. What was he so sad
about? Was it the fact that he was someone who had graduated from university and gone on to reach the rank of lieutenant in the Imperial Army, only to become a suspected
criminal, a laborer with a hand towel wrapped around his
face pushing a cart?

Recently he had realized that since coming to Himeji he
had gradually changed into someone quite different from his
previous self. One day, as he was hauling his cart along the
road, he had noticed a woman, probably out shopping, walking a few paces in front of him. She was carrying a makeshift
bag, made from what had once been the Japanese national
flag. It appeared that she was using it to carry potatoes, but

when Takuya saw this, rather than feeling anger, he had just looked away. Maybe he was starting to change with the times too, like the young woman walking hand in hand with the U.S. serviceman. Smoking American military-issue cigarettes no longer felt the least bit strange. All that remained was the fear of being caught by the American military. Maybe the tears were a sign of how delicate his nerves had become after all this time on the run.

When he got back to the workshop he said nothing to Terasawa about the accusations. He had explained about the two black market dealers approaching him on the road and trying to get him to steal from the match factory, so if he told Terasawa about the stolen matches there was a chance his boss would think that he had given in to temptation and actually committed this crime. Furthermore, the lack of evidence meant it was highly unlikely that the match factory manager would ever mention the incident to Terasawa.

The next day, Takuya hauled a load of boxes to the match factory as usual. Requesting a change to another task would only increase the match factory manager's suspicions of him, and if he told Terasawa about what had happened in order to be relieved of his delivery duties, the odds were good that his boss would take steps to protest Takuya's innocence. Terasawa's connections with the police being what they were, it was possible that he might even ask them to lend a hand in clearing Takuya's name.

Definitely, the right way to proceed was to continue doing deliveries, he told himself. To guard against further accusations, every time he arrived at the match factory now he stopped in front of the office and waited until one of the workers came out to escort him. When he went into the warehouse to unload his boxes, he always asked the stores clerk to accompany him, and if for one reason or another the clerk had to go back inside Takuya waited outside, leaning on the empty handcart, until the man came back and verified that everything was in order. Nonplussed by this approach, the clerk was sometimes sarcastically servile, but Takuya kept his replies short and impassive and remained unperturbed. Sometimes he would bump into the factory manager, and when their eyes met the manager would just keep walking, a decidedly uncomfortable look on his face.

The power outages were as frequent as ever, so to maintain production levels they started operating the machines before dawn. Takuya got up earlier too, to lend a hand carrying the pressed timber sheets and the striking paper. This summer there were many more fireflies than the previous year, and little specks of light flickered everywhere around the workshop.

The heat abated and the first signs of autumn appeared.

One day in mid-September, coming back from his deliveries and wanting to take a short rest, Takuya pulled his empty cart up the embankment between the road and the river. The breeze felt refreshing against his skin, which was moist with sweat from his toil, and a panoramic view of the countryside opened up in front of him.

As he sat down against the cart and wiped his face and neck with his hand towel, he spotted something blue down in the expanse of reeds between the river and the embankment. It looked like a pair of trousers. Straining to see through the rustling reeds he made out a pair of feet protruding from the trouser legs. Maybe a young couple was there, seeking to enjoy themselves away from prying eyes. As the reeds swayed and hummed in the next strong gust of wind Takuya got a clearer view of the blue cloth of the trousers, then he caught sight of the man's shirt and the back of his head. He was obviously alone.

Takuya lit a cigarette. The reeds bent over again with the next gust of wind and the man lying in the reeds was exposed to view once more.

Each time the wind blew strongly enough to move the reeds, Takuya found his eyes drawn to the man. The sweat on his face was almost dry by now. In the distance he could see a train slowly pulling out of the station just this side of Himeji Castle. There was no one to be seen anywhere near him. The only person visible was some distance away along the embankment, a woman dressed in a dark work kimono, bent over picking wild vegetables.

Maybe this man had been doing the same and was taking a rest before starting again. Takuya remembered how he used to pick bamboo shoots and parsley in the woods and fields around his village, and thought that if there were something edible down among those reeds, perhaps he should go and pick some for himself.

Hat in hand, Takuya got to his feet and walked down the embankment and onto a little path through the sea of reeds. They were so high that each time the wind blew, the fluffy tops would brush against his face.

Before he had taken many steps along the winding path a faint sickly-sweet smell brought him instinctively to a halt. The black, swollen feet of a dead body were poking out of the blue trousers. From a distance it might have seemed as though the man was taking an afternoon nap, but the terrible smell of decaying flesh wafting in Takuya's direction was unmistakable.

Waving his hand in front of his nose at the stench, Takuya watched as the wind flailed the reeds against the man's body. The man lay facedown, his shirt pushed up to reveal the reddish-black skin on his back.

Takuya edged backward two or three steps before turning around and scurrying a few more paces back down the path. The sickly-sweet smell of death still clung to his clothes, and as he hastened up the embankment he was hit by a wave of nausea.

Back beside his handcart, Takuya retched as he stared at the blue cloth down among the reeds. Had the man been murdered, or had he starved to death? Takuya had only seen the man's feet and part of his back, but he guessed that the man had probably been at least middle-aged. He knew that he should report it to the police, but of course that was the last thing he intended to do. Being questioned by the police was just too risky.

The dead man has nothing to do with me, he thought. Eventually that woman picking wild vegetables, or maybe some children playing in the reeds, would find the body. If the man had simply collapsed and died on his way somewhere, his body would be carried away and disposed of.

Takuya lifted the handle of the cart and started walking. The revolting smell persisted, clinging to him. He retched again and again as he walked down the road. This smell was different from the one that had wafted up from the shallow graves when they had exhumed the decapitated bodies to destroy the last evidence of the fate of the American fliers. That smell had been something akin to wet, rotting cardboard, but it was equally pungent. Maybe there was a difference when a corpse decomposed in the sun.

Despite having no proof, Takuya somehow sensed that the man had died a natural death. But if that was so, why had he wandered off the road and down into the reeds? Had he been so hungry that he'd remembered his childhood days and gone searching for birds' nests? Or had he ventured down the embankment to look for wild vegetables? The thought of that poor man lying there dead, facedown among the reeds, deeply affected Takuya.

He tried to picture the families of the men who had been executed in that clearing in the bamboo grove. They would have had parents, maybe even brothers and sisters. Their families would have mourned their deaths and no doubt despaired at the fact that there were no remains on which to focus their grief.

As a crewman on a B-29, the man whom Takuya had beheaded had been party to the slaughter of countless Japanese, but the clear memory of the man in his mind included nothing of what Takuya imagined a murderer might look like, no suggestion of anything criminal. He had just been playing his part as a cog in the wheel of the American war machine in its attacks on the Japanese mainland, and even if that had resulted in the slaughter of civilians, it was unlikely that he felt any guilt about his part in the process. To him, there may have been only a tenuous connection between the bombs that tumbled out of his plane's bomb bay and the carnage down on the ground.

Takuya mused that his involvement in the executions was essentially the same in nature as the actions of the man he had killed, in that both were merely carrying out their duties as military men. The difference was that whereas the killing committed by the American had been by bombing, which precluded directly witnessing the bloodshed, Takuya's act had involved wielding the sword with his own hands as he beheaded the flier. The fact that the American had killed countless people as opposed to Takuya's one victim brought him some comfort.

Takuya shook his head and frowned. He wished he had never seen that blue cloth. As recollections of that afternoon in the bamboo grove swirled inside his head, he felt ashamed of his loss of nerve. These days he hardly ever checked his pistol to make sure it would be ready for that moment of truth if he was cornered, and he even doubted he'd have the courage to pull the trigger if worst came to worst.

The reeds waved this way and that before bending right in unison as a gust of wind blew from downstream. Takuya fixed his eyes on the ground and pulled the cart off down the road.

Temperatures dropped with each passing day. There were no articles in the newspaper about any murder, and as the body in the reeds must have been found by now, the authorities must have decided that the man had died a natural death.

Takuya delivered his cartloads of matchboxes, his routine unchanging from one day to the next. He had attached a long canvas strap to two points on the deck of the cart so he could move it more effectively, and once a hard knot of muscle formed under the skin on his shoulders, pulling the cart was no problem at all.

The first colors of autumn could be seen on the low hills near Himeji. Fine weather continued, with pleasant days followed by glowing red sunsets.

One day toward the end of autumn, when the reds and golds of the surrounding hills had begun to mute to softer yellows and browns, Takuya saw something that made him stop in his tracks and stare down the road. A convoy of four U.S. Army trucks, their canvas canopies rolled up, were moving toward him, kicking up clouds of dust.

He had often seen American trucks and jeeps trundling along the main road and over the reinforced concrete bridge just downstream from the rickety old wooden bridge he pulled his cart over, but never once had he seen them using this old pathway. The road was barely wider than the wheel-span of a large truck, making it impossible for two vehicles to pass each other. Maybe they were lost, or maybe they had decided to make a shortcut. There were no side paths to push the cart off into, and all that separated the road from the paddy fields on both sides was a narrow ditch.

He knew that the trucks were coming toward him at a considerable speed, but for the life of him he couldn't think of what he should do. His load of matchboxes stuck out on both sides of the cart, so if he didn't move it off the road there was no way the truck would be able to pass.

For a second he thought of turning around and heading for the last crossroad, but that was almost a kilometer back down the road, so there was no way he could make it in time. There was nothing to do but push the cart to one side of the road and hope that the trucks would be able to squeeze past. He summoned all his strength and hurriedly pushed the cart back a few meters to a spot on the side of the road where it was slightly wider than where he had been standing.

The sound of the trucks' engines and tires grew louder as the front vehicle closed rapidly on him. The sunlight reflected off the windshield so he couldn't see inside, but he could see an elbow sticking out of each of the windows.

The truck's horn blasted the air for what seemed an age, leaving his ears ringing. The full width of the road was taken up as the convoy bore down on Takuya and his cart. Fear seized him at the thought that the driver of the truck might not slow down at all, and would instead choose to smash both the cart and Takuya out of the way. The truck's tires seemed enormous, and the chassis with its white star on the side was far higher than any Japanese vehicle he had ever seen.

The sound of the horn was followed by the screeching of brakes, as the truck halted ten meters short of the hand-cart. Takuya clasped the bar tightly as he stood his ground. Shouts of surprise came from the soldiers sitting on the truck's rear deck and heads poked out to check why they had stopped so suddenly. Seconds later the truck was engulfed in the cloud of dust floating up from behind.

A fresh-faced young soldier leaned out the window on the passenger side, yelling something and gesticulating excitedly at Takuya to get out of the way. Evidently enraged, he shouted the same thing again and again with increasing urgency.

Takuya moved the cart. His vision seemed to blur for a

moment as sweat poured down his forehead. He maneuvered the cart forward and backward to get it as far off the road as he could.

The truck's horn rended the air once again before the vehicle started to roll forward. Edging the cart back, he looked up to see a husky, red-faced man sitting behind the steering wheel. The man leaning out the window on the passenger side was still furiously shouting something at Takuya. The chassis of the truck closed on him, and the wheels kicked up little stones as they turned.

Realizing that it was impossible to keep the cart up on the road, Takuya stepped down into the ditch, pulling the handcart with him. One of the wheels slipped down off the road and Takuya leaned over sideways trying to keep the cart from toppling over. He threw all his weight against the cart's metal bar and just managed to stop the weight of the load from tipping the cart into the rice paddy.

The truck rolled forward on a course which would take it within inches of Takuya's cart. The soldiers on the flat deck behind the cab, both black and white men, seemed to be laughing as they looked down at Takuya. They all had submachine guns slung over their shoulders or resting against their knees as they stood peering down over the side.

As Takuya concentrated all his might on keeping the cart from slipping into the paddy field, he pitched his gaze diagonally up at the Americans. Maybe this looked comical to the soldiers, as a gale of laughter erupted from them. This was the first time he had seen foreign military up close since the afternoon of the day the war ended. Every one of them seemed to be smiling.

As the lead truck passed him and moved off down the road, the second vehicle approached slowly. Once again the flat deck was full of soldiers looking down at Takuya and his cart perched precariously at the side of the road. A round-faced man with mousy-colored hair leaned out the passenger window, smiling widely at Takuya. He couldn't have been much more than seventeen or eighteen years old. The cab went past and the deck came level with Takuya. Again the soldiers smiled down at him, their eyes seemingly genial. Takuya could sense a fawning, obsequious expression coming across his own contorted face.

Suddenly one of the soldiers thrust his upper body forward and swung the steel helmet he had been hiding behind him down onto Takuya's head. The lack of anywhere to retreat, and the speed with which the helmet was wielded, made the blow impossible to avoid. The other soldiers on the flat deck must have been waiting for that moment, as a loud cheer went up from them. Takuya caught sight of a black soldier giving the culprit a few congratulatory slaps on the shoulder as he felt himself and the cart slowly tipping over sideways into the rice paddy. The load of matchboxes spilled into the water and Takuya felt his face slap hard into the mud.

The soldiers' jubilant faces quickly moved out of view, and the remaining trucks accelerated down the road now that the obstacle had been ejected from their path. The clouds of dust settled as the noise of the trucks' engines faded into the distance.

Barely conscious, his eyes almost shut, Takuya's first thought was to see this as an officer of the Japanese army being insulted by a lowly American soldier, but for some reason this didn't anger him in the slightest. He just couldn't fathom the grinning looks on the young soldiers' faces, their joyful animation as they celebrated Takuya's difficulty. He felt that the soldiers smashing him over the head with a steel helmet was part of some frivolous game, like the bomber crews whiling away their time inside the B-29s by flipping through pornographic magazines and listening to jazz.

Some time passed before he slowly opened his eyes again. There was no pain but his ears were ringing as though a hundred cicadas had got inside his head. He tried to get up, but the side of his face was stuck to the mud and wouldn't move. His vision seemed to be all right, as he could see the bar of the cart directly above his head, as well as the canvas strap hanging down on top of him. Beyond these he could see the clear blue sky, with only a few delicate clouds.

A man dressed in peasant clothes appeared. Takuya felt himself being lifted and dragged out of the paddy field and up the slope, where he was helped into a sitting position on the side of the road. Some more men, probably ten in all, appeared around him. Some were trying to push the cart up out of the mud, and others were carrying his spilled cargo back up onto the road. A man wearing shorts was asking him something, and while Takuya could sense himself replying, the sound of his own voice was drowned out by the ringing in his ears.

He looked up at the blue sky and the clouds moving across it. There were women in work clothes among the crowd. Takuya could feel someone holding him in an upright sitting position.

People were milling around the handcart, stacking the load back into place. The cicada-like ringing seemed to echo from one side of his head to the other.

Terasawa appeared in front of him, talking frantically. Again he felt himself answering but unable to hear his own reply. Kameya's face came into view, and Takuya felt himself being lifted onto the flat deck of the truck. The glare of the sun made him squint.

He closed his eyes.

Chapter Eight

Takuya spent three days recuperating in bed.

"You poor thing," said Terasawa's wife every time she put some food down beside his pillow. The ringing in his ears was gone, but he still had a splitting headache.

Evidently a farmer working in a nearby field had seen Takuya toppling into the rice paddy with his handcart. The people who came to his assistance after the trucks left had noticed the company name painted on the cart and sent someone to report the incident to Terasawa, who had rushed to the scene with Kameya in the truck.

"We told the police, but they just nodded and said that when it comes to the Occupation Forces, there's nothing they can do," explained Terasawa in a despondent tone.

Takuya couldn't imagine pulling the cart again. If U.S. Army trucks had chosen that road once, they might choose it again, and if he got in their way a second time the same thing could happen again. He sensed a strange malevolence in those cheerful Americans. Their physical size equally overwhelmed him. Thinking of how intimidated he felt now, he couldn't believe that just two years ago he had the nerve to actually stand up and behead one of their countrymen.

When Takuya asked timidly if he could be switched from deliveries to a job in the workshop, Terasawa agreed without a moment's hesitation. He said that he understood Takuya's reluctance to get back out on the road, and that another man had been asking for a job doing deliveries.

For four days Terasawa's wife nursed the swollen wound on Takuya's head with antiseptic. Five days after the incident, Takuya came back to work again on light duties, and two weeks after that, when he was fully recovered, he started on heavier duties, carrying pieces of timber around the workshop.

By now the hills in the distance were covered with a white blanket of snow.

Orders for matchboxes went up with the increase in the black market production of matches. Production capacity was pushed to the limit, and to compensate for the time lost during the day because of power interruptions, they started up the machines in the workshop before dawn.

At the end of December, Terasawa's wife's niece, a well-built twenty-five-year-old by the name of Teruko, came to live with them to help with the housework. She got up early in the morning to help Terasawa's wife boil the sticky concoction they used as glue each day. In addition she helped with the cooking, washing and cleaning, and went out to collect the week's rations.

A bathroom was added on to the house and hot water

was generated by burning the scraps and sawdust from the workshop. Terasawa let the staff who lived away from the workshop take turns soaking in the new bathtub after work. He also followed rises in the wage market, and increased his workers' wages as often as he could. At the end of that year, Takuya's live-in wage was raised to one thousand three hundred yen a month.

Kameya sometimes spent his spare cash down in the brothels near the station, returning late at night.

"Do you want to come down sometime?" he asked Takuya, holding up three fingers to indicate that three hundred yen would buy the services of a young lady for an hour.

Takuya smiled and said nothing.

Lugging timber around in the workshop was hard work, but not having to venture outside removed a weight from his mind. As had been the case when he'd been pushing the handcart, most days he kept a small towel wrapped around his face, more for function than disguise now.

In his free time Takuya gazed at the white walls of Himeji Castle or tried to imagine what was happening in his village back in Shikoku. Almost two years had passed since he left home. He wondered what his parents and brother and sister had done during that time, and whether or not his father and mother were still in good health. They must be wondering what had happened to him too. The police would be checking their mail, so sending them a letter was too risky. But all the same, he wished he could put their minds at ease with the knowledge that, for the time being, he was still alive and safe.

As New Year's approached, Terasawa bought a stack of

greeting cards and, after stamping each of them with the company seal, got Teruko to address them, which she did in immaculate, precise handwriting.

Takuya toyed with the idea of sending a New Year's card to his parents. He could write Terasawa's company address, he thought, but of course he would use a false name, something new, neither Kiyohara Takuya nor Higa Seiichi. At first glance his family would think it strange to be receiving greetings from a stranger, but they'd soon recognize his handwriting and realize that he was safe and well, living in Himeji.

After thinking it through this far, Takuya suddenly changed his mind. Maybe he was slowly starting to cave, he thought. When he'd left his parents' home, Takuya had told himself that there would be no return, and that he would never see his family again. He had known that evading the authorities hinged on cutting the bonds with his hometown, and that was as true now as it had been two years earlier.

But as time passed, Takuya's resolve started to waver. Sending New Year's greeting cards was so ritualized that receiving one from someone with whom you normally had very little contact was nothing out of the ordinary. Surely the police wouldn't notice his one card among the dozens of others. He pondered a little longer, convincing himself that there was no risk involved. Letting his family know that he was still alive was something he just had to do.

After getting one of the company-stamped cards from Terasawa, Takuya thought hard about what to write. Something as bland as possible would be best, and addressing it to his younger brother rather than his father would make it safer still. He wrote "New Year's Greetings" at the top, followed by "Wishing you and your family all the best for the year to come." They were very nondescript words, but he was sure that his family would read between the lines and recognize his message.

That night, Takuya went to the mailbox in front of the makeshift ration distribution center. There was a chance that a member of his family might try to visit him at the address on the card, but surely they would realize that this could be fatal for him.

He headed back home with an extra spring in his step at the thought that even a tenuous connection was about to be made with his family.

At dinnertime on New Year's Day, 1948, Terasawa brought in five bottles of beer and a large bottle of sake for them to drink with their meal of rice cakes and vegetables boiled in soup. He even obtained some dried fish to supplement the meal. By all accounts match production in the area was increasing by leaps and bounds, and Terasawa's production of boxes, and therefore profits, was also rising. By this stage he had increased the number of staff to almost twenty workers.

Terasawa often spoke of hearing rumors that the match market was about to be freed up later that year, with the old wartime rationing and control regulations possibly being abolished. He told them that while the overall quality of the matches was still inferior, production levels were basically meeting demand, so the regulations were becoming pointless. Terasawa said public discontent was running high over matches that frequently snapped or failed to light properly, and that government offices in Tokyo and Osaka were starting to handle appeals from citizens' groups for something to be done about the situation.

"There's certainly something farcical about making matchboxes when more than half of what goes in them is going to break anyway," Terasawa lamented.

The front page of the morning newspaper on New Year's Day contained a long message to the Japanese people from General Douglas MacArthur, supreme commander of the Allied Powers, in which he laid out a plan for Japan's future as a nation. Takuya scoured it for mention of war criminals, but found nothing.

After the New Year's holiday came to a close, however, the newspapers featured lengthy articles almost daily recounting the proceedings in the Tokyo trials of class A war criminals. Takuya read through every one of them, but since that article the previous September about the imprisonment in Sugamo of the high-ranking officers, there had been no further mention of the POWs held by the Western Regional Command, something which worried him intensely.

While he had long since recovered from the physical damage caused by the encounter with the American soldiers, emotionally he was far from healed. The pitiful feeling of helplessness he had experienced as the helmet smashed down on his head was still rooted in his mind. It was a feeling less of humiliation than of having been absolutely crushed in defeat. Everything they did seemed lighthearted, he thought. If they caught him they would probably make a comedy out of leading him to the gallows and placing the noose around his neck. He remembered how the Americans adorned the B-29s with caricatures of naked women and pictures of flames painted on the fuselages to show how many raids they had taken part in.

On his job carrying timber around the workshop Takuya kept a lookout for anyone approaching from outside. Houses were being built in the vicinity of the railway station, and the boundaries of this new residential area were gradually pushing farther out.

With the price of materials increasing at a frightening pace, Terasawa decided that the best thing would be to stock up on timber and striking paper and, as the existing warehouse was already full to capacity, to build another one next to it.

It appeared more and more likely that the sale of matches would be freed up soon, and an article in the newspaper on the twentieth of January reported that a special ration of matches was to be given to each household. Families with three members could buy two small boxes, those with six people four boxes, ten people eight boxes, and ten boxes could be purchased by households comprising ten or more people. The price was set at one yen twenty-three sen, and normal ration coupons for household goods would suffice. This was proof that production levels were finally starting to meet demand.

Maybe the news that matches were going to be removed from the list of regulated goods was encouraging more operators to start manufacturing, for the number of strangers coming in to buy large quantities of matchboxes had increased considerably. Thick wads of notes were handed over in exchange for cartloads of matchboxes. The buyers, dressed in all sorts of clothes, were obviously black marketeers, and none of them knew much at all about the product they were looking to buy. Every time these strangers approached Takuya worried that they might be plain-clothes policemen.

With the drop in temperature came occasional light flurries of snow. The icy winds that blew across Himeji robbed the feeling from Takuya's hands, and that winter he again developed painful chilblains on his ears, fingers and toes.

The new houses built near the station hid the lower part of Himeji Castle from view, but the white towers and donjons stood out in stark relief against the clear blue of the winter sky.

Toward the end of January the newspapers were dominated by articles about the poisoning of twelve workers at the Shiina-machi branch of the Imperial Bank, but in early February Takuya found one that mentioned the Western Regional Command. On February second the legal department of the U.S. Eighth Army announced the names of twenty-eight people, comprising sixteen military personnel, including the commander in chief of the Western Regional Command, and twelve staff of the faculty of medicine at Kyushu Imperial University, who had been charged and would be tried together publicly by the Yokohama Military Tribunal. The charges were divided into the three broad categories of vivisection, cannibalism, and the unlawful execution of B-29 crew members, with a note at the end of the article to the effect that Professor Iwase of Kyushu Imperial University had already taken his own life.

Takuya had secretly hoped that the trial of the seven officers from the Western Regional Command, including the commander in chief, who had been held in Sugamo Prison since September 1945, had already ended. Now he knew that in fact it was just about to start, and that the number of people charged had increased to sixteen. The article he had read almost a year and a half ago had mentioned seven suspects incarcerated in Sugamo Prison, six of them high-ranking officers, and the other, Lieutenant Howa Kotaro, the only one who had actually taken part in the executions. That the number of suspects had increased to sixteen meant that another nine of the soldiers who had participated in the executions must have been arrested and charged.

Takuya had taken part in only one of the three executions, so he didn't know for sure how many people had been involved altogether, but he surmised that it must have been around fourteen or fifteen, meaning that including himself there were still four or five men at large. Shirasaka had mentioned giving Lieutenant Hirosaki demobilization papers and telling him to flee, and Takuya had done the same for his friend Himuro in Osaka. If these two men were still at large, then another two or three more must be on the run.

SCAP would have wanted to start the trials, and would have instructed the Japanese government to arrest the remaining suspects. The government in turn would have entrusted the police with the task, which they were no doubt doing their utmost to carry out. Again Takuya felt as though the net was somehow closing in around him.

He started to feel uneasy about having sent the New Year's card to his family in Shikoku. Using a false name was one thing, but maybe he shouldn't have used a card with his real address in Himeji printed on it. But then again, if

the police had been suspicious about the card they surely
would have sent someone to Terasawa's workshop by now.
He assumed that the fact they hadn't was proof that the
card had slipped past the censors unnoticed.

Takuya tried to imagine the lives his comrades were
leading as fugitives. Like him, they would have assumed false
names and endeavored to change their appearance, and
would probably be leading secret lives somewhere as laborers. They would no doubt pay just as much attention as he
did to the newspapers, and would have seen this article.
How wonderful it would be, thought Takuya, if they could
all evade capture.

The class A war criminals' trials entered their closing
stages, and toward the end of February there was further
mention in the newspaper of those in the Western Regional
Command. The article first covered the charges against
those involved in the vivisection of eight captured fliers in
the Faculty of Medicine at Kyushu Imperial University, then
went on to describe how after the experiments, the livers of
the dead airmen had evidently been extracted, marinated in
soy sauce, and served at the officers' club of the Western
Regional Command. Takuya hadn't heard anything about
livers being eaten, and thought that it must be some kind
of mistake.

Accompanying the indictment was an explanation of
the background to the charges that further increased Takuya's anxiety. The names of those charged were preceded by
the statement that although those in the Western Regional
Command had tried to conceal the truth by stating that the
eight fliers who died on the operating tables in Fukuoka had

been killed in the atomic bombing of Hiroshima, "the full story had finally been revealed after hundreds of interrogations had been carried out all over the country." Takuya thought this testified to the rigor of the investigations undertaken by the Occupation authorities.

After reading this article Takuya decided it was almost a miracle that he hadn't been caught.

The police had probably already traced his movements as far as his uncle's house in Osaka, then on to Corporal Nemoto's on Shoodo-shima, and from there to his friend Fujisaki in Kobe. They would have been unrelenting in their questioning, and while each of his friends would no doubt have admitted to giving him shelter for a short time, the fact that he was still a free man was obviously due to the fact that Fujisaki and his family had not let on that they introduced him to the Terasawas.

The temperature started to rise as spring approached.

"Do you want to try your hand at keeping the accounts? You seem to write pretty well, and I think my wife and niece are right when they say that lugging wood around the workshop doesn't really suit you. They're always on me about it," said Terasawa to Takuya as he sat taking a break on a pile of wood.

Takuya didn't know what to say.

"I remember you saying that you finished high school in Okinawa. The warehouse is in full operation and stock is streaming in, so we need to keep a proper inventory of things. Want to give it a try?" said Terasawa, offering Takuya a cigarette.

He could sense the goodwill behind Terasawa's offer.

His boss might only have finished primary school, but

he treated his workers with an innate generosity that formal education could not teach. He had led a hard life and was extremely demanding when it came to work, but his kindness ensured that a proper balance was maintained. He implied that the idea behind the offer wasn't his, but Takuya had no doubt that Terasawa had thought it all up himself.

The thought of changing jobs made Takuya uneasy. Moving wood around the workshop allowed him to stay in an isolated environment, while if he were to look after the company accounts he would be obliged to go out into the public eye to arrange deliveries and collect payment from clients. He wanted to turn down the offer, but could think of no good excuse.

The prospect of not having to toil away in the workshop was certainly appealing. Although he had been a sportsman during his university days, laboring required a different sort of physical and mental hardness that was starting to take its toll. Deciding that it might seem peculiar if he turned down Terasawa's kind offer, Takuya consented to changing jobs.

Beginning the next day he sat behind a desk in the large concrete-floored space in the front part of the house. Obviously there could be no more wrapping a hand towel around his face while he worked, nor could he wear his mountaineering hat all the time. He felt exposed and unnerved without what he now realized had been, at least in his mind, crucial elements of disguise.

Terasawa came in and handed over some money, telling Takuya to go and buy a new pair of glasses to replace the ones he had repaired with a piece of string.

Glasses were the only means he had left to make his

face less recognizable in a crowd, so he willingly took the money from Terasawa and headed off to an eyeglass shop in an area of town which had largely survived the fire raids. There wasn't much to choose from, but he picked out some dark brown, horn-rimmed glasses and asked the shopkeeper to fit them with quite strong lenses. He tried them on and looked in the mirror on the counter. The rims of the glasses Fujisaki had given him had been relatively thin, so they hadn't made much difference in the way he looked, but these new ones altered his appearance considerably. On the way back to the workshop he tossed his old glasses onto a pile of rubbish by the side of the road.

The two women made quite a show of their surprise upon seeing Takuya, and Terasawa commented jokingly that he looked like a completely different person, which of course eased his fears somewhat.

Takuya set himself conscientiously to his new job. The accounts book Terasawa gave to him was nothing more than a large exercise book with the word "Accounts" written at the top. While he thought he should hide the fact that he had a degree in economics by keeping the books as simply as possible, he knew that he would have to use some basic bookkeeping practices in order to maintain the accounts properly. He ruled some blue and red lines on the pages and organized them into workable columns.

Terasawa was impressed when he saw what Takuya had prepared.

"When I say high school, it was a business school after all," said Takuya, looking a little embarrassed at the praise.

Terasawa's niece brought cups of green tea to Takuya's desk midmorning and midafternoon. She also who told him that amid the desolation a charred plum tree had actually started blooming. Two little clumps of blossom had appeared on one branch sticking out from the blackened trunk, and quite a few people had come to see this. She added that she had noticed couples standing under the tree looking up at the pink flowers.

Teruko often whispered to him that she would be glad to mend any of his clothes, or do other little jobs for him.

On the eleventh of March, Takuya read in the newspaper that the trial of those involved in the vivisections at Kyushu Imperial University had begun at the Yokohama Military Court. The article described how three hundred people, including foreigners, the families of the accused, and reporters from Japan and overseas had packed into the public gallery, and how the accused, the public prosecutors and other lawyers had filed into the court, followed by members of the military tribunal. After one of the public prosecutors read out the charges, each of the accused, including the commander in chief of the Western Region, had pleaded not guilty, and the day's proceedings were closed after the chief prosecutor made his opening address to the court.

Six days later Takuya came across an article that, in its own way, indicated the probable fate of the accused from the Western Regional Command. It reported on the sentencing of naval garrison personnel on Ishigaki Island who had been involved in the execution by decapitation, and subsequent bayoneting of the corpses, of three American fighter crewmen. The chief of the military tribunal had sentenced two of the forty-five accused to imprisonment with hard labor, and found another two not guilty, but had sentenced the remaining forty-one men to death by hanging.

Logically speaking, no more than three garrison soldiers had actually beheaded the American fliers, so the others must be the officers who had ordered the execution and those who had bayoneted the corpses. That the list included many soldiers ranking corporal or below served to confirm this, the officers undoubtedly having ordered the bayoneting to prepare the soldiers for the battles to come. Such practices were almost routine in front-line units, and there was no place for the will of the individual soldier to intervene in the process. Nevertheless, it was SCAP's position that several dozen soldiers should receive the death penalty regardless of whether they had been acting on orders from their commanding officer to mutilate the dead bodies. By this reasoning, Takuya and those of his comrades who had actually beheaded B-29 crew members could expect nothing less than the gallows.

He often woke up in the middle of the night and struggled to get back to sleep, worrying about how someone he had passed in the street had looked at him, or how a man standing on the street corner seemed to be peering curiously into the factory area. Since taking over the office duties he had to make regular trips to the bank and to clients in order to receive payments for boxes. Occasionally, he had gone as far as the railway station to arrange for the shipment of an order of matchboxes by freight train. Every time he left the confines of the company premises, the thought that he was stepping into public view unnerved him. At times he thought that for his peace of mind he should take his pistol with him, but he knew that the nerve he would need to actually use it had long since vanished, so it stayed in his rucksack.

Takuya started to think that being attached to the Western Regional Command Headquarters had been a stroke of very bad luck. The other graduating cadets had been scattered to postings throughout Japan and overseas. Within the anti-aircraft defense corps, some had taken up positions with ack-ack units and others had gone to command electronic aircraft detection groups. If only he hadn't been assigned to headquarters, he thought, he wouldn't be on the run, and would probably be sitting in an office somewhere, content with his lot.

He thought back to the time when the lieutenant from the legal affairs section had told him to pick out two sergeant-majors to take part in the executions, and regretted having offered to do his part too. He had volunteered from a feeling of outrage toward those who had carried out countless incendiary raids, as well as not one but two atomic bombings on Japanese cities, seeing the execution of the B-29 crewmen as a natural and indisputable response to such acts of barbarism. But after the war there had been no adverse media comment about the bombings, the primary objective of which had been to slaughter defenseless civilians. SCAP censorship probably had played a part in this, but even so, the average person in the street was just as reluctant to say anything. Women offered their bodies to American soldiers for money, children groveled in the streets for candy, and men bought what the Americans didn't need to sell for their own profit. They must have erased from their minds any memory of the houses being burned to cinders and the lives lost in the firestorms. Not an iota of hatred about what had happened seemed to remain among the populace.

Takuya too now came to the realization that his anger toward the American military had all but evaporated. Did the time after a war act as some sort of filtration process, whereby all memories and experiences were expunged from the present and relegated to the past? All that remained in Takuya's mind was the undeniable fact that he had beheaded a POW and the relentless anxiety of being on the run.

He started to rethink the meaning of the badges he had worn as an officer in the army. Wearing an officer's badge was an article of faith, a sign that one was not afraid of dying, and Takuya had held true to it during his days in uniform. However, since leaving the army, the fear of death dominated his every moment, and the fact that such a change could occur in the two short years since he left his parents' house seemed incredible to him. Whenever he went out on business he took the lesser-used roads and walked with his eyes cast slightly downward. If he had to go to the Sanyo Line freight station, he furtively slipped the duty station worker a box of matches from Terasawa, smiling obsequiously and acting as ingratiating as he could in order to avoid giving the impression that he'd been an officer in the army.

Down on the embankment the cherry trees were blossoming, and crowds of people were said to be flocking in for a festival which was being held at the Ryuumon Temple near the sea. Slowly society seemed to be moving back toward normality.

On a day when they knew that the power was to be off, Takuya went with Terasawa and the others to the beach to collect shellfish. The women got up early and cooked some rice with soybeans to use for making rice balls. One of the day workers and his family joined them, and Kameya drove them all to the sea in the truck.

They crossed the bridge over the Ishikawa River and drove through the residential area of Shirahama, where many of the match factories were located. The beach was on the edge of town, not far from the little fishing port of Mega, so they could see fishing boats heading back in after a day out at sea. Men and women in sedge hats were working in the belt of salt fields stretching out on one side.

At this first view of the sea in two years Takuya relaxed immediately. It was a beautiful calm day, and in the distance he could see a number of small islands, each covered in a lush blanket of green. A school of fish must be just off to the west, as the water was agitated with the fish breaking the surface. Seabirds took turns plunging out of the sky into the mass of fish, or sat bobbing up and down on the water's surface.

There were crowds of people there that day, all bent over scraping away at the sand. Here and there, the sun's rays reflected brightly off puddles of sparkling clear water.

Takuya and the others dug away at the sand with metal clamps they had brought from the workshop. They found small clams everywhere, but occasionally, to everyone's delight, they uncovered a really big one. Every so often, Takuya straightened up and stretched his back, surveying the area around them. At the water's edge, he could see little waves curling white at the top before dropping onto the shore. The color of the sea was slightly greener than how he remembered it near his hometown. Off in the distance a black freighter slowly threaded its way between the islands.

Terasawa sauntered over to him, metal clamp in hand and an old straw hat on his head.

"Higa," he said, as he bent over to scrape at the sand. Takuya turned to face him.

"My wife asked me to speak to you about this. Um . . . What do you think of her niece Teruko? To marry, I mean. You know what our situation is. Losing our son in the war means that we don't have anyone to take over the business after us. My wife likes you, you know," said Terasawa, as he dug some little clams up and placed them neatly on the sand.

"Teruko seems to have a soft spot for you too, so why don't you think about it?" said Terasawa. Then he stood up straight, picked up the clams and walked off toward the bucket.

Takuya wasn't surprised. In fact, he had almost expected such an approach. On more than one occasion Teruko had flashed her platinum-capped teeth at him in a way that betrayed the feelings Terasawa had alluded to, and the gleam in her eye when she looked Takuya's way had not escaped him either.

Teruko was a straightforward, pleasant young woman. Her sturdy, buxom presence had certainly served to remind Takuya of the opposite sex. No doubt she would make an admirable wife. Terasawa had implied that they wanted Takuya to consider taking over the company, and he did not doubt that the Terasawas would make ideal in-laws. Maybe marrying their niece, having a family and living out the rest of his days in Himeji wouldn't be such a bad idea.

But after a few moments he shook his head. If he were

to marry Teruko and become Terasawa's adopted son, he could not keep his past a secret. A commitment to marry the niece would have to be predicated on his telling them the truth about himself. Getting them to understand his situation must come first, he thought. But Takuya knew that he couldn't bring himself to make such a confession, and that therefore his only choice was to turn down Terasawa's offer.

At lunchtime, they all retired up onto the grassy dune beyond the beach to sit on straw mats and unwrap rice balls. Teruko sat on the edge of the bank and placed a hand towel neatly on her lap before starting to eat her own lunch with chopsticks. Terasawa kept them entertained with funny stories and Teruko covered her mouth with her hand as she laughed happily at his jokes.

In the afternoon, the line of waves breaking on the beach crept closer as the tide started to come in, shepherding the people with their buckets full of clams back toward the grassy dune. When the sea had reclaimed all but the last few yards of sand, Takuya and the others retreated up the slope and loaded the day's haul of shellfish onto the truck.

Off they went. Teruko sat holding on to the edge of the flat deck with one hand as she pushed the hair off her face with the other.

That night, after he crawled into his futon, Takuya told himself that the time had come for him to leave the Terasawas. He'd been with them for two years now. Staying in one place was never wise for someone on the run, and the fact that he had been with the Terasawas for this long was obviously the main reason behind the suggestion that he marry their niece. If Takuya were arrested now, the authorities would suspect that Terasawa had given him shelter despite knowing what he had done. He decided to leave Himeji before he burdened Terasawa with repercussions from his past.

The next day, on his way back from a visit to the bank to deposit the week's receipts, he dropped in at the local employment agency. If he were to look for a different job, it would be best to avoid the cities and instead hide somewhere, like in a coal mine up in the mountains. Spending time in the bowels of a mine, away from prying eyes, would surely bring him peace of mind, he thought. Men and women were going in and out of the agency, and inside a throng of people lined up in front of the workers standing behind a counter on the other side of the room. Waiting his turn would require more time than Takuya had that day, so he decided to come again the next morning.

As he turned to leave, he saw a poster beside the door advertising for laborers in the Ikuno mine. Almost certainly they needed to advertise like this because many people were unwilling to work there.

That night he casually asked Kameya about the location of the Ikuno mine and learned that it was a silver mine, further inland, to the north of Himeji.

Looking at the map on the wall above his desk, Takuya thought it seemed like an ideal place to hide. It was right in the middle of Hyogo Prefecture, about halfway between the Harima Sea and the Sea of Japan. The symbol on the map indicating the exact location of the mine showed that it was in a gorge between two lines of mountains. A quick look at the railway timetable told him it was just under an hour and a half from Himeji on the Bantan Line. Being up in a heavily wooded area meant that if the police did come to arrest him, it would not be too difficult for him to evade them by slipping away into the forest. Working underground he would never need to be seen by anyone apart from his co-workers.

Suddenly Takuya felt extremely uneasy about being in Himeji. If he continued to parade around town in broad daylight, before long the police would recognize him. Also, with the bombed-out areas gradually filling up with new houses, more people who knew him might move back into the city, which obviously increased the likelihood of his being identified by the authorities. At the same time, he couldn't help but be worried about Fujisaki's family. They knew that he was working at Terasawa's workshop, and if the police tracked him as far as the Fujisakis they might well crack under interrogation and divulge his whereabouts to the authorities. That the Fujisakis knew his whereabouts was a danger he was only beginning to appreciate fully now. The only way to circumvent this potentially disastrous situation was to distance himself from the Terasawas and to keep his move to the Ikuno mine a secret.

Takuya felt himself losing his composure. At times he was completely immobilized by the premonition that the police were about to appear and arrest him.

Three days later, when the power supply was off, Takuya went to the employment agency to get the forms to apply for work in the Ikuno silver mine. When he returned to Terasawa's house, he slipped the forms between the pages of his account book and, checking that no one was likely to disturb him, furtively started filling them out. The figure for mine workers' wages on the forms was several times higher than the average wage in Himeji.

When Takuya went into the living room that evening, the sound of running water told him that Terasawa's wife and their niece, Teruko, were in the kitchen doing some washing. Terasawa was smoking a cigarette as he read the newspaper spread out on the low table in the middle of the room. Takuya sat down on the other side of the table, his legs folded under him in formal style, and without beating around the bush said that he wanted to quit his job. Terasawa lifted his eyes from the newspaper and stared in bewilderment at Takuya.

Takuya saw straightaway that Terasawa was hurt. Two years had passed since the Terasawas had taken him on. Their warm support was the only thing that had saved him from starvation.

"Is this because I asked you about Teruko? If that's the case, don't worry about it. Forget I ever mentioned it," said Terasawa remorsefully.

"That isn't the reason," Takuya replied instinctively.

"Well, what is it then?" said Terasawa, looking him squarely in the face.

Takuya was at a loss for words. He regretted that he hadn't at least concocted an appropriate excuse for quitting his job. If he allowed Terasawa to think that the talk of marriage was the reason, Teruko would be needlessly offended. Of course he bore no ill will toward the Terasawas, and he did not want to see them hurt.

"You know I don't have anyone to take over for me, so I just thought that it might be good if you and Teruko got together. But if you're not keen on the idea it's no big deal. Are you worried about your parents? If so, why don't you get them to come to Himeji? I know it might not be so easy to leave Okinawa these days, but...." Terasawa pushed his glasses back up the bridge of his nose, the women's laughter from the kitchen seeming to finish his sentence.

Takuya looked away and hung his head. He could not bear betraying Terasawa's kindness.

He flushed with a sudden urge to confide in Terasawa. He could feel himself starting to panic, and fidgeted uncontrollably as he looked up at the ceiling. He took a deep breath to try to calm himself down, but felt his face turn red, as though all the blood in his body were rushing to his head. In his mind he could hear two opposing choruses of voices, one telling him that it was wrong to hide the truth from Terasawa any further, the other that he shouldn't do anything on an impulse which could not be rectified afterward.

Terasawa sat looking dejected, saying nothing.

"To tell you the truth...," Takuya began. As he spoke, the voice of caution seemed to repeat itself over and over again in the back of his mind. He felt himself break out in a cold sweat. Nevertheless, once he had uttered the first short sentence, the words flowed as though they had been a script waiting to be articulated. It was almost as if his mouth were moving independently of his mind. He could feel a faint nervous spasm in his knees start to spread through the rest of his body.

Terasawa's gaze was fixated on Takuya's face, his expression one of utter astonishment. Though his fear of the possible consequences of his decision was undiminished, Takuya continued with his confession, a powerful surge of emotion driving him on.

Takuya felt his eyes moisten as he finished his story.

Terasawa sighed, and his hands shook slightly as he filled his pipe with tobacco and struck a match to light it.

"So that was it? From the day I met you I thought you weren't just some ordinary guy off the street," he said. He sighed again, more deeply this time, but then turned his gaze back to Takuya as though he had just decided something, and said in a hushed but forceful tone, "You did well to own up to that. Leave it to me. I won't say a word, not even to my wife or niece. Wherever you go it would be dangerous. Best to stay here, I'd say. I'll make sure you're safe."

Takuya bowed deeply, said nothing as he stood up, and returned to his own room. A wave of fatigue came over him as he sat down on his futon. While he had been happy to hear Terasawa's kind words of support, he agonized that the punishment might not stop at him if his true identity were discovered. Speaking about his past against his better judgment was proof that he had come to rely too heavily on Terasawa's goodwill. Takuya resolved to stick to his plan to go up to Ikuno and hide away in the depths of the mine.

He had decided to return the forms for the job at the Ikuno mine on the next day the workshop was closed due to power outages, but when that day came he could not bring himself to step out of the gate and go to the employment agency. In part, he did not feel determined enough to shake himself free from his dependence on the Terasawas, but the main reason was his apprehension at being unable to imagine what life would be like underground in the mine. He could no longer find the mental fortitude necessary to push himself to move again.

The rainy season started.

Dressed in a long raincoat, Takuya trudged around the streets collecting payments and taking them to the bank. Terasawa's attitude toward him had become slightly more respectful of late, and whenever he saw Takuya helping to unload incoming materials, he called over one of the other workers to do it instead.

A few days of thunderstorms brought the rainy season to an end. With the government having announced that the regulations covering the sale of matches would be lifted in autumn, a large number of would-be manufacturers started up businesses, which led to a dramatic increase in the demand for matchboxes. As orders began coming in from factories in the Kobe area, Takuya found himself increasingly busy organizing large consignments to be shipped there by freight train.

One day Takuya plucked up the courage to go to the black market and buy himself a pair of blue trousers, a shirt, some secondhand black shoes and a felt hat. A change of clothes was one thing, but he couldn't bring himself to go further and visit the barbershop. The thought of sitting in the barber's chair, his face exposed for all to see, made him continue letting Kameya cut his hair with the electric clippers.

Whenever he left a piece of clothing out in his room, Teruko would take it away and return it later that day nicely washed and ironed. Terasawa's wife was obviously behind this, but Takuya chose to say little more than a casual thank-you each time he found the clothing back in his room.

Fine weather continued and the temperature steadily rose. The number of power lines in the area around the workshop increased, and they could often hear cicadas clinging to the pole beside the gate to the company grounds.

At the end of July match manufacturers had managed to obtain a small quantity of white willow from Hokkaido, so good-quality matches were being produced again. As more goods circulated in the market, the skyrocketing prices that had continued since the end of the war started to ease, and the freeze on access to savings was removed. On top of this, reports appeared in the newspapers that the price of vegetables and seafood was starting to fall below the prices regulated by the government. The meals at Terasawa's gradually improved, and the dining table was occasionally graced by large bowls of rice mixed with real barley.

Takuya noticed that articles about the war crimes trials had all but disappeared from the newspapers. Once in a while there would be some mention of the trial of a class A war criminal, but it was never more than the briefest of coverage. Terasawa had obviously kept his word about not telling his wife or niece about Takuya's past, as there seemed to be no noticeable change in their attitude toward him.

The summer that year was unusually hot.

On the twenty-eighth of August, Takuya found an article in the newspaper reporting that a verdict had been

delivered in the case against the men involved in the vivisections carried out at Kyushu Imperial University. Three
medical staff from the university, the commander of the
Western Region, and a total of five staff officers from the
tactical operations center were condemned to death by
hanging, while two other university staff and two headquarters staff were sentenced to life imprisonment. It closed by
stating that the trials of those involved in the execution of
B-29 crewmen would commence very soon.

Takuya sensed that the Allied administration was moving into the final stages of dealing with Japan's part in the
war. The military tribunal's adjudications would close with
the trials in Tokyo of the class A war criminals and those
staff of the Western Regional Command involved in the
execution of POWs. Takuya mused that after these trials
were finished, the danger of capture might abate as his pursuers became less zealous.

Early the next morning, Takuya was overseeing the shipment of a consignment of boxes. A very large order for various sizes had come in from a match manufacturer in Kobe,
and Takuya had to organize its transport by horse-drawn cart
to the freight station, and then its loading onto the train.

He stood on the platform at the Sanyo Line freight station, checking that everything was in order as the cargo was
loaded into the freight car. The workers were stripped to the
waist, their back muscles glistening in the sun and their arms
and chests speckled with pieces of straw packing stuck to
the sweat from their toil.

The man in the guardroom stuck his head out the window and called out to Takuya that there was a telephone
call for him from Terasawa. He told the men to stop loading

until he got back, walked over to the hut and put his hand in through the window to take the receiver.

Terasawa's hollow-sounding voice came over the telephone line, telling Takuya to drop everything and run for it. "Go to Okayama, I've got a friend who makes matchboxes there who will help, he said. He blurted out the address of the place before telling Takuya that two detectives from a city near his hometown had turned up at the workshop together with one from Himeji Central Police Station, and had left hurriedly when Kameya said that Takuya was at the freight station. "Run for it! They must almost be there! Go to Okayama!" said Terasawa, now almost shouting into the telephone.

"OK," Takuya replied, and he leaned in through the window to replace the receiver. He turned and looked toward the road leading to the workshop. All he could see was a horse-drawn cart slowly moving along the parched dirt track, and an old woman dressed in disheveled clothes with a baby on her back.

Terasawa's words imploring him to flee rang in his ears, the name and address of the man in Okayama echoing inside his head. If I go now everything will be all right, he told himself, amazed at how calm and collected he was. As he stood beside the guardroom, it occurred to him that he wanted to check with his own eyes that someone had actually come to arrest him. For a moment he couldn't believe that he could be so deliberate at a time like this, but he told himself that there was still time to wait and see them before making his escape.

A man wearing an open-neck shirt appeared a short distance down the road. Two other men quickly followed, one of whom crossed to the other side, picking up his pace as he approached the platform. The second man had close-cropped gray hair, suggesting that he was much older than the other two.

Takuya couldn't understand why he hadn't turned and run already. It was almost as though his joints had locked and his feet were set in concrete. He knew that all he had to do to escape was to jump down onto the tracks and thread his way to safety through the lines of freight cars. Nevertheless, he stood glued to the spot, watching the three detectives hastening toward their goal. The tallest of the three men looked quite young, not much more than twenty or twenty-one years old.

Takuya was at a loss. A feeling of inertia seemed to have come over him, as though the mental strain of two years on the run had disappeared, leaving nothing but a feeling of lassitude. Even if he evaded capture, he would doubtless end up being caught somewhere else, he thought. Maybe he wasn't as good at being a fugitive as he had thought. He had done all he could to stay at large, and he had no strength left to push himself any further.

Enough, he told himself. The three men walked into the station, casting studied glances at everyone, until almost at the same moment all three recognized Takuya.

One of the younger men clambered up onto the platform. The other made to seal off the path to escape by walking farther down the footpath and stopping in front of the freight car. The gray-haired man walked over toward the guardroom and stepped up the stone path to the platform to stand in front of Takuya.

"Takuya Kiyohara?" he said. Takuya nodded, watching

dolefully as the detective pulled out a set of handcuffs. He told himself over and over that this was all right, this was the way it was always going to end.

His father was there waiting at Himeji Police Station. As soon as he saw Takuya walk into the room he hung his head and started sobbing uncontrollably. He was still weeping as he began to explain himself in beseeching tones. He told his son that the police investigations had been relentless from the day after Takuya had made his escape, with all of his family, relatives, friends, and even his teachers from primary and high school being interrogated one by one. Within weeks of Takuya's disappearance, the atmosphere at the municipal office had soured so much that he had quit his job. A month ago he had been taken into custody for another round of interrogation, the police insisting that he must know where Takuya was hiding. He described how the police had told him that the three other men from headquarters had been arrested after their parents had confessed their whereabouts, and that they were all trying to put the blame for everything on Takuya. His interrogator had kept telling him that because of this, Takuya must receive the heaviest sentence, and the only way to prevent it was to bring him before the court as quickly as possible.

As they had decided that Takuya's father was not going to try to escape, they had let him sit outside and sun himself in a spot where they could see him. Not wanting to be a public burden, he spent much of his time outside, weeding the police grounds as payment for the meals they provided. His father had realized that the false name on the New Year's card had really been Takuya, but fearing that writing a reply would lead to disaster, he had gone no further than to copy the address in Himeji onto the reverse side of the paper attached to the straw festoon adorning the family's Shinto altar in the living room, burning the greeting card after he had done so. After being held for about a month, and increasingly worried about what his interrogator had said about Takuya's remaining at large leading to a heavier sentence, he had told the police about the address written on the festoon.

"What have I done? I wish I were dead," Takuya's father sobbed, burying his face in his hands.

Early that evening, some sushi rolls were delivered to the holding cells by one of Terasawa's workers. Two other men were being held in the same cell as Takuya, so he shared the food with them.

Later that same night, he was handcuffed and taken to Himeji Station by two detectives. As he walked in he saw his father and Terasawa standing beside the ticket window. Terasawa handed the detectives some cigarettes and matches before fixing his forlorn gaze on Takuya.

The police must have contacted the station beforehand, as there were seats reserved for them on the train. Takuya sat between the two detectives and looked out the window as the train slowly moved away from the platform. The moon was out and the sky was clear, so he could make out the profile of Himeji's White Egret Castle, but before long that faded into the distance and disappeared.

The next day, just after eleven o'clock in the morning, the train pulled into Tokyo Station, and from there Takuya was taken directly to the Tokyo Metropolitan Police Station. After a brief round of questioning he was put into a cell. When asked how he had acquired the pistol and ammunition, he said nothing about Shirasaka, instead saying that he had brought them home to Shikoku after the war ended and had buried them in the forest behind his parents' house.

After breakfast the next morning he was taken on foot to SCAP headquarters. His interrogator was a twenty-seven- or twenty-eight-year-old American officer who spoke good Japanese, asking him about his rank and posting during his years in the army. He pulled out the wanted poster they had used in their search, smiling as he said, "You're just a little boy here." It was a photograph of Takuya's face, enlarged from the class photograph taken when he graduated from high school. They must have got the original from one of his classmates, he thought.

Later that day Takuya was driven through the main gate at Sugamo Prison in a U.S. Army truck. A burly military policeman escorted him into a room off the courtyard, where he was made to strip down to his underwear before being photographed and fingerprinted.

From there he was led down a long corridor into a cell. The American military prison guard pushed the steel door shut with his foot and locked it. The prison clothes Takuya had been given had the letter "P" stenciled in black on the back of the shirt, both arms, the back of the trousers and the front of each trouser leg.

On the second of September, with a second-generation Japanese-American army sergeant acting as interpreter, the questioning conducted by the public prosecutors and lawyers began. It didn't take Takuya long to comprehend that what Shirasaka had said about the commander of the Western Region and other high-ranking officers trying to evade responsibility was obviously true. They were all insisting that the executions had been carried out arbitrarily by junior officers and their men rather than because of any orders from above. This of course flew in the face of what Takuya knew to be true. The deputy chief of staff, the colonel in charge of the tactical operations center, the headquarters legal officer and a number of headquarters medical officers had all been present at the executions, which should surely remove any doubt as to whether consent had been granted by those at the very top echelons of command.

Apart from one small window at the back, Takuya's cell was defined by concrete walls and a heavy steel door. He spent most of his time sitting there quietly by himself, but at bath time, twice a week, he had a chance to see the other prisoners, among them some of those who had served in the Western Regional Command.

When Takuya bowed to higher-ranking officers they did little more than casually acknowledge his presence before looking away. He wasn't sure whether this was because they were indignant at what they viewed as his cowardice in fleeing in the face of arrest, or because they felt pangs of conscience at the thought that their statements about ordering the executions had compromised Takuya and the other more junior men. Their long confinement seemed to have weakened them physically, as their faces looked gaunt and pale.

Lieutenant Hirosaki, who had been given blank identification papers by Shirosaka, and Lieutenant Himuro, whom Takuya had advised to escape from Osaka, were there too. Both men described in hushed tones how they had let their parents know where they were hiding and how this had ultimately led to their arrest. As had been the case with Takuya's arrest, the parents of these two men had broken under the pressure of interrogation, divulging their son's whereabouts on the assumption that they were thereby helping to avert the worst of punishments. Apparently this had been a calculated scheme to round up the last fugitives.

Himuro told Takuya that a former colonel from the tactical operations center of central command had insisted in court that the indiscriminate bombing of Japanese cities and towns by the U.S. Army Air Force was a violation of international law, and that the people responsible for such attacks were the ones who should be brought to justice. Takuya was impressed by the man's courage, but at the same time, knowing that criticism of the American military in front of a military tribunal could only lead to the heaviest possible penalty, he realized that he could never bring himself to say anything so provocative when his turn came to speak in court.

About a month after Takuya entered Sugamo Prison, he happened to pass the former commander in chief of the Western Regional Command in the corridor as the old man carried his meal on a tray back to his cell. Maybe it was because he had lost so much weight, but in his baggy prison clothes the former commander looked frail and ordinary, a completely different person from the one Takuya remembered. The intimidating presence he had in his lieutenant-general's uniform was gone, leaving behind only a haggard old man.

On the eleventh of October, in the military court in

Yokohama, the first public hearing was held in the trial of those from the Western Regional Command. Takuya was one of thirty-five accused, including the commander in chief. They all pled innocent to the charges against them.

The public hearings were a long process. Takuya and his fellow accused traveled each day by bus through the black market area in front of Shinjuku Station, down Shibuya Doogenzaka, through Oosaki and Shinagawa to the military court of the American Eighth Army in Yokohama. Upon arriving at the courtroom they would eat a simple midday meal from a mess tin while sitting on the floor in the make-shift holding room, make their appearance in the courtroom and then return by bus to Sugamo Prison. As a precaution against suicide, before they were returned to their cells when they got back to the prison they were made to strip naked to allow an MP to check their ears, noses, mouths and anal orifices to make sure they were not bringing back any poisons.

Every time Takuya attended the court sessions he was astounded that every one of the high-ranking officers from headquarters persisted in completely denying giving any orders to carry out the executions of the American fliers. In the face of determined questioning from the public prosecutor, even the deputy chief of staff and the colonel in charge of the tactical operations center, both of whom had actually witnessed executions, were adamant that no orders had been issued from above to dispose of the POWs. The only thing that concerned these shadows of men in prison clothes now was saving their own lives. That this would mean compromising the lives of others meant nothing to

them. They were different people now. The poise and as-
surance these men had demonstrated when they were in
uniform was gone.

From all appearances, they seemed terrified by the prospect of death. Their faces were ashen and their replies to
questions were halting, as though they were afraid that
choosing the wrong word could be fatal. There were some
among them whose voices trembled with fear as they spoke.
The expression "strung up" was being used in Sugamo to
mean death by hanging, and it was clear that these men
were choosing their words very carefully in a desperate attempt to avoid being "strung up" themselves. Takuya
couldn't help but notice that when one of the American
military prosecutors directed his gaze at any one of these
men, they literally stiffened with fear, their every word of
reply filled with apprehension.

From time to time thoughts of regret entered Takuya's
mind for not having escaped at the freight station, but he
always returned to the conclusion that fleeing would only
have served to postpone the inevitable. The more contact
Takuya had with the prison MPs, the American military
prison guards, and the judges, prosecutors and lawyers sitting
in court, the more he came to the realization that America's
omnipresent military had total control of the country. Even
if he had managed to evade his pursuers at the freight station, the Americans' control of society was so comprehen-
sive that his capture would have been only a matter of time.

From other inmates, he learned that about a month earlier the commander of the Tokyo *kempeitai*, Oishi Kojiro,
had been incarcerated in Sugamo Prison. He had managed
to stay one step ahead of the authorities until they discov-

ered that he was working in a coal mine and moved swiftly to arrest him. Many of Takuya's fellow inmates said that Oishi's staying at large so long was proof that his *kempeitai* background had equipped him well for stealth and deception, but the fact that even someone as careful as this could be captured brought home the inevitability of his own arrest.

Takuya, struggling against the fear of death as he spoke, testified in court that his own subordinates, the two sergeant-majors, had taken part in the executions only because of his orders. Shortly after this, a major posted to Fukuoka from Imperial Headquarters gave evidence to the effect that Takuya's participation in the executions was in compliance with orders he himself had given, and that these orders had of course originated at the very top of the chain of command in the Western Region, a statement which directly contradicted the testimony given by the highest ranking officers. It seemed as if any suggestion that the U.S. Army Air Force's indiscriminate incendiary raids on Japanese cities might have been a violation of international law had been ruled out from the start, as the defense lawyers made no mention of this in any of their statements.

On the twelfth of November, Takuya heard that verdicts had been reached in the trials of the class A war criminals, and that seven of the defendants, including former prime minister Tojo Hideki, had been condemned to death by hanging. Another sixteen, including former navy minister Shimada Shigetaro, had been sentenced to life imprisonment. Two men were given fixed terms of imprisonment. Only seven received the death sentence, which was less than Takuya had expected, giving him a faint glimmer of hope that he might escape the noose.

Day after day, he and the other defendants rode the bus from Sugamo Prison to the military court in Yokohama. No one spoke along the way, so there was nothing for him to do but cast his mournful gaze out the little windows at the outside world, or hang his head and close his eyes, thinking of the past. Occasionally he visualized himself stepping out of the command center and seeing Fukuoka consumed by flames, or remembered the sight of the two B-29s heading toward Nagasaki, then that shrill voice over the radio from Ohmura air base minutes later, reporting the devastation of the city. But these images were now no more than vague memories from days long gone by. There wasn't a hint of emotion involved in their recollection. The anger he had once felt toward the American bombers who had obliterated Japan's cities with incendiaries was all but gone.

By the time the American soldier wielding the steel helmet knocked him unconscious as he clutched his handcart on the edge of the paddy field, he had probably already joined the rest of his countrymen living in a new, postwar world, he thought. Even then he had felt no hatred toward them, only an obsequious feeling of terror. And now, in his hazy memory of it all, his strongest feeling was relief that he'd been lucky enough to get away as lightly as he had. He remembered the fawning look he had directed toward the American soldiers on the deck of the truck just before being struck with the helmet, and knew that the same expression had become a virtual fixture on his face since he had entered prison.

They were allowed to wash themselves in the bath twice a week, but most of the time the MP guarding them screamed for them to get out of the bathtub after what seemed like only a few moments. Takuya and his fellow inmates would strip while they waited in the corridor, ready to rush into the bathroom when the MP gave the word, and shave and wash themselves frantically in the short time available. Some sat there leisurely washing themselves, but more often than not Takuya was flustered by the guard's shouts, and left before he could soak in the bath. In the morning, too, he leaped out of bed the moment he heard the guard's shrieking voice and the crash of a boot against the steel cell door. Not a day went by when Takuya did not feel intimidated by his captors' overpowering physical presence.

He often thought about his father, reduced to a sobbing wreck in the police station. He had aged dramatically, the skin of his face loose around the jowls. Takuya sent two postcards to his family. Outgoing messages were limited to one hundred fifty characters, but nothing that required more space to write about came to mind, so this posed no problem. His father had spoken of wanting to be dead, but Takuya was reassured knowing that his strong-willed mother and loyal brother and sister were there to provide support.

Most inmates had family problems. Anyone accused of being a war criminal sullied the family name, so the relatives of those in Sugamo were not received kindly by those around them. Takuya had heard of marriage arrangements for sons and daughters being called off, job offers rescinded and children being refused entry into schools and universities because their father was in Sugamo. The wife of Takuya's friend Himuro had returned to her parents' house while her husband was on the run, and filed for divorce as soon as she heard he was in Sugamo. Like so many other inmates who had been married, Himuro put his seal on the papers and sent them back as requested.

There were even cases where the parents or wife of an inmate had been so distressed that they had committed suicide. In the early weeks, as many inmates succeeded in taking their own lives, the Americans had instituted considerably more rigorous body searches and left the corridor and cell lights on through the night. As a precaution against the transfer of poison or razors, those who were yet to be sentenced were refused visits from people outside the prison.

On two occasions, from inside his cell Takuya sensed fellow inmates being taken out to be executed. Apparently notification that the sentence was to be carried out always occurred on Thursdays, when the prisoner was moved to a special cell for his last night before being executed the next day. That summer, five new sets of gallows were constructed in the execution compound.

One Thursday Takuya overheard a prison guard calling out the name of an inmate in a cell a few doors down from his. He heard the door being unlocked and the man stepping out into the corridor, saying his last farewells to the men in adjacent cells. The footsteps soon faded out of earshot and silence was restored after the steel door in the corridor leading to the adjoining wing was shut behind them. Takuya later heard that the man was executed the next day.

About two weeks after that, Takuya again heard someone quietly bidding the other inmates farewell, then breaking out into an old Imperial Army song as he disappeared down the corridor. This man was one of four hanged the next day.

News traveled quickly around Sugamo on the twenty-fourth of December that seven people, including former prime minister Tojo Hideki, had been executed the previous night. There were showers that day, and through his cell window Takuya could see raindrops against an otherwise clear sky.

The trial of those from the Western Regional Command was entering its final stages.

Takuya felt as if he were playing a part in a bizarre stage play. It was as though each of the accused were frantically trying to climb on top of the others to keep from drowning. As each day passed the atmosphere among the men became more tense, their expressions betraying a growing desperation. Takuya was no different from the others, aware that he was tied into a life-and-death struggle with the rest of the accused. When he sensed another defendant's answers to the prosecutor's questions being framed to compromise his own position, and therefore edge him closer to the gallows, Takuya felt himself stiffen and his mouth go dry. When he in turn made a statement, he could almost feel the other defendants' gazes burning into the back of his neck. By this stage, like all the other accused, Takuya was focused on nothing but his own chances of survival. Any difference in status that had previously existed between superiors and subordinates had long since disappeared. It was every man for himself.

When he was alone in his cell he would sometimes imagine the moments before his own death—the noose being slipped around his neck, the trapdoor falling open and his body dropping half through the hole with a jolt. If only he could avoid the pain that must come the moment before death, he thought, hoping that it would all end the very instant the trapdoor swung open. When Takuya thought of the minutes before stepping up to the gallows, he was filled with trepidation. He wondered if he would be able to hold himself together long enough to walk up the steps unassisted. Those who kept their composure to the very end would be eulogized, he told himself. He too must keep his dignity and stay calm until the moment he succumbed.

He recalled the scene in the bamboo grove before the American fliers were executed. While they must have been terrified by the prospect of death, they all did exactly as they were told, walking off through the undergrowth and kneeling down to await their fate. Was it pride, or maybe even vanity, he thought, that stopped them from causing a commotion? The instant the sword touched the man's neck, his body had jerked upward, as though his legs had unleashed the last action of his mortal coil. Would something similar happen when a man was hanged, Takuya wondered, and were the stories true about mucus and urine being released at the moment of death?

That night Takuya got no sleep, tossing and turning for hours on his straw mattress. It was rumored that suicides among inmates yet to be sentenced were on the rise, and as Takuya's sentencing approached he too felt that if the opportunity arose, he would like to end it all himself.

The deliberations in court drew to a close, and it was announced that the sentences of those from the Western Regional Command would be passed on December twenty-ninth.

That day Takuya was taken from his cell, handcuffed

and led out into the rear courtyard. Some inmates were already standing in neat lines, others were being led out by MPs to join the assembly. Many had bloodshot eyes and puffy faces, so it was obvious that Takuya was not the only one going without sleep.

They were ushered onto a waiting bus, and escorted by jeeps at the front and rear carrying armed MPs. When everyone was seated the bus moved off, picking up speed once they left the Sugamo compound, driving through the streets of Tokyo and then down the main road toward Yokohama. Takuya gazed out the window along the way, but nothing caught his eye.

Eventually the bus came to a halt in front of the court building, from where they were all led into an anteroom. Takuya avoided looking at the others, instead staring down at the polished wooden floor.

After a short wait an MP told them to move out of the room. When Takuya got up from his chair his knees and ankles felt strangely weak, as though all the strength in his legs had drained away. They were made to form a line and file down the corridor, the commander in chief's diminutive figure walking in front of Takuya. The former lieutenant-general's close-cropped hair was now completely white, as thin and soft as baby's down, and the skin on his neck hung loose, deep wrinkles moving ever so slightly with each step.

As always, their handcuffs were removed in the corridor before they filed into the courtroom. A large United States flag took pride of place high up on the wall behind the judge's seat. Below it was a framed photograph of President Truman, flanked by photographs of General MacArthur,

Supreme Commander of Allied Powers in Japan, and General Walker, commander of the United States Eighth Army. Takuya and his fellow accused remained standing as the lawyers, public prosecutors and judge entered the court. Out of the corner of his eye he could see an MP in a white helmet standing beside the door behind the seats for the defendants. The U.S. Army colonel in charge of the proceedings started to speak, at first addressing the court, but soon looking down at the documents in front of him as he read out the verdicts in a monotone. Takuya sat motionless and stared at the deadpan expression on the man's face.

The colonel looked up again and, turning his head slightly toward the defendants' seats, began to speak. The interpreter repeated the verdict in Japanese.

Takuya recognized the commander in chief's name despite the colonel's exotic American pronunciation. His heart pounded as he stared at the colonel's lips reading the charges, the verdict and the sentences. Takuya understood very little of the English, but knew that it was a guilty verdict and recognized the words "death by hanging" at the very end. The interpretation that followed confirmed that he was not mistaken.

Suddenly Takuya was overwhelmed by a feeling of suffocation, as though a trapdoor had swung open underneath him and a noose were closing on his neck. The deputy chief of staff's name was read out in a perfunctory tone amid a familiar-sounding stream of English, and again the words "death by hanging" rang in the court. In quick succession, the names of the other high-ranking officers were read out, including that of the former colonel directly in charge of the tactical operations center. All of them were sentenced to death by hanging.

His knees started to tremble. His body shuddered, and staying on his feet became a painful struggle. The sentences of the soldiers from Ishigaki Island who had beheaded and then bayoneted the bodies of three American pilots came to his mind. Forty-one of the forty-five men accused had been sentenced to death. Takuya and his comrades from the Western Command had killed a total of thirty-three fliers, so it went without saying that their crime was much worse than that of the coast guards, and therefore the words "death by hanging" would surely be read out after each of their names.

As they moved down through the ranks, next came the lieutenants. Both legal affairs officers were condemned to death, and after their names and sentences were read out, Takuya recognized the name of Lieutenant Howa Kotaro. He had thought the fact that Howa's mother had been killed in the fire raids on Fukuoka might have been seen as an extenuating circumstance, but again the words "death by hanging" rang out.

By now Takuya had lost all hope. His own action had been no less extreme than those of the two legal affairs officers or Lieutenant Howa. His name would be next, he thought, but instead the name of the young officer cadet was read out in the same American pronunciation, again followed by the death sentence. Takuya's head started to spin. His legs went numb and his knees felt as though they would buckle any second.

Next came the name of the staff officer who had ordered

Takuya to take part in the executions. The set English expressions describing the charges were read out in the same somber tone, but the words at the end were different. Takuya was sure that rather than an expression mentioning "death," he heard the word "life." As he struggled to understand the difference, the interpreter translated it as a "life sentence."

Himuro's name was read out next. Takuya concentrated as hard as he could on each individual word, and again he picked out the expression "imprisonment for life."

"Ta-ku-ya Ki-yo-ha-ra," said the chief of the military tribunal. Takuya gazed intently at the colonel's lips. His sense of time seemed to have deserted him as the space between one moment and the next seemed like an eon. The charges were read in full and again Takuya thought he heard the word "life" among the words explaining the sentence.

Another wave of shaking came over him and he felt a chill run down his spine, then barely controllable nausea. The culmination of years and months of unrelenting suspense had passed in an instant. He was not going to be strung up after all. A wave of emotion pushed the other physical sensations into the background, but for a fleeting moment, until the interpreter confirmed it, he thought that maybe he had misheard his sentence.

The remaining defendants' sentences continued to be announced in the same monotone English followed by the interpreter's Japanese, but by now the words were no longer registering with Takuya. He stared at the American flag, at the same time repeating to himself the words "life sentence."

After a short while the tenor of the announcements

seemed to change, and the words "not guilty" could be heard following the charges.

Realizing that the English announcements had come to an end, Takuya returned his gaze to the chief of the military tribunal. The American colonel shuffled his papers into order on his desk and rubbed his cheeks slowly with both hands.

Suddenly a voice could be heard from down in front of Takuya. Incredulous, the chief of the tribunal turned to see what was happening.

Takuya could just make out a muffled sobbing two rows down, as well as the sound of someone breathing hard and trying to keep back tears. Looking toward the front, Takuya saw a little old man moving forward from the line of seats, his head quivering slightly.

The old man was pleading tearfully that he hadn't given any orders to kill POWs. His voice trembled as he spoke. Obviously the strain had got the better of him, for he stood ramrod straight, almost as though someone had inserted a board down the back of his shirt.

Takuya felt ashamed to see this old man groveling before the court, insisting to the members of the tribunal that while he might have been sentenced to death in the earlier trial of those involved in the vivisection of POWs at Kyushu Imperial University, and had now received the same sentence in this trial, he had never given anyone orders to do such things, and that this decision was regrettable in the extreme.

Takuya felt as though he had witnessed something he would have preferred not to see, and looked away. He shut his eyes, but could still hear sniffling sounds from the former commander in chief. The old man Takuya had respected as a famous general was now openly weeping.

A different American voice said something in English, which the interpreter quickly translated as the announcement of the end of the proceedings.

Takuya and the others turned to the right and, after being handcuffed once again by the MPs, filed out of the courtroom.

In the makeshift holding room down the corridor, they were given their evening meal in army-issue mess tins. Takuya had no appetite, but somehow he knew that he had to eat. He dug his spoon into the white rice mixed with barley and chewed away at the pieces of tasteless dried fish.

Three hours after leaving Tokyo they were back on the bus to Sugamo. The sun was starting to set and the western sky was tinged with red.

Out of the left side of the bus Mount Fuji was visible off in the distance as they crossed the Rokugo Bridge over the Tama River. With the sun sinking behind it, the snow on the mountain took on a light shade of purple.

Chapter Nine

Takuya was moved into a different cell to begin serving his sentence.

Soon after New Year's in 1949 his father and brother came to visit him. Through the three layers of heavy wire mesh separating them Takuya had only a blurred view of their faces, but he could see his father blinking uncomfortably, wiping his eyes repeatedly with a handkerchief. Seeing them stare at the handcuffs and the leather band wrapped around them made Takuya feel decidedly uncomfortable.

When their time was up an MP came over and led Takuya's two visitors out of the interview room.

In the end nine people, including the commander in chief, were sentenced to death, five to life imprisonment, one to forty years of hard labor, four to thirty years, three to twenty-five years, four to twenty years, one to ten years, and one to five years. Seven were found not guilty. Evidently four of the men who had taken part in the executions, Howa being one of them, were sentenced to death because their involvement was judged to be voluntary, whereas Takuya and the others who received various prison terms were deemed to have been acting in response to orders passed down the chain of command. That night, the nine men sentenced to death were moved to another wing of the prison.

Takuya spent his days uneventfully, going along with prison routine. Having avoided the gallows, he started paying greater attention to prison life. The food was dreadful. The staple component of most meals was a rice sludge made from what the other inmates said could only have been chicken feed, and the soup that sometimes accompanied it was little more than miso-flavored water with a few tiny pieces of vegetables in it. On the rare occasions they were served bread it came lightly buttered, the fat already starting to separate. Eating, getting up and going to bed took place at set times. When Takuya thought of how he'd managed to avoid the gallows, his face relaxed. He might be destined to spend the rest of his days in prison, but he was happy to be alive.

Just after the rainy season started Takuya's younger brother came to visit again. He said their parents and sister were well, and that with the sale of sake having been liberalized a month earlier their father was now enjoying a drink every night before going to bed. He went on to announce cheerfully that he'd received a raise at work.

Takuya listened patiently before telling his brother not to come anymore. With their father having left his job, it couldn't be easy for his brother and sister, so the money needed to get from Shikoku to Tokyo and back was better spent on keeping the family fed, he said. His brother nodded from the other side of the steel mesh dividing screen.

Newspapers were not allowed in Sugamo. Instead there was a simple mimeographed tabloid put together by the inmates, but this featured nothing more than wood-block prints depicting prison life, some satirical verse, the occasional cartoon and a column of letters to the editor. There were effectively no sources of information about life in the outside world.

Several days of hot, humid weather set in.

One evening, through his cell window Takuya caught sight of fireworks bursting one after another in the night sky. A voice from the next cell told him that it must be from the river festival at Ryogoku. There was no sound with them, but the brightly colored strands of light seemed to trace flower petals in the darkness before trailing away to nothing. When two or three went off at once the night sky was illuminated with splashes of brilliant color, soon followed by an audible sigh from those watching from the cells. As Takuya stood staring out his window at the fireworks, he thought that at last the confusion that had followed defeat in the war was starting to dissipate.

Autumn came and went and the temperature dropped.

Takuya hadn't smoked since entering Sugamo. There was an allocation of five cigarettes a day for those who wanted them, and the guards walking up and down the corridor would light them if asked. But Takuya felt so nervous about calling the guards over that before long he had lost any desire to smoke.

One day in the third week of November, when Takuya was on his way back to his cell with a tray of food, the old man walking beside him started talking.

"You guys were really lucky, you know," he said calmly. The man was a former colonel in the Imperial Navy who had been sent to Sugamo on a life sentence just after the prison was opened.

Noticing Takuya's puzzled expression, the man began to explain what he meant.

In the early trials, he said, many people had been condemned to death for little more than slapping prisoners of war, and only after two years had the punishments started to get lighter. He said things had changed markedly after the forty-one navy coast guard troops from Ishigaki Island were sentenced to death in mid-March 1948, almost three years after the surrender. The judgment of those from the Western Command in the last of the war crimes trials, with most of the accused escaping the hangman's noose, was proof that the American position on war crimes had changed dramatically. United States policy toward Japan was at a turning point, he explained, with the Americans moving away from treating Japan as a former enemy, and instead trying to entice her into their camp as a friendly player in the increasingly complicated political situation in Asia. This new stance, he said, was manifesting itself in all sorts of areas, one of them being the handling of war criminals.

Before the war, this man, now well on in years, had been a naval attaché at the Japanese Embassy in Washington, and at the time of the surrender he was working as an intelligence officer at Imperial Headquarters.

"Do you follow what I'm saying?" he asked, smiling faintly.

He told Takuya that after graduating from the Imperial Naval Academy he had studied at a university in the United States, and that since he spoke fluent English he was acting as a liaison for the American military authorities with former Imperial Navy personnel in Sugamo. Obviously, it was through his ongoing contact with the Americans that he had detected this subtle change in direction, and as he had some knowledge of world affairs in general he was able to make the connection between American policy toward Japan and the effect this had on the issue of war crimes.

Takuya thought the man's observations were probably very accurate. There was certainly no doubting the fact that punishments had become much less severe with the passage of time, as his own case illustrated. As the man said, luck had indeed been on Takuya's side.

On reflection, he realized that there had even been a change in the attitude of the American prison guards. The ones who had treated the inmates with spiteful severity had suddenly disappeared, replaced by more pleasant, cool-headed characters. The MPs were much more lenient about the inmates' time in the bath, and occasionally even winked affably at the men. The food situation throughout the country must have been gradually improving, as the quality of the prison food seemed better, and the time inmates were allowed to spend outside was extended.

On the twenty-fourth of December, Takuya was reminded of just how perceptive the former navy colonel's conclusions had been. That night, the Christmas message from the U.S. Army colonel in charge of Sugamo was pasted to the wall in each wing of the prison. It detailed a number of improvements for the inmates as well as specific reductions in the sentences of those serving shorter terms. These were to go into effect immediately. Two days later forty-six men were released on parole, followed by another sixteen on the thirty-first of December.

The atmosphere in Sugamo became even more hopeful in early 1950. In the first week of March, the prison superintendent announced parole for all inmates serving short sentences, and rumors immediately started circulating that sentences might even be reduced for those in for life or still awaiting execution. This proved to be the case, with reductions of sentence announced for all those remaining on death row. Word spread around the prison that all nine men from the Western Regional Command who had been condemned to death, including the former commander in chief, were to have their sentences commuted to life terms.

Thirty-four of those involved in the executions on Ishigaki Island had their death sentences reduced to prison terms, so including the Ishigaki garrison commander, former navy colonel Inoue Otsuhiko, only seven people remained on Sugamo's death row.

Everyone expected that they too would be reprieved, but early in the evening on the fifth of April, these seven men were notified that they were to be moved to cells in a different wing of the prison, in preparation for the carrying out of their sentences. Two days later, at thirty-two minutes after midnight, Colonel Inoue and three others were hanged, followed to the gallows twenty-five minutes later by former navy lieutenant Enomoto and two others. The Japanese prison chaplain told the other inmates that after they had eaten a meal with the men they had made their way through the rain to the execution yard singing the "Battleship March."

When the Korean War broke out that June, the American approach to the occupation of Japan was further relaxed, and one after another the remaining inmates had their sentences commuted. Takuya was no exception, and his term was reduced from life to fifteen years.

Around this time, Takuya found himself considering the war crimes trials in a new light. By rights, a trial should represent the precise application of the law, with the verdict being the strictly impartial result of due process. But the war crimes trials seemed to be heavily influenced by world affairs, with the severity of the sentencing varying greatly from one trial to the next and the original sentences often commuted within a short time of being delivered, which surely threw into question their legal foundation, and suggested that judgments were made by the victors however they saw fit. While it pleased Takuya to know that many condemned men had escaped the gallows, and to have had his own sentence reduced, he couldn't help but think that these trials had been nothing more than an arbitrary set of judgments, distant in the extreme from what he imagined a trial should be.

With the escalation of the conflict on the Korean Peninsula, the pace of changes in Sugamo accelerated. American prison guards dispatched to the front were replaced by Japanese staff, which brought more dramatic improvements in the conditions for the inmates. In September of the following year, 1951, the San Francisco Peace Treaty was signed, and once it came into force the administrative responsibility for running Sugamo was transferred to the

Japanese government, which soon allowed stage shows and even sumo wrestling troupes to entertain the inmates.

Takuya closely followed the bewildering changes happening around him. People were being released one after another, and five-day paroles offered to anyone who chose to apply. Inmates were even allowed to leave Sugamo during the day to work in the city, and before long the prison gate was witnessing a veritable commuter rush in the morning and early evening. By this stage Sugamo was no longer a prison in the true sense of the word.

About this time Takuya heard that the former commander in chief was receiving treatment in the prison hospital for a neurological disorder. A short time later word went around that the old man had died in the middle of the night, filling the air with bloodcurdling screams of agony before he succumbed. The news aroused no emotion in Takuya. It was as though he were hearing of the death of some old man with whom he had no connection.

Takuya chose neither to seek work in companies during the week nor to go on work parties outside the prison, and he did not apply for five-day parole. Those who worked in companies during the week brought back newspapers as well as stories of the changes in the outside world, but Takuya scarcely ran his eyes over the headlines, and paid little attention to the other men's gossip. The regular stage shows held little appeal for him, so Takuya spent his days quietly in his cell. Such entertainment was supposedly organized as a special favor for the inmates, but this "benevolence" only served to annoy Takuya.

In early November of 1954, he noticed an article in the newspaper forecasting a rice harvest of around four hundred million bushels, the largest in history. The food in the prison was now all Japanese, and in both quality and quantity it had tangibly improved.

Early in January of 1955, Takuya's father died of tuberculosis. The prison officials encouraged Takuya to go and visit his family, saying they would grant him special parole, but he stubbornly refused their offers, finding their displays of sympathy nothing more than an unwelcome intrusion.

In a letter from his younger brother, Takuya read that the attitude of the people in their hometown toward war criminals had completely changed, the general opinion now being that these men were in fact victims of the war, and that while it might have been an unofficial offering, the town officials had sent the family a condolence gift after the death of Takuya's father.

Takuya ripped the letter up and threw it away. He knew that the expression "victims of the war" was in common usage, but still felt that these words were of no relevance to himself. He wrote a reply to his brother, stating that having beheaded an American POW he in no way fell into the category of victim. When he remembered once having read an article describing war criminals as "enemies of mankind, utterly repulsive beasts of violence," he felt an overpowering bitterness toward those who, in the space of seven or eight short years, could simply change their minds on such a crucial issue. It annoyed him that his brother could be foolish enough to pass this on as though it were good news.

The release of the class A war criminals who had avoided the death sentence continued, and the less than two hundred inmates remaining in Sugamo were all moved into the same wing.

In February of 1957, nine years after he had entered Sugamo Prison, Takuya was released on what was termed "parole."

He felt no sense of elation as he stepped out through the prison gate. The first thing that struck him was how many well-dressed men and women were out walking on the streets. From the window of the streetcar he could see rows of houses and newly constructed buildings, neon signs everywhere and all kinds of automobiles on the neatly paved roads.

Everything he saw made him feel uncomfortable, as did the thought that he was now thirty-seven years old, with the prime of his life behind him. Merely looking at the streets and the people on them made him angry.

Just after nine o'clock that night he boarded the express train bound for Uno, from where he would take the ferry across the Inland Sea to Takamatsu in Shikoku, and change again to the train for Uwajima. In his pocket was an envelope holding the money he had been given by the Demobilized Soldiers Bureau to cover the cost of returning home.

All the seats in the train were clean, and with few people on board he had no problem finding a place to sit. In the row in front of Takuya, a young woman sat slumped against the shoulder of the man sitting next to her, and diagonally across from him on the other side of the carriage a middle-aged man was pouring himself a glass of sake. Outside, neon lights lit up the streets beside the tracks.

Takuya wiped the lenses of his glasses, clouded by the steamy air inside the carriage. His nearsightedness seemed to have worsened in the last few years.

Leaning against the metal window frame, Takuya closed his eyes. His younger sister had missed her chance to find a husband when she was still in her twenties and had married a widower the previous spring, while his brother had married three years earlier and now had one young child. In her last letter, Takuya's mother had recommended that he get married as soon as he left prison, even going as far as to enclose a young woman's photograph for him to consider, but he had sent it straight back without any comment. Marriage held no appeal for him. All he really felt like doing at the moment was lying down and resting on a tatami-matted floor.

From time to time he opened his eyes and gazed drowsily out of the window.

Eventually the first signs of dawn came and the sun started to rise.

Takuya left his seat to wash his face and clean his teeth in the washroom at the end of the car. When the train reached Osaka Station he stepped down onto the platform and bought a boxed lunch at the nearest kiosk. Trains came in and departed from the other platforms, with waves of people rushing up and down the stairs.

As the train approached the outer suburbs of Kobe, for a brief moment Fujisaki's face flashed in front of his eyes. The train rumbled on through Akashi and Kakogawa.

Thoughts of Terasawa and his wife came to his mind. Takuya had sent them two or three postcards in his early years in Sugamo and had received letters of reply with gifts of rice crackers, but their correspondence seemed to have dried up a number of years ago.

He turned his head to look out the window again. Fields

had been replaced by rows of houses, and Himeji Castle had come into view off in the distance. It almost seemed to rotate slowly as the train drew nearer on the last curve of track into the city. Heavy gray snow clouds hung low in the sky.

The idea of returning home was less and less attractive. If he went back to his parents' house, his mother would probably weep at the sight of him and his brother and sister would likely be just as tearful. He would have to go pay his respects at his father's grave and talk to the relatives and friends who would gather to welcome him back. The prospect of all this was still annoying to him, something he preferred to put off as long as possible.

The train slowed as it approached the station. Takuya took his bag down from the luggage rack above his head, put on his overcoat and walked toward the exit.

As he stepped down onto the platform he noticed that the station had been completely refurbished, with new benches and kiosks on each platform. He walked out onto the street. The area in front of the station was packed with shops and large buildings. All the roads seemed to be in good condition, and a wide tar-sealed boulevard stretched directly from the station to the castle's soaring walls. The green of the pine trees surrounding the castle stood out in stark contrast to the gleaming-white plaster walls of the donjons and towers, and the light brown of the stone buttresses provided a distinctive outline against the surrounding scenery.

Gazing toward the White Egret Castle as he walked, Takuya headed along the road beside the railway tracks, and crossed over them at the first intersection. Before long he passed the employment agency he had visited years ago. Still on the same spot, it was now a larger, permanent structure, surrounded by rows of houses probably built as part of a municipal housing project. There were new houses and shops on both sides of all the streets he passed, so Terasawa's factory would have been enlarged and the old house knocked down and replaced.

Takuya walked down the tarred road until he got as far as the pachinko parlor, where he stopped. Almost ten years had gone by since he had left Himeji. Terasawa and his wife would be old by now, or they might even have died while Takuya was in prison. Their niece would have been adopted as a daughter, then would have married and taken over the business.

Takuya tried to imagine what meeting Terasawa would be like after all these years. All they would have to talk about would be how things were in the past, and once that was over conversation would quickly dry up. He had sent Terasawa a postcard expressing his gratitude and had received a reply, so maybe that was where he should leave it. Indeed, if they had adopted Teruko and she had married and started a family, she would probably feel obliged to offer little more than a perfunctory welcome. The prospect of having to make conversation with Teruko's husband hardly inspired enthusiasm.

He took a deep breath before turning around and walking back down the road toward the station. The idea of getting off the train and visiting Terasawa seemed ludicrous to him now. That part of his life was too long ago, over and done with now. As he stood at the railway crossing a Tokyo-bound train gradually accelerated away from the platform and past him to the right. As the last car passed, the arm at the crossing lifted and Takuya walked back across the tracks and down the road to the station.

Inside the station building, he stepped up to a kiosk and bought a box of matches. An ukiyoe-style picture adorned the label on the top of the box. When he turned the box over he found the name of a match factory in Shirahama, Himeji, printed in small characters. The matchsticks had a healthy luster to them, and their vermilion-colored heads were all the same shape and size.

He struck one. The match didn't break and the head ignited cleanly on the first attempt. Enticed by the paraffin soaked into the wood, the flame slowly moved along the stick. It was a small, brilliant light.

He blew out the match and tossed it in a trash can, then looked up at the big timetable above the ticket window to find the next train heading west.